No Such Happily Ever Afters

Emma L Chester

Copyright © 2024 by Emma Chester

All rights reserved. No part of this book may be reproduced in any manner whatsoever without written permission except in the case of brief quotations embodied in critical articles and reviews.

First Printing, 2024

For my Savior, Jesus Christ
The author of my story and the reason we can hope in a happy ending.

For my family,
You are the reason I am here; you are the reason I am me; you are the reason I know there is such a thing as "happily ever after".

NO SUCH HAPPILY EVER AFTERS

1

I immediately knew it was a mistake coming home for the holidays when a turkey wrecked my car.

Okay, so maybe I was the one who wrecked my car, but the turkey started it.

That wasn't the explanation I gave the towing company when I called them though, sitting fifteen minutes outside the town of Pinecrest, Connecticut in a snowbank.

Already, I am close enough to the city to see the twinkling of Christmas lights and the warm hues of goodness and cheer – it's disgusting.

It makes me long for the busy streets of New York where preparation for New Year's Eve has already begun, and the safe walls of my small two-bedroom apartment I share with an old friend from college.

Or rather... acquaintance considering the fact that she and I have hardly spent anything other than eight hours together in the apartment... when we are asleep.

I replay the last twenty minutes in my head, wondering how everything went so terribly wrong: I was driving along the empty, two-lane road, cleared of any ice or snow (hence the snowbanks) when out of nowhere, a turkey appeared in the middle of the road!

Even though Thanksgiving was a week ago, the wildlife in Pinecrest didn't seem to get the memo.

I was able to slow my car down before hitting the bird, assuming it would spook and move on.

It didn't.

While it has definitely been a few years since I last graced the winter wonderland of my hometown, I can't recall a time when a startled animal in the road *didn't* move. And yet, this turkey remained in the middle of the road, pacing back and forth between the two lanes.

Impatiently, I honked the horn.

I wasn't late to meet my parents, but I felt I had stayed away long enough to justify at least arriving on time.

The honking only seemed to anger the turkey, who stopped its pacing in front of my car and began circling me.

There was no moving forward, and no moving backwards, as the bird walked laps around my 2010 Sedan. Honking again only resulted in the turkey furiously pecking at my window and attempting to jump on my hood.

Having had enough, I decided backing up and going around the bird was the only way to solve the problem. So, I threw my car in reverse and began gradually backing up... until the turkey began to chase me.

Horrified by the sudden pursuit, I continued to drive in reverse, hoping it would give up.

As I glanced around me (I'm still unsure as to whether it was to cry for help or avoid a wreck) I let the wheel slip, and plowed rear-end-first into a wall of snow.

The turkey watched me triumphantly when I let out a cry of frustration and used my single bar of cell reception to pull up the number of the town mechanic. I didn't recognize the voice of the lady on the phone, but Debra seemed nice enough. Her lack of familiarity reminded me of the fact it's been nine years since I've been home.

When I texted my parents to let them know I'd be a few minutes late, my message was met with skepticism and cautious messages of concern. Quite frankly, I don't blame them. In the nine years I have lived in New York, I haven't come home since my sophomore year of college, and only twice have my parents visited me: once when I moved into my apartment, and then again for graduation.

Those isolated events aside, all other accomplishments, holidays, and anniversaries have been celebrated over FaceTime and phone calls, using my career as an excuse to stay away.

I don't think I ever truly meant to cut my parents out of my life, just the memories and feelings they brought with them. And as time passed, I began to wonder if I had somehow silently conveyed this, with my dwindling updates and increasingly shorter calls.

Next to no communication became the standard for our relationship, and no one seemed to care enough to change.

Despite this, the years of birthdays I've missed, and the calls I've dodged, this was one celebration I couldn't avoid.

* * *

As I continue to wait for the tow truck, I pull the wedding invitation off the dash. Running my fingers over the silver embossed words, I notice how they contrast against the smooth cream parchment. Tiny glittery snowflakes litter the invitation, making the names appear as if they are resting on a plush bed of snow:

RSVP for the union of Aiden Oliver Marshall and Rosalind Caroline Hart, the 29th of December.

I look now at the little serrated edges, rough from where I tore off the response section to mail back my reply:

Circle yes or no.

I shouldn't have said yes. I realize this now, sitting here in the snow.

Even though my brother and I talk more regularly than my parents and I do, I haven't even met his fiancé, who could never seem to get off work long enough for a trip upstate.

Surely, they wouldn't want me there to taint the day with my... "unpleasant demeanor" (some might say I am an acquired taste).

But I love my brother – he is the only one who couldn't accept my desire to disappear and insists on monthly calls – sometimes even visits to New York.

For one reason or another, he's been there for me. Reading over publishing contracts to make sure I get the best deal possible, constantly recommending new bars or clubs for me to go to in hopes I'll meet someone (in the off chance I would ever emerge from behind my laptop long enough to do so) and asking me about the books I'm reading just to make conversation.

And because I love him, I think maybe this whole revelry would be better without me.

I almost consider shoveling myself out of the snow so I can turn around and get back to New York before I ruin everything, but the bright red Chevy approaching stops me from moving.

I laugh under my breath at the abomination of Christmas cheer driving towards me: shining in a cheery red, white, and silver, it sports garland wrapped around varying parts of the truck and a wreath attached to the front grill.

I get out of my car, trying to escape the wall of snow I've trapped myself in, and wait for the truck to idle to a stop.

A tall man with broad shoulders gets out. The standard mechanic jumpsuit clings tightly to his body, showing off his strong arms and solid build – it makes me want to tug my beanie further down my head, suddenly self-conscious about the disheveled leggings and oversized sweater I snagged from the men's section of a department store during Black Friday sales.

I feel the snow squish beneath my boots and my cheeks redden at the stripey fleece socks peak out from the top of them. As he walks towards me, his bright blue eyes crinkle and he breaks into a blindingly white smile.

"Is that *the* Harper Marshall?! I don't believe it!"

The deep baritone voice startles me, almost as much as being recognized by the mechanic, but he is sweeping me up in a bear hug before I can recognize who this golden retriever of a human is.

I can feel the heat radiating throughout his body, and it makes me want to turn about 15 shades of red. When he sets me down, I manage to get a better look at him.

"Charlie Grant?"

He hears the confusion in my voice, and it only makes his smile broaden. His skin is a warm ivory, and the acne he had in high school has cleared up, replaced now with the beginnings of a beard.

"Yes ma'am! Wow, I didn't know you would be back in town. Come back for Aiden's wedding early?" He is eager to talk, and less than eager to acknowledge the bright blue car stuck in the snow.

"No, I just enjoy getting my car stuck in the snow on random highways this time of year." He seems shocked by my sarcasm. "You're a mechanic?" I try to change the subject, somewhat stammering and remembering I haven't seen this man in nearly a decade.

Charlie merely seems surprised at my question, as if for a moment he forgot.

"Indeed, I am," he says with a nod, "which means you probably want me to get to work on your car? Sorry for getting distracted, I am just *really* surprised to see you."

Sarcasm having failed I try for a different approach: honesty.

"What's so surprising about seeing me? I'm from this town, same as you." My voice teeters on biting, coming out more defensive than I mean for it too, but who does Charlie Grant think he is? Making assumptions about whether or not I should be back in town and when.

He shrugs his shoulders unfazed by all my attempts at keeping people at bay (which usually works).

"I mean, it's been what, nine years? Jeez, you look really great."

He says everything in one breath, shaking his head as if the very notion of life both excites and mystifies him.

I try to soften myself, having forgotten about the jarring friendliness and unnecessary politeness of people who live in small towns, and the fact that I used to be one of them.
I also choose to ignore his very blatant compliment (that is probably a lie), and gesture to the car behind us.

"Yeah, I got stuck in the snowbank and can't get out. I don't do much driving in New York, so I probably don't have the world's highest quality tires, and the roads are slick, so I guess I just slid into the bank."

Charlie's smile transforms into a mask of concentration as he begins surveying my car, suddenly a professional.

"How did you run the back end into the snow anyway?"

I debate making up an excuse before remembering a part of Charlie's "golden boy" personality also includes being a human lie detector.

I roll my eyes as I explain, "A turkey chased me down the road".

He quirks up an eyebrow before asking, "A turkey chased you... in reverse?"

I sigh not wanting to share my humiliation with anyone else, but he presses, "Come on, you know if I am going to give you a fair assessment of the situation, I need to know some context clues."

I think about giving him a context clue of my own, New York style, knowing what he's saying is not entirely true and he's just looking for something to give me a hard time about, but I also am beginning to suspect he won't help me until I tell him.

"There was a turkey in the road, and he wouldn't move, so I backed up to go around him and he started chasing me! While I was driving in reverse, I ran into the snowbank, and now I'm stuck."

Charlie busts out laughing, taking a few minutes to catch his breath.

"It's not funny!" I protest, "It's ridiculous actually!" My futile justification only makes him laugh harder.

"You mean to tell me, you haven't been home in, what? Ten years? And the minute you get within a 20-mile radius of Pinecrest you meet Terry?"

I shake my head in disbelief, not even bothering to correct his math.

"It has a name?!" I shout incredulously.

Charlie nods along as if this is the most logical explanation in the world. "Terry the Turkey. He's notorious for stopping traffic right outside of town. No one will claim him, and we don't know where he comes from, so we just leave him out here to terrify tourists."

Quietly I argue, "I'm not a tourist."

"But you definitely wouldn't say you're from Pinecrest either, would you?"

Something in Charlie's face catches me off guard, stopping me short. For once, I don't have a response. I can't tell if it's disappointment or anger written on his face, things I wouldn't have expected from him of all people.

It makes me want to return it with a look of disdain all my own.

I may not have the fancy black baggage or sleek designer shoes, but to small-minded townspeople like Charlie, I might as well be the villain in a Hallmark movie: the small-town girl who ran away to the city and forgot her roots (i.e., the worst kind of human - because who would want to ever leave Santa's village?).

After a beat of chilling silence, I ask if he will be able to help me, or if I should just begin my hike on foot.

"Though a tempting sight to see, I'll just hook you up to the tow truck and bring it to the shop. It'll be easier to assess any damage there."

He takes my nodding as compliance before getting back into his truck and backing it up, lining the hook and chain up with my bumper.

He moves with deft precision, connecting the vehicles, and when he's done, he guides me over to the passenger side of the truck and opens the door for me: a gentleman to his core.

"Your chariot, my lady".

* * * *

I study Charlie as we drive silently towards town: the same sandy blonde hair, only shorter; the same baby blue eyes only creased with time; the same athletic build, only possibly more muscular than he was at 18. Light-blonde stubble scatters his face.

All around, he looks older – like a picture diverged, then overlaid on top of one another: past and present colliding.

No wedding ring – and yet, his eyes hint at a long life, thoroughly lived by a young body. Sunspots from long summers, and tired creases from hardships I've never been told about.

It all makes me wonder what he's been up to since graduation.

In high school, Charlie was a three-sport varsity athlete, playing football, basketball, and baseball. He was also class president and close runner-up for prom king (he was beaten in a tie between my brother and a band kid).

Charlie and Aiden had been best friends since they were toddlers in Sunday school and remained nearly inseparable since. And because of this, Charlie practically lived at our house growing up, often bringing with him his mom and younger sisters.

Even as kids, people knew Aiden and Charlie were special.

That was the thing about growing up in a small town: everybody knew everybody, and everyone knew the "dynamic duo".

Light and dark, mischievous and good-natured, one wreaking havoc and the other following behind to clean up the mess.

Aiden was typically the schemer, and Charlie followed shortly behind to ensure maximum damage had been carried out.

They created chaos in class, serenading whichever cheerleader they were trying to go on a date with (an obsession started after they watched *10 Things I Hate About You*), getting their classmates to laugh, seeing who could sweet talk their way out of the most homework – and when they'd land themselves in detention, our teachers would good naturally harass them while the boys fulfilled their punishment with total compliance.

It had been frustrating growing up under their shadow, being known as "the little sister of the great Aiden Marshall".

They were the golden boys of Pinecrest High School, and I was merely the circle of light that flashes in the dark after you've stared at something far too bright for too long.

Which is why, despite the three of us being what most would consider "close" growing up, I cut almost all communication with Charlie after he graduated.

He was Aiden's best friend – not mine, and I assumed he didn't want his friend's weird little sister texting him after he moved.

They in turn made leaving easy for me.

Despite the frustration it often filled me with, I couldn't deny that Aiden and Charlie deserved every ounce of attention they received; they were both heavily involved in sports, clubs, and our youth group growing up, and were raised with nearly impeccable manners.

It was what made loving them easy as well.

That even if their star-like qualities were infuriating, there was still something that made you want to have at least one of them in your sky.

I had always assumed Charlie would follow in Aiden's footsteps: running with one of the sports scholarships I'm sure he was offered and using it as a one-way ticket out of this town (I know for a fact he at least had a chance to play baseball at Vanderbilt, with the charm to succeed in any career he could want). It's what Aiden did.

He went to law school and ended up working at a big firm in Chicago.

And yet, here Charlie is, driving me in his pickup truck like we are teenagers again, coming home from school.

"Penny for your thoughts?"

Charlie's voice breaks my reverie and I realize now not only have I been quiet for most of the ride, I've also been staring at him.

"Why are you the town mechanic?"

I don't hold back with Charlie. It's one of the perks of knowing someone your whole life: despite our time apart, he's no stranger - he's more like distant family.

"Because I like working with cars," he replies smartly.

I narrow my eyes at him, willing him to give me more detail.

"Then why work on cars in *Pinecrest*? You could go anywhere. You could have been *anything*."

He shrugs his shoulders as if the fact he's never left one of the smallest towns in the United States isn't a big deal.

"I did go somewhere; I just came back." He focuses harder on the road and tightens his grip on the wheel, indicating those are the only details I am getting for now. "How is the big city anyway? Everything you always dreamed of?"

"And more," I say.

He nods like he knows, and a part of me is beginning to think he does.

"You always did want to get out here; you weren't like the rest of us." He smiles wistfully as if recalling a fond memory, catching me off guard.

"What's that supposed to mean?"

Charlie pauses for a moment, the heat desperately trying to come out of the car vents is the only sound between us, harmonizing with the tires driving through slush.

I watch the buildings blur by as we enter Pinecrest, and I see absolutely nothing has changed since I left.

"You always talked about being a famous writer in some major city and that's exactly what you became. You worked hard in high school; you went to your dream school - you made it happen. Now you have five different books published, are topping every bestseller list, and you haven't looked back, which is more than the rest of us can say."

Charlie's knowledge of my life shocks me; I didn't think he ever paid me much attention. My silence causes him to glance at me: our eyes locking in a moment before I glance away.

"Don't be so surprised, I like keeping tabs on everyone," he says with a brief laugh.

There's a dancing Santa in the window of the general store, and a literal horse-drawn carriage passes us on the road (the horse's name is Karl, and his still being alive doesn't surprise me as much as it should).

"So, the rest of us? Does that mean everyone stuck around after high school?" I ask.

He rolls his shoulders and turns onto my street before answering.

He's not the only one allowed to change the subject.

"Pretty much. Kate and Matthew got married, have three kids, and moved into the old Andrews place. Sarah convinced Bethany to help her run a small bed and breakfast on the edge of town. Donovan helps his dad with the diner and will probably take over once Sammy retires. Margaret married a guy in the Navy, so they stop by when they can. Blake tried to make it as a country singer but moved home from Nashville about two years ago and helps run the radio tower. Your brother is an engaged lawyer in Chicago. I'm the town mechanic who still lives on his parent's property. And you're a successful novelist living in New York... that should cover it."

He rattles off names and I try and place them to memories from high school.

A flash of Matthew crowd-surfing at a football game emerges, and I see Bethany and Sarah performing a duet in the spring musical. I almost laugh at the image of Donovan pantsing Aiden at graduation. I close the door on my memories as Charlie pulls into my driveway, the truck comes to a slightly alarming, shudder, of a stop.

"What are you doing back in town anyways?" He asks me. I cock my head at the challenge in his tone.

"You guessed it earlier: I'm here for Aiden's wedding."

Charlie purses his lips while thinking. He's playing with me. It's what he's always done. Annoying the younger sibling is practically in the job description for "friend of the older sibling".

"No. If you were just here for Aiden's wedding then you could have waited at least two or three more weeks. Your brother's wedding is after Christmas."

I shift in the seat, attempting to make myself appear more aloof, busying myself with unbuckling to get out of the car.

"Yeah, I'm aware, but did you ever consider maybe I'd like to spend Christmas with my family for once?" I reply in a tone equally as patronizing as the tone he used with me.

"No."

There it is again, the completely disarming seriousness I never noticed before, or maybe just hadn't existed until now.

"Someone grew up honest," I tell him, wondering what happened to the mild-mannered, people-pleasing boy from our youth.

"You haven't wanted to spend a single holiday, let alone Christmas, with your family in over five years Harper. Why would you start now?" He pauses and I swear those crystal eyes see right through me as something comes together in his mind: "How's your next book coming along?"

I make another move to get out of the car, but he jumps out before I can even open the door. Suddenly he's holding the door for me with an extended hand, reminding me exactly where those manners are.

He helps me out of the truck and grabs my suitcase from the backseat, but I manage to beat him to my laptop bag, scooping it up from the passenger side where it had been resting at my feet.

"Thank you," I mumble as we walk towards the door.

He holds my luggage in one hand and knocks with the other, and I wonder if he will have completely forgotten about the subject of my next book by the time I'm inside, but of course, he hasn't, and he won't.

"You're here working on your next novel, aren't you?"

I brush a stray hair behind my ears while nodding. It's as I open my mouth to speak that the front door gets flung open.

There is a flurry of arms, hugs, shouts, and kisses on cheeks as my parents welcome me home.

I hear them praising Charlie and scolding me, and I feel the wagging tail of my parents' golden retriever Sleet, eager for the attention I'm getting at the moment.

"Oh, we are just so thankful for your help Charlie. Harper, what on earth happened?!"

Two sets of warm brown eyes are trained on me, crinkles creasing their faces as my mother looks up at me, worry painted clear on her face.

When my parents finally step back, I am able to really take them in for the first time in a while: my family has never been known for our height, but it feels like somehow my mom has shrank. Her hair is still a thick mousy brown bob, streaked through with silver, opposite to my dad, whose hair is nearly completely gone. A crown of gray curls alludes to the messy black mop I know my brother now wears, and weight crowds my father's midsection.

They've aged, and I didn't even know.

Charlie saves me from myself, answering for me when he realizes I'm too stunned to speak. "She got into a little tussle with Terry."

My father throws up his arms like Charlie did only moments ago as if this is the simplest thing in the world.

"Well, there's your problem! What were you thinking, picking a fight with Terry?" Ignoring the charming warmth in my father's eyes, I opt for going on the defense.

"I was thinking there is no such thing as a turkey named Terry who chases cars outside of town!"

"Well, you would know if you came home every once in a while." My mother says it quietly, but it still hits a nerve, reminding me of the bitter sting of one of the last times I came home... a time I try not to think about often.

Charlie clears his throat to break the building tension, and it makes me breathe a sigh of relief as my parents turn their focus back to him.

"Oh, we've been so rude! Do come in and warm up, Charlie dear," my mother offers, stepping out of the way for us to come into the house.

Charlie offers my mother a soft smile but politely declines. "I've got to get Harper's car back to the shop to see if the snowbank caused any damage. I can call you sometime next week to give you an update?"

Three pairs of eyes are trained on me with expectance as I agree to the arrangement, making me wonder if I've somehow agreed to more than just a phone call.

When Charlie begins to walk back towards his truck it dawns on me: he won't have a way to reach me after all this time.

"Hey, wait! Don't you need my number?" I shout. He turns around looking confused.

"Why? Has it changed since freshman year?"

"No," shrugging his shoulders he tells me he's good: he still has it saved from when we all first got phones in junior high.

"You still have my number?" I ask dumbfounded.

Breaking into a smile, he hauls himself into his truck, "Of course, Harper Marshall. Everyone needs to have a resident turkey chaser on speed dial."

I roll my eyes as he winks at me before pulling off, leaving me alone to face my parents.

I turn around to see them staring at Charlie dreamily, not even looking at me until his truck is out of sight and back on the main road.

I swear, it's like they don't already have a son of their own.

"Charlie is such a sweet boy," my mother says with a sigh. I blanch a little as she follows it with, "And you know he's still single, right?"

"And you know he's like a brother to me, right?!"

Another frustrated sigh escapes my mother as she tells me, "I wasn't suggesting anything, I was only letting you know. These are the types of things you would know if you called more often, or visited once in a while," the dog pawing at my leg stops me from responding.

If this is how my whole trip is going to be, I might have been better off staying in the snowbank.

A shiver races down my spine as I realize how cold and tired I am. I had to leave the city early this morning in order to make good time, and all I want now is to go inside.

"Can we go in the house?" I plead as gently as I can muster.

I don't want to fight with my mom, not now at least.

Without another word, she leads us into the house.

The scent of warm cinnamon and cardamon greet me, as I survey the old Marshall place.

Unlike my parents, it hasn't changed a bit in my absence.

The same old fading carpet lays across the floor beside the large rock fireplace, an eclectic collection of lamps acting as lighting in the living room, and the old wood floorboards still creak beneath my feet.

I watch Sleet lumber into his bed beside Dad's favorite chair and try to determine if there are any new titles on the ornate bookshelves covering the walls. Wincing, I see the shelf still proudly dedicated to me, my books lined up in a row next to a picture of me when I was eight.

The sounds of a kettle whistles from the kitchen, and I know it means it's time for my parents' "pre-dinner cup of tea". It's a tradition in the Marshall household, and one I took with me to New York, thoroughly disturbing every roommate I've ever had.

"Tea is ready," my mother's voice carries from the kitchen to the foyer, and my dad offers me a soft smile before disappearing into the kitchen.

"I think I'm going to go up to my room for a minute."

No one responds, except for Sleet, whose only acknowledgment is a gentle whine as he lays his head down in his bed.

I shake my head and begin to lug my suitcase up the stairs; as I walk, I survey the pictures lining the walls leading to mine and my brother's bedrooms.

One captures Charlie and Aiden in pre-school covered in paint. Another is Aiden and I playing in a pile of leaves. I remember Aiden getting his license, as I pass a picture of him in front of the DMV, and my first car wreck as I pass a picture of me smiling with a cast on. I laugh to myself when I see the three of us: Charlie, Aiden, and I all piled up in the living room watching a scary movie. Our eyes all glow red from the flash, and I have two sets of bunny ears from both boys.

Homecomings, proms, graduations, and holidays. Family picnics, Christmas cards, and beach vacations all hold a place on our walls.

What some would consider cluttered, my mother calls "high-quality decorating", and for the most part, I agree.

I've never been one to print out pictures or hang things on walls, but I don't blame my mom for doing so. It keeps the memories alive, so even if you don't appreciate it in the moment, you still have something to hold on to when it's all gone.

Stepping into my old bedroom feels like stepping into a time machine: so little has been altered since I left all those years ago.

But this seems to be the thing about Pinecrest, doesn't it?

Nothing changes. The houses, the photos, the boys. They remain in the same state you left them, no matter how long you're gone.

It does strike me that there isn't a speck of dust anywhere. My mom cleaned my room for me.

Something within me aches at the careful precision of her signature touch. It's the same skill she applies to picture placement, cookie decorating, and the town library she works at.

Swallowing hard, I set my suitcase by the edge of my bed and sit down.

The box springs still squeak and the quilt smells of childhood. Gently, I run my fingers over the marker stains, and lay my head on the pillow, sinking into the familiar shape my body made for 18 years. My eyes snap open as my phone buzzes in my pocket for the third time in an hour. Upon opening the screen, I see it: another email notification.

I want to close my eyes. To be absorbed by the ancient mattress, or eaten by Terry for dinner, or trapped in the car with Charlie who seems to know me all too well. He knew something was up.

Taking a deep breath, I steady myself, and brace for the inevitable.

It won't be a surprise because I already know what the email will say. Tapping on my agent's message, I begin to read:

Harper, I hope this is finding you well!

I was so happy to hear you were taking a trip to get away and write! Your voicemail made your remote little cabin out west sound so lovely.

I did want to remind you of your deadline: the publishing house is getting a little anxious, and there's only so much more I can do. They need a new novel before the year is up, so they can go ahead and start marketing.

Just something in your usual Harper style, I know you said you had a few chapters done already – maybe go ahead and send them on?

Best wishes,
Lauren Dales

The "few chapters" are just pages of me smashing the keyboard. And lately, the "Harper style" isn't coming too easily.

In fact, it's not coming at ALL.

And it hasn't for a while, but Lauren doesn't know that. Neither does my publishing house, or my roommate.

But Charlie Grant does.

He's right, I have writer's block. And if something doesn't change by New Years, then I am majorly screwed.

2

That night I sleep restlessly, anxiety keeping sugar plums from dancing in my head.

I'm not really sure how or when I got so far behind with my writing, but I do know at some point it just stopped.

The ideas that always used to come so easily, dissipated from my head like I had been yanked from a fog I didn't even know I'd spent my life walking in. The things that used to inspire me didn't anymore; no coffee shops, museums, or songs could bring back the ideas that used to plague me.

I used to beg for my mind to be silent, even for a moment, and now that I'm alone with myself, I hate the feeling.

So, when the invitation for Aiden's wedding came in the mail, an idea began to form: the first time I felt inspired to write was in this very bedroom. Maybe by coming back, I could find inspiration again, but so far, the only thing "inspiring" is how many cups of coffee I can drink while staring at the clock on the wall of our kitchen.

I didn't tell anyone I was coming to write. They don't need to know I, of all people, am at a loss for words.

I can picture Aiden and Charlie's mocking grins, just like they used to in high school when I'd hide out in my room, making worlds of my own, and they'd storm in after football practice.

They would yell and run around, and I would act frustrated because my "creative process" had been disturbed (my "creative process" consisted of me blasting a lot of Coldplay while I wore one of my dad's sweatshirts).

My mother wouldn't be thrilled to know I was here for work either, begrudging me the entire time to "be present with the family".

All the while, Lauren believes I've gone to a cabin out west to work on my already half-completed manuscript because I don't have the guts to admit I have been struggling.

Now, I find myself pacing the kitchen alone, killing time, grasping for any straws that might resemble ideas, while waiting for my brother, and his blushing bride-to-be, to get into town.

Aiden and Rose both live in Chicago but are taking a break from the busyness of the holidays to get married before New Year's.

How Aiden convinced his soon-to-be-wife to get married in the middle of nowhere, I'll never understand, but this place has always been special to him. From what I can tell through our phone calls, he comes home every chance he gets, and obviously still keeps in contact with Charlie.

I check my watch again, counting the hours in my head till I'm supposed to meet them at *Written Comfort,* our favorite coffee shop.

During my last phone call with Aiden, he explained to me this trip would be a brief one; just long enough for me to meet Rose and her bridesmaids, help them get settled in, and then head back to the city.

Rose is an up-and-coming interior designer, and apparently Christmas is an incredibly busy season – which is why the bridal party is coming early: to finish preparations for the wedding so Aiden and Rose can wrap up their work affairs.

Aiden and Rose will be back for Christmas Eve and will stay till their wedding. Then they'll jet off on their honeymoon.

I survey myself in the mirror once more, wiping some smeared mascara from under my eyes, and adjusting the collar of my sweater. I've never met Rose before, outside from hearing her soprano tone from the other side of the phone, and I want to make a good impression.

Even though I often come across as "callous", I've never had a sister before; in fact, I've hardly even had girlfriends. Instead, I've always settled for being surrounded by boys and sports teams.

It had never occurred to me that Aiden would ever really settle down with someone either. He was always on the move: adapting, changing, growing, chasing after whatever goal he set his eyes on. But now he's found his new goal: Rose.

I remember him calling me after his first date with her, telling me he had just met his wife. At the time I had thought he was being ridiculous; Aiden was always the type to fall hard and fast, get bored, and move on. He put his entire capacity for hard work and commitment towards becoming a partner at the law firm he works for, but something about Rose opened him up.

A week after their first date he bought the engagement ring, sending me a picture of the glimmering rock; I was proud of him for waiting till their six-month anniversary to pop the question.

I'd be lying if I said a part of me didn't envy my brother: how easy it all seemed to be for him – because deep down I suspect there will never be a ring on my hand.

Which is good, because it's not like I've ever wanted one...

* * * *

The scent of warm gingerbread cookies greets me as I enter the small brick building of *Written Comfort*.

I close my eyes and take a deep breath as the door jingles, allowing the scent of old books and nutmeg to wash over me, christening me with the smells of familiarity.

The warmth from the old-fashioned wood-burning stove thaws my fingers after the walk here: I firmly believe no matter how drastic the chill, *Written Comfort* can thaw just about any frozen heart… and fingers.

Opening my eyes, I take in the small second-hand book shop and smile at the young children gathered around the display case of desserts residing in the far corner of the café.

Edison bulbs illuminate the room and coffee hangs in the air, adding to the warmth of the atmosphere, and I run my fingers along the spines of a large bookcase sitting near the entrance. I pick up a copy of *Call of the Wild*, noting the scribbles in the margins of the old paperback – this is what I love about this place: every book has its own story.

Being one of the only coffee shops in town, as well as the only bookstore, I spent a lot of time here in my teenage years. It helped me realize a vanilla latte paired a lot better with a book than the boxes of apple juice my mom used to give me at the library did.

Aiden beckons to me from a plush blue velvet couch nestled against the wall, and beside him I see the person who must be Rose.

She is a stark contrast next to my brother, with his rich ebony curls and trimmed beard, standing somewhere around a lanky six feet (an unusual trait for a Marshall). His counterpart best resembles a sugar plum fairy, with nearly luminescent blonde hair and eyes the same stormy color as a winter sky before the first snow.

Her petite lips form a warm smile reminiscent of spring - something my brother and her have in common.

I feel my own smile break out as I walk over to them, Aiden standing to crush me in a hug. Rose follows with a surprisingly strong hug for such a small woman.

Once greetings have been exchanged and introductions made, we take our seats, me sitting opposite of them in a matching blue velvet chair to their couch.

Rose squeezes my hand, letting out a small squeal, "I am so happy to finally meet you, Harper! Aiden has told me so much about his brilliant little sister – I already feel like we will be best friends!"

If it were anyone else, I would assume she was lying through her teeth, but the look on her face is so genuine I know she means every word she says.

I feel a warmth deep inside, a comfort, knowing Aiden found her.

I squeeze her hand back, "While I don't know if brilliant is the best word to describe me, I am happy to finally put a face to the name. You have no idea how grateful I am to finally have a sister."

Aiden beams between us, watching. I can't help but laugh as I look at him: he's always been the brightest spot in our family, so full of laughter and warmth, and as he stares at Rose, the stupidest grin threatens to splinter his face in half: he's found his perfect match.

"It's good to see you Harper, it's been too long," he tells me.

I know Aiden is serious when he says this, it's been nearly six months since he was able to make his last visit.

"What have you been up to?" He asks, "How's the writing stuff going?"

I run a hand through my mousy blonde tresses debating how much to reveal to my brother. What was the last thing I told him?

"Um, it's going good. Just slow this time of year, nice to have a break," I offer.

Rose rolls her eyes, setting down the mug she's taken a sip from.

"I wish! It feels like everyone and their mother wants to either redecorate their homes for Christmas or sue somebody."

"Hey, nothing says "Happy Holidays" like "I'm taking you to court"," Aiden says laughing at his own joke.

"I swear, the longest we've seen each other since Thanksgiving was the flight over here," Rose nestles closer to Aiden as he kisses her on top of the head, and for a moment I feel like I'm intruding on something private. I smile at them before excusing myself to go order a drink.

I return a few minutes later, coffee in hand, counting cup five for the day. I can hear my doctor chastising me in the back of my mind about how I need to cut down on my caffeine consumption before it gets the best of me.

"So, the flight over here, how was it? Did you get settled in okay?" I ask.

Aiden's smile falters as he leans back onto the couch, wrapping his arm around Rose's shoulders.

"About that... we aren't getting settled," he hedges. I know the confusion is clear on my face because Rose adverts her eyes, suddenly fascinated by the foam atop her cappuccino.

"What do you mean you aren't getting settled? I knew you were leaving soon, but I thought you would at least be here a few days. And what about your bridesmaids, I thought they were supposed to be here to finalize everything for the wedding?"

It's Aiden's turn to inspect his lap, picking at a spot I know doesn't exist.

Rose wrings her hands as I look between the two, but the awkwardness and explanation are postponed by a familiar voice.

"Well look at this! If it's not my two favorite Marshall siblings, back under one roof!" Charlie sits in the chair to my right, grinning ear to ear like *we* are his Christmas present.

Aiden lets out a deep breath, obviously relieved at the sight of his best friend. "Charlie! It's good to see you, man!" He exclaims, "This is actually perfect; we needed to talk to both of you anyway."

"Both of us? What does that mean?" I press, hoping to finally get a straight answer. Charlie's smile doesn't falter for a moment as I pepper my brother with questions.

This is the way it's always been with our trio: I the inquisitor, Aiden the accused, and Charlie the jury.

"Hey, you must be Rose, it's a pleasure to meet you," Charlie says, shaking Rose's hand and asking about the flight over as I sit impatiently, awaiting an answer.

My leg begins to shake, growing tired of the pleasantries.

"Look, I'm sorry to break up this lovely meet and greet, but I'd still like to know what you needed to tell us," I ask. My voice comes out more brash than intended, but I am swimming laps in the anxiety pool wondering what is going on.

Rose offers me a sympathetic smile, causing a sinking feeling in my gut.

"So, as you know, the original plan was for my bridesmaids to come down with us today, get settled in, and leave them to finish off the details for the wedding," Charlie and I nod our heads in unison as she continues, "but there's been a bit of snag. My maid of honor came down with a bad case of chicken pox," I cut her off.

"Chicken pox? Is that even a thing anymore? Who gets chicken pox these days?!" Charlie laughs at my incredulity, while all Rose and Aiden can do is shrug their shoulders.

"I suppose so, but there's more. Two more of my bridesmaids have had problems come up with work, so they won't be able to make it till the day before the wedding, and my fourth bridesmaid went into labor, so she is completely out of the picture for the foreseeable future."

The chasm in my gut deepens.

"I'm sorry to hear about your bridal party, but where does that leave me and Charlie?" I ask cautiously – I don't like the direction this is going.

Aiden joins the conversation, adding, "As you might know, Charlie is my best man, and you're in town for the next month." I nod my head yes, as Rose takes back over.

"And when Aiden and I began talking about it, I thought, who better to join my bridal party, than my very own sister-in-law!" I know my smile is now completely gone. "Which would work perfectly since you and Charlie have known each other for so long, and obviously know Aiden well, and you aren't working right now!" I shake my head in disbelief, trying to protest against a losing argument.

"Rose, I would love to help you, but you and I just met. I won't know where to even start with helping you finalize your wedding."

She shakes her head, obviously learning from her fiancé's tactics in the courtroom.

"But that won't be a problem: there isn't anything *new* for you to do! All you have to do is make some choices we've already arranged!" Smiling broadly as if her plan is coming together, she presses on, "We have the venue lined up already, all you have to do is choose between some flower arrangements, pick a cake flavor, pick up a few last-minute items, and maybe polish off with some decorations. I don't want anything extravagant – I just want to marry your brother. Everything else is just extra, but the extra can't be done without some help."

I stammer a little, my mouth trying to work out a response.

"We'll do it," Charlie replies for the both of us.

I look at Charlie, wondering if he is joking... he is not.

His once smiling face is now covered in determination and sincerity as if he has been tasked with protecting the president of the United States.

"Really?!" Rose's face has broken into a blinding smile, and Aiden is biting his lip in anticipation.

"You guys really are the best!" Aiden exclaims. My brother shakes Charlie's hand as he and Rose stand, mentioning something about needing to see Mom and Dad, make their rounds, and drop off Christmas presents before their flight tomorrow morning.

Charlie and I stand as well, coffees in one hand and phones in the other, exchanging numbers with a girl I've met once, whose wedding I've now been tasked with planning.

"I don't know how I'll ever make it up to you, but this really does mean so much to me!" Rose hugs me once more, as Aiden pulls on his coat, and somehow, I can't help but feel as though I just got played.

As quickly as everything began, it ends, leaving Charlie and I surrounded by the stories from our childhood, looking to write the story of my family's future.

* * * *

Outside *Written Comfort* I take a few deep breaths to steady myself, trying to process everything.

Now, not only am I expected to pull a manuscript out of thin air by the New Year, but I'm also in charge of planning my brother's wedding. Or, at least, "parts of it".

"Don't you just *love* love?" Charlie has a soft smile on his face when he breathes in the fresh winter air as if he is tasting December for the first time.

I give him my dirtiest glare in response.

"Woah, I haven't seen that look since, what? Junior year Pre-Calc? Yes, it was definitely then. I borrowed your homework without asking first. You were *pissed*," he says with a laugh, sticking his hands in his pockets.

"No, you *cheated* off my homework without asking, and I was justifiably disgruntled," I argue, defending my past self.

"Disgruntled? What an interesting word to describe a high school-aged Harper, who was practically foaming at the mouth."

I contemplate the merits of screaming as my cheeks begin to warm.

"Can you stop talking about high school for five minutes?! Just take a second to realize what you've gotten us into!"

It's not fair to take out my stress and frustration on Charlie, but he's here, and he's looking like every golden boy, from every Hallmark movie ever, and it just seems so easy to chew him up and spit him out.

His smile hardly faltering only infuriates me more.

"What's your deal anyway Turkey Chaser? Is your new book giving you fits?"

I release another groan of frustration and an eye roll before storming away, my boots crunching the little piles of snow on the sidewalk as I stomp up main street.

I hear Charlie jogging to catch up with me before I see him by my side, this time looking legitimately concerned.

"Come on, I thought it would be fun for us. The times we did stuff together growing up were far and few between, but whenever they did happen, they were pretty epic! Besides, isn't it like every girl's dream to plan a wedding?"

"Not this girl's!" I practically shout.

I've stopped long enough to face Charlie, or really, glare up at him.

"And why is that?" He asks.

"Because I don't believe in happy endings!"

"I know," he replies calmly.

The understanding in his answer catches me off guard. Wordlessly, I stare at him panting, unsure of what to do now, with my argument swept out from under me.

"I know," he says again. His deep voice is tender, making something in me quake.

"You know?" I manage to stammer out with confusion.

Charlie steps back from me, breaking apart any confusing haze surrounding us.

"Yeah, I've read all your books, you have a tendency for the dark and morose."

I swallow hard and start walking again at a slower pace, Charlie matching me step for step.

Of course, he's read my books.

"I guess so."

"I mean, do any of your main characters make it to the end alive?" His question makes me laugh a little.

"For your information, Arthur happens to survive to the end of *The Pecking Order.*"

"Only after his family died in a car wreck!" It surprises me how well Charlie knows my work.

"It was poetic justice!"

"In what way?!" He demands with indignation.

We continue to bicker playfully as we walk down the street, debating the morality and supposed justice in each of my books. Finally, Charlie concedes.

"Fine, I suppose I shouldn't be fighting with the author of the book on the proper ending for a story, but seriously, why no happy endings?"

I shrug my shoulders, and I feel it, the same tightness in my chest I get every time I think about a "happy ending". The same seasick, rolling waves of fear that creep in whenever I consider changing my ending.

"Because happy endings aren't real."

Charlie looks at me like I've grown a third head, so I take a sip of coffee before preparing my defense.

"Look at the world around you," I say while gesturing to the street with a grimace, "Okay, so maybe not Pinecrest. New York for example: I walk around every day and see only a handful of the 80,000 men, women, and children who are homeless. All you have to do is open any kind of news app or turn on a TV, and you can see your fair share of war, disease, and famine."

Charlie doesn't make to immediately cut me off, so I continue, "People die every day from hunger, car wrecks, sickness, and every other kind of misfortune. Not to mention the day-to-day strings of bad luck people endure: lost keys, broken phones, failed assignments, and crappy internet connections. These happy endings where the guy gets the girl, and the shoe fits, and Shadow comes home just aren't real, and I sell people realities – not false promises."

I hate the small victory I feel when I see the stunned look on Charlie's face as if I've also told him I ate a basket of puppies for breakfast.

"First of all, wow. Lot to unpack there, going to put a pin in that and return to it in a moment. Second, how dare you bring up my favorite childhood movie like that! You know *Homeward Bound* has always given me chills!"

I can't help it; I laugh out loud at Charlie's pouting lip. We walk for a few minutes in silence, giving my evident pessimism a moment to set in. Finally, Charlie breaks the silence by asking, "What happened?"

He seems deeply troubled, thoughts tumbling around in his mind.

"You may not have been the most positive person, or "beam of sunshine" growing up, but the Harper I used to know was a dreamer. She tried to see a silver lining, even if the sky was filled with clouds."

I give him a long look, and I wonder if I could tell him the truth, tell him what really broke me, but I shake my head dismissing the idea.

"I don't know. I guess the city opened my eyes. I grew up."

"Growing up doesn't have to mean losing all faith in humanity though," he urges, "there may be a lot of dark in the world, but there are little bright spots too. Those are the things you have to look for, otherwise life can become pretty bleak."

I nod my head in compliance. I'm tired of debating the reality, or rather lack of, happy endings.

"Wise words Mr. Grant," I oblige, thinking we can move on, but he's not done yet. We've almost walked to my house when he begins again.

"Besides, with freedom, books, flowers, and the moon, who could not be happy?"

"Oscar Wilde had some equally wise words," I admit. Charlie shakes his head.

"No, not Oscar Wilde, Marjorie Grant. Come on, you have to remember my mom quoting that to us all the time growing up?"

I do remember.

His mom had that quote on at least three different plaques, scattered around their house. She even gave me a bracelet with the quote on it for my 15th birthday.

"I do remember. How is your mom anyway? It's been forever since I've seen her. I'd love to visit her sometime, catch up with her and the girls for old times' sake."

There he goes again, the closed-off look. I almost press this time, simply to know what has happened, and why no one has told me.

"She's good. They're good. The girls would appreciate it, I'm sure they'd love to see you."

Charlie's younger sisters Aria and Beckett would be in middle and high school by now.
I suppress a shudder at the realization that Marjorie would probably have aged as much as my parents – the evident passage of time in people is something I'm going to have to get used to.

"Great, I'll have to come by one day." He hesitantly smiles at my words as we approach my driveway.

"Sounds good, you can do that one day while we are out wedding planning and you're avoiding your writer's block." I punch him in the arm, and his smile turns downright wicked.

"Hey, you never mentioned why you read all of my books," I tell him. "I don't recall you being much of an avid reader in school. Is Charlie Grant secretly my number one fan?"

He shrugs his shoulders before leaning against my mailbox.

"What can I say? My mom made me do it. I actually started reading more a few years after graduation, got pretty into it, picked up your books for some unknown reason, and decided they weren't complete and total trash for a downtrodden weirdo."

He's poking fun at me now. I roll my eyes for what feels like the millionth time.

"Not downtrodden – just realistic. And only like half a weirdo." He rolls his eyes because he knows I will simply never let him win. "So, you guys have like some sort of book club?"

Charlie chews on the inside of his cheek mulling over the answer, "Something like that."

I nod in understanding. "Mysterious. Okay, I can get on board with a secret Grant family book club, especially if it means someone keeps buying my books."

Furrowing his eyebrows Charlie asks if I've been having trouble with sales.

"You know, this isn't something we have to get into right now. Thanks for the concern though." I begin to make my way up the driveway, ignoring the unintentional puppy dog eyes Charlie gives me.

"Harper wait," I turn around to see him fumbling for something to say, "Uh, your car will be ready soon."

I nod my head, assuming as much.

"Thanks, Charlie."

"So, I was wondering if you wanted to do the first thing for Aiden and Rose's wedding the same day? When you come to get your car, we can go after."

"Okay, sounds fine," I agree.

"Um... alright. I'll see you then." His sudden nervousness makes me want to giggle – what does Charlie Grant have to be nervous about around me? I can no longer suppress my smile when he kicks a pebble with his toe.

"See you soon, Charlie," I offer as means of escape.

He waves goodbye and begins walking away from the driveway, pausing again to turn back around.

"And Harper?" I raise my eyebrows in response.

"It's good to have you back."

3

Three more days of unfruitful, creative attempts pass before Charlie calls the house to not only let me know my car is ready, but we are scheduled to go to a cake tasting on Thursday as well.

I dread it, but I am being promised free food, so how terrible could it really be?

The night before the tasting, I text Rose and Aiden to determine their favorite flavors so I can be prepared in some capacity, and by lunchtime on Thursday I'm setting off for Charlie's shop to pick up my car.

A friendly-looking receptionist greets me in the office, calling down to the garage for Charlie. With a wink, she tells me he will be up in just a few minutes.

"Are you a friend of Mr. Grant's?"

My jaw almost falls to the floor at the mere notion of someone not immediately recognizing who I am, before remembering I hadn't been able to place her voice on the phone either.

"Um, yes, an old friend," I offer stiffly.

Debra smiles sweetly at me as if we are in on the same secret. Now what secret, I'll never know. With a glance around the office, I note a picture of her and what I assume are some grandchildren, hanging on the wall.

Seeing me eye the picture she says, "Matthew and Lizzie, they're nine and six - my son's kids," I smile and nod in response. "Do you have any of your own?" She asks.

Another jaw-dropping moment: no one has ever considered me the type to have kids before.

"Me? Oh no, I'm not married," I hurriedly explain. Debra nods understandingly.

"Where are you from, dear?" She now asks in a butterscotch-sweet tone.

The garage can't possibly be this far away.

"New York..." I think about Charlie's comment the other day: *"You wouldn't say you're from here though, would you?"* before amending my answer: "Well, technically here. I haven't lived here for a long time though."

"New York! How exciting!" Debra exclaims. "What do you do out in the big city?"

After telling her I'm a novelist, she asks if I've written anything she would know.

No, I assume she wouldn't have; something tells me my work isn't the type of thing sweet little grandmothers like to discuss over knitting club meetings.

"And how long have you and Mr. Grant been seeing each other? He never told me he had such a successful girlfriend."

Leave it to Mr. Charlie Grant himself to walk in right as she asks this, leaving my mouth gaping and face red.

"What did I miss?" He smiles hesitantly at Debra who melts in his presence (he always had a way with old people).

Growing up, Charlie was old people catnip.

Shockingly, I do not share this trait.

"Oh, nothing. Just getting to know Debra here," I manage to stammer out.

"You two have a lovely time now!" Debra calls out as she swivels her chair back to her computer and begins furiously typing as if her life depends on it.

Another smile and Charlie grabs his jacket from the coat stand before opening the door for me.

* * * *

"Did Debra just invite you to join her backwoods death cult while I was closing up shop?" Charlie asks abruptly, ten minutes into our car ride.

"What!?"

"I'm just trying to figure out what could have possibly happened while I was shutting everything down, to make you turn so many shades of red," he pauses, "and I've been trying to figure out how to join for like six months now, so an insider's advice would be appreciated."

I swat him on the arm, rolling my eyes. Charlie, however, finds himself hysterical, obviously having no change in humor since we were 15.

"There were no backwoods death cults sadly, although it would have made for some great research experience."

"Speaking of, ready to talk about that novel of yours yet?" He presses with a smile.

I shake my head nope and continue to rattle on about the pros and cons of joining in on occultic activities.

"On the one hand, you'd have your life pretty much mapped out for you. But on the other, you probably couldn't have a ton of contact with the outside world."

Charlie rolls his eyes at me, humoring my attempts at distracting him. I settle down as he flicks on the blinker, turning off the main road, to get to the best bakery in a 50-mile radius.

"Alright, well if you don't want to talk about it, it's fine. You can open up when you're ready." He says it like he's placating a stubborn toddler, which in many ways I suppose I can be. "What were you and Debra talking about though?"

Running a hand through my hair, I avoid his eyes while responding, wondering why I feel such embarrassment over something a dozen people tried to tease us about when we were growing up (because no one in this town believes a guy and girl can simply JUST be friends).

"You and I mostly. Where I'm from, what I do, how we know each other. She's a sweet lady, where'd she come from?"

Charlie tells me she moved here from Florida after retiring from a bank three years ago and couldn't live the retired life for too long before she asked if they were hiring at the mechanic. Now, she keeps the books, schedules appointments, and works reception – and takes a whole lot of stress off of Charlie.

"If you're nice enough, she'll give you a butterscotch candy from her purse," he adds.

I don't doubt that she would, I think as my laughter fills the car.

When we reach a comfortable silence, I turn on the radio, tuning it to a station I know we both liked growing up. We hum along for the rest of the car ride.

My humming softens as I listen to Charlie singing quietly and ever so wonderfully off-key.

Gosh, I forgot Mr. Hallmark can't sing to save his life.

And yet, there's something soothing in the confidence with which he warbles away, familiar in its strangled tone.

Relaxed, I trace a smile in the corner of the window with my pointer finger, where the heater has fogged up the glass. When I look over, I notice Charlie is smiling at me. It's infectious, and I can't help but smile back before glancing out the window again.

****

We reach *Sweet Treats* after another ten minutes in the car, and the smell of confectionery sugar greets us as we open the door.

Fluorescent lights hang from the ceiling, and the white walls are decorated with pictures from events the company has catered.

Sally comes out from behind the cupcake display case to run over and hug us as we walk in the door, and before my startled self can realize it, I hug her back.

Aiden, Charlie, and I spent many afternoons here when we weren't at *Written Comfort* (one of the downsides of growing up in a small town, is you're limited to how exactly you can spend your free time) and Sally viewed us all as her second family.

She had a son who was a few years behind us in school, so seeing the boys at football games was a regular thing.

If anyone in Pinecrest ever wanted a cake for a special occasion, they came to *Sweet Treats*, not just because it's one of the few gourmet bakeries in the area, but because it's the best.

Of course, if you were in need of a quick pick up and a bargain, then the generic sheet cake from the *Stop & Shop* would suffice, but for a wedding cake? You go see Sally. And I'm certain Aiden probably made some kind of blood oath to Sally after graduation: if he ever got married, he would come to her.

"How are you, sweet angels?! I haven't seen you in so long!" Sally squeezes me tight again before guiding us to the back where a table is set up for sampling.

"I'm good, just in town for Aiden's wedding then back to New York."

I think Charlie might grimace at my mention of going back to my real life, but I ignore it, in favor of trying to calm the sudden turning in my stomach at the sight of the white cakes and groomsmen toppers.

I smooth down the non-existent wrinkles in my sweater as I try to look anywhere other than the table Sally has so kindly decorated: rose petals and white lace, little china plates and fake wedding rings, hearts, and tiny brides held tightly by their groom.

This was meant for Aiden and Rose. This was meant for Aiden and Rose. This wasn't meant for me. Breathe.

I repeat the words over in my head, swallowing hard as I take my seat. Charlie smiles at me oblivious to my internal panic, slipping my jacket from my shoulders, and hanging it on my seat.

As I shift in my chair, Charlie and Sally shoot the breeze, talking about the previous football season, church, and the retirement party she is catering for Donny Jones.

"Okay, so when Aiden and Rose - such a lovely girl by the way – had their original consultation, they told me they wanted a tiered chiffon cake, with two layers, so I made you two some of our most popular flavors for the chiffon cakes, and thought you could sample it, and once you decide on a flavor, we can begin talking designs."

Sally then carries out the tray with cake slices, and a quick count tells me I only have to make it through five samples before I can leave.

The warmth of the ovens, with the scent of the sweet sugar; Charlie's closeness in the folding chair beside me, and Sally sitting across the heart-covered table is just too much, and I can feel sweat sliding down my back, making me wonder if it's too soon to ask for a glass of water.

I swallow hard, trying to still myself, and mentally recite the flavors I spent the morning trying to memorize: something mildly sweet, maybe with fruit.

I suppose Aiden and Rose want a little taste of summer for their winter wedding.

Charlie slides the first slice in front of me, before taking a delicate bite himself. I watch him chew, a satisfied look on his face, before mimicking him.

The coconut cream tastes like a solid lump in my mouth and I cough a little.

"Hey Sally, would it be possible for us to get a glass of water?" Charlie flashes her his golden boy grin before she disappears into the kitchen. I can hear the sink running and cast a hesitant glass at Charlie. "What is going on with you?" He stares me down hard, as if his eyes are capable of piercing into my brain and figuring out what thoughts are making me sick to my stomach.

"Nothing, I'm just not a big fan of the whole wedding cake thing."

"No happy endings AND no wedding cake? Who hurt you?" He says, horrified.

"The tiny grooms: they offend me. I feel like there isn't enough representation in the cake topper community." He rolls his eyes at my self-satisfied smile.

"Seriously, are you okay?" He asks, eyes searching mine for an answer. I try to brush him off with dismissive affirmation, but he presses: "I can't help you, if you don't let me, Harper."

When he tries to soothingly stroke my knee, I push his hand off.

"I know, but I never said I wanted your help."

Charlie doesn't say anything, he merely resigns himself with a nod, acting as if no words were ever exchanged, as Sally returns with two tall glasses of water.

I take a long sip, wishing it were possible to fast forward through this whole trip: the new novel, the wedding, my bonding time with Charlie. I wish I could just go back to New York, and act like this was all a strange dream about turkeys.

A bite of classic vanilla is plain and pleasing to my palette. Strawberry is too sweet.

German chocolate serves as a cure for any kind of chocolate craving one could have, but Aiden has never been a chocolate lover. Lemon finishes off the sampling with a refreshing twist, and I wonder if it's possible to grow tired of eating cake.

Marie Antoinette mocks me in the back of my mind.

"'Let them eat cake', said no one ever," Charlie declares. I do a double take wondering if maybe I said something out loud.

A timer dings from somewhere inside the kitchen, and Sally instantly brightens as Charlie and I rub our stomachs.

"Do you think you have room for one more slice?"

We exchange a hesitant glance, and my stomach mimics a whale, attempting to process all the sugar I just consumed. Charlie reads this expression, and all I can do is watch in horror as his grin turns devilish.

"Absolutely! What did you have in mind?"

Sally claps excitedly before running back into the kitchen, leaving me with the urge to punch Charlie in his perfect face.

I suppress a laugh, thinking of a time when we were little when I did just that.

"What are you thinking about?" He asks, noting my expression.

"Oh nothing,' I say with a happy sigh, 'Just the good old days".

Charlie nods, clearly confused, when Sally emerges from the kitchen carrying a cake.

My mouth goes dry staring at the two-tiered masterpiece, coated in a light dusting of powdered sugar and candy snowflakes, a winter-themed bride and groom top it, surrounded by white chocolate hearts.

It smells of fresh spices and gingerbread, and the saccharine scent of oranges and cream cheese icing.

It is wintertime love on display, and I'm worried I might puke all over it.

"I'm sorry, I just need some air," I gasp before shoving back my seat. It scrapes against the linoleum eliciting a screech as I rush for the door at the front of the store.

The heels of my boots click against the floor, echoing through the silent building, only broken up by the bell above the door jingling as I burst into the crisp mid-day sunlight.

As the door closes behind me, I hold my hands behind my head taking long, deep breaths.

I will not be sick. This is not about me. This is not about me.

I close my eyes, counting to ten, ignoring the bell on the door ringing behind me.

"What is wrong with you?!" Charlie demands, "I'm serious this time, Harper. Enough of this beating around the bush - I want to know why you can't seem to manage to sit through a cake tasting."

I turn around slowly, seeing Charlie's steely blue eyes pinning me to where I stand.

"I told you, it's just hard to get behind something you don't believe in."

"What marriage? Happy endings? Your own brother's happiness?" He fires off at me, "I thought surely, you of all people, could put aside your own *selfish* discomfort to help somebody out."

"I can!" I whine, sounding like the child I am.

"Can you? Because so far, I haven't seen it."

His words come out bold and unafraid, premeditated words he has thought about before.

"You wouldn't understand," I try to tell him.

"I wouldn't?" He says, his voice filled with fire, "Well, I don't know how they do things in New York, and you know it may just be the "small-town bumpkin" in me, but in Pinecrest we don't dramatically run out of bakeries every time we are faced with an issue we don't like, we don't leave home and never look back, and we help out our brothers when they ask. But I guess you've forgotten all about that haven't you?"

My response gets caught in my throat, threatening to rip its way out, and I almost let it, if only to know what my mouth can't seem to say.

Charlie's words strike me like a blow, causing tears to prick in my eyes.

He's said all the things I've thought since the moment I came home: that this town is too small, that I've been gone for too long to be brought back – that deep in my core, I'm selfish.

Charlie's face softens while I try to push the tears back, blinking my lashes rapidly. He doesn't say a word as he waits for me to compose myself.

Patient Charlie. Always so kind, even when angry. Even when arrogant, or wrong, or right, he's patient. I take a shaky breath before stammering out.

"You wouldn't understand what it's like to be surrounded by reminders of the happy ending you don't have: a constant reminder of the things you don't believe in, and can't believe in, because the world hurt you too many times – some wounds just can't be healed."

For a moment, nothing happens.
And then: he snaps.
He shuts down.

He gives me the same look he wore in the truck when I first arrived, and I wonder what is going on inside his mind: the mind I used to think I could read like an open book, or at least a skimmed-over cover.

"Get in the truck."

His voice is cold, despite the look of complete brokenness fracturing his eyes.

"What?"

"*Get in the truck*," he commands, his voice deathly quiet – like it's taking all of his willpower not to explode.

He casts a glance back at the bakery before reaching into his pocket to toss me the keys.

"Get in the truck and start it, while I let Sally know we will be taking the coconut cake. You said you wanted to see my mom, didn't you?"

I nod my head yes before he continues.

"Okay then, I think it's time to pay Mama Grant a visit."

I don't protest as he walks back in the store, leaving me alone in the parking lot.

* * * *

An uneasy feeling settles on me as we drive around the outskirts of town in silence. This isn't the way to Charlie's house.

"Taking me to be the next sacrifice for Debra's death cult?" I offer. He offers me a weak smile in response to my joke. "I thought we were going to see your mom?"

"We are," he says, his grip shifting on the wheel.

I don't remember Aiden ever mentioning the Grants moved, but I guess it's possible.

He flips the blinker up, driving even further from the main road, toward the Old Chapel.

Its fellowship hall had burned down in '79, and they didn't have enough funds to rebuild, so the congregation moved to the newer church in the town square, leaving the Old Chapel sanctuary for events: funerals, weddings, and baptisms if people so wished.

"You never mentioned moving?" I ask cautiously, treading the thin ice of this conversation like one trying to traverse a frozen lake: not knowing how far out you can step before the ground gives way.

"We didn't," he replies softly. The knot in my stomach twists tighter as Charlie pulls into the parking lot of the dilapidated building.

It's quaint in a pretty-abandoned-building sort of way, with its patchy paint job and ivy vines. A thin layer of snow coats the cemetery in the back, never being cleared of the fresh winter powder.

The vision of Marjorie picking up some part-time work briefly crosses my mind before I realize that if she needed a job, she would be at the library with my mom.

When Charlie puts the car in park, I make no move to get out, and neither does he.

He turns the truck off.

My mind can't process what's happening, why we are here, and what he is trying to say.

I search his face, trying to read the inscrutable look he wears.

The thing about Charlie Grant is he hides his feelings just as easily as he wears them. Or at least, he used to.

He was either an open book, or he was breaking inside, and you would never know the difference till he wanted you to.

Always opting for honesty, I've never seen him try and hide something from anyone until now.

After a shake of his head and a quick breath, he opens the door, coming around to open mine.

A dozen jokes about ax murders flit through my mind, but they all die on my lips when I lock eyes with Charlie. I feel the inner turmoil radiating off him; torn between letting me in and blocking me out.

"Let's go," his voice is barely above a whisper as he offers me his hand.

I take it, closing the truck door behind me, letting him guide me towards the cemetery.

We walk an invisible path in the snow, a trail of footsteps long since buried, but memorized in Charlie's head. He tightens his grip on my hand, and I feel the callouses on his fingers, knowing we are both desperate for comfort from whatever we are about to face.

My mind feels static, like snowfall, or a blizzard, or blinding bright light, so I focus on the feeling of Charlie's hand in mine.

It's the hand I held a dozen times crossing the road as a little girl, during prayers before supper, getting out of trucks, out of fear in the dark: hands I know.

They're different now than when we were kids; harder and stronger, stained with oil from cars I've never seen, but familiar all the same. The shape, the fit, his fingers against mine; they are something I've always known.

A memory flashes through my mind of middle school. When I was a scared little sixth grader, and Charlie and Aiden were fearless eighth graders and we all made a pact: no matter what was going on around us, all we had to do was grab the other's hand, squeeze it twice, and we would know we were going to be okay.

I would find the boys after tests gone wrong, or mean girls in the hallway, and I would see them grab for each other after lost games and fights with fathers.

I always knew it wasn't for them, so much as it was for me, but they did it anyway because they were my self-appointed protectors.

No matter how much we fought, how long we stayed apart, regardless of the distance – we were going to be there for each other.

Or at least, we were supposed to be before I cut everyone out.

Now, winding through headstones, I squeeze Charlie's hand twice: strong and hard, trying to protect him from the inevitable evil of the world I failed to see.

He stops in front of a headstone towards the corner of the cemetery where the newer graves are located. Atop it, sits an angel, and below it, an inscription telling of: *Marjorie Grant, beloved wife, mother, and friend, may she rest in peace.*

We don't say anything for a while. We just stand there in silence, letting it sink in.

At some point, Charlie drops my hand.

I try to wrap my mind around it, try to connect the image of my friend, so alive and full of life, who often baked me cookies after school, and recommended books for me, to the body six feet underground.

Charlie snaps out of his trance, crouching down closer to the earth.

"Hey Mama, you'll never guess who finally came to see you." He looks over his shoulder at me, and I see the wistful look in his eyes. I mimic him, crouching down so I'm eye level with the headstone, and I feel a tear trickle down my cheek. I wipe it away and try to muster up a smile for the woman who used to be like a second mom to me.

"Hey, Mrs. Grant. I'm sorry it took me so long to get back here. I never knew... *I never knew*. How did I never know?"

I'm not asking Charlie so much as I'm asking the world, and my family, and myself.

I should have known something was wrong when she stopped getting brought up in conversations, but then again, I stopped asking.

I got so caught up in myself that I never stopped to consider that even though people stay the same in our memories, time still passes outside of us.

Charlie tells his mom about the girls and how their dance class is going (they're apparently in the annual Christmas recital). He tells her about Aiden's wedding too and lets me talk about Rose.

"You would really like her. She's sweet, smart, incredibly pretty, and I'm sure she has to have the patience of a saint to put up with Aiden."

Charlie laughs at that.

"She and I are going to be friends Mrs. Grant. You would be really proud of that, wouldn't you? I never had many friends in school you know, but I want to make things right this time," I confess.

Charlie tells her about work, and how things are going at the shop – I learn that he's apparently a part of the PTO at the high school and they've begun plans for the school dance.

I try to stifle the stream of tears pouring down my cheeks, but as Charlie settles back in the grass taking a seat, I know it's okay for me to cry.

"The craziest thing lately Mama, has got to be this newfound attitude of Harper's," the joking is evident in his tone as he talks to the headstone like we are merely sitting down for coffee with his mom. "I mean, she goes to the big city for a few years and seems to think she's hot stuff. You would have a good time setting her straight. At least she hasn't gone and covered herself in tattoos or something crazy – she's still our Harper deep down."

Another lump forms in my throat, and I know my nose is running, but I can't fight it anymore. A sob escapes past my lips, and a tear streaks Charlie's face.

I stammer out apologies to Charlie amidst my gasping cries, because this shouldn't be about me, but as he moves closer to me, holding me to his side, I know that Charlie Grant would hold the crumbling pieces of my world together if I so much as asked.

He could put Atlas to shame.

After so many gasps and sobs, I don't know who I'm apologizing to anymore, I just know my friend is gone.

My friend is gone, and I'm left here with her son, who was my friend that I've now neglected for years, and I'm ruining his shirt with my tears.

He runs a soothing hand down my hair, over my back; tries to comfort me while I know he's hurting, and all I can do is hug him a little harder.

At some point, I manage to run out of tears, and I apologize for how selfish I've been.

"It's okay. You didn't know," he says shaking his head.

I nod my head in agreement, but I couldn't disagree more.

How did I get so far from who I once was?

How did I not know?

"How did it happen?" I manage to whisper the inevitable question I'm not entirely sure I want the answer to.

Charlie sits up straighter, and his hand falls from my shoulder to the ground. A winter chill blows across the cemetery, and I wipe my face again, no longer caring whether my face is red and splotchy, or my eyes bloodshot.

"I did go away to college you know... I got a baseball scholarship to play at Vanderbilt. Nashville may not have been New York, but it was still a lot more city than Pinecrest, and I loved it."

He sighs, his mind heavy with memories, "I started dating a nice girl my sophomore year, I made new friends, I visited Aiden in Chicago on breaks, or I'd come back home and visit. I loved playing college ball; I was *good* at it. Maybe even major league good. I managed to catch the eyes of a few scouts, and we started talking about my future. I was getting a degree in business marketing with zero plans on using it, but junior year things changed."

It never occurred to me that Charlie might have had a life like mine.

I always knew he was meant for more, but I never thought he would take the chance and chase the life I lead.

Be a pro-baseball player and have a beautiful girlfriend, and friends to go with it.

"Mom started talking about some pain in her feet, and we didn't think anything of it," he continues. "She was always chasing after us anyway, pain was expected, and arthritis runs in her family."

Charlie swallows hard, trying to keep the emotion out of his voice as he tells me, "The pain began spreading to her knees; she said it was like a dull ache – like she could feel her body weakening. Then her fingers would go through these stages of just *numbness*. She said it was like her muscles weren't working right."

He loosens a long breath as he swallows again, trying to force the words out of himself.

"If we had listened to her sooner then maybe there would have been something we could have done."

A few tears slip out his eyes, but I don't move. I fear any sudden movement might make him stop, make him retreat into himself in the way he does, try and shield me from the harsh reality of his world like I'm a kid again.

"The doctors diagnosed her with Lou Gehrig's disease towards the end of my junior year.

She put a brave face on for us, but Dad and I knew the truth. There's no treatment for ALS: it's a terminal illness. It's just a slow and painful death, and the worst part is you don't know how long the pain will last."

I watch him rake a hand through his hair, trying to erase the memories.

"I spent my summer going back and forth between training for baseball and caring for her, but Harper... she declined *so* fast. Or at least July was the first of several declines. We didn't know, didn't have a clue what we were doing or supposed to be doing, I just knew my time with my mom was limited. So, I dropped out. I quit the team, canceled my courses, and came home to care for her."

"What did your dad do?" I ask.

Growing up, Charlie's dad never would have won an award for parenthood.

He worked long hours, he was short with his kids, and he liked alcohol just a little too much. Never anything abusive, but certainly not the model parent, always walking the thin line of life's vices.

I suppose that was why Charlie was so close with his mom, and why they were always at our house.

In the duration of time I have known Charlie, I've actually only seen the inside of his house four times, one of which was interrupted by a fight between his parents.

Now, I realize, the reason Charlie became the man he is was most likely because of that: do the opposite of everything his dad did, take care of your family, be a model citizen, and show up for people.

"He actually turned over a new leaf, as shocking as that is," Charlie admits. "He stopped drinking, backed off on his hours at work, and really tried to be there for Aria and Bex. Which left me to care for Mom."

Charlie leans back on his hands, replaying the last few years of his life in his head: "Around the start of senior year my girlfriend dumped me: she couldn't handle the constant back and forth between Pinecrest and Nashville, and she decided I came with just a little too much baggage. Or maybe it was the fact I wasn't going to be a major league baseball player anymore that really turned her off. I didn't exactly have time to dwell on it."

Charlie readjusts, taking to ripping little handfuls of grass from the frozen ground like he can't get comfortable with the words coming out of him, and I feel a flush of anger at this girl I will never know for leaving him when he needed someone the most.

Just like I left them...

"How come no one ever said anything to me? I could have helped," I say. Charlie's smile is rueful as he shakes his head.

"Help with what? Watching my mother fade slowly? Listening to my dad cry himself to sleep? You couldn't have helped. This disease isn't like that."

He's not angry with me, he's just sad, and I can feel my heart shattering for him.

I want to pick up the little broken bits and hand them to him, give them as an offering for all the ways I've failed; use my brokenness to patch all the little holes in him.

Charlie Grant is my friend, and he deserved more than this.

"No one told you, Harper, because *I* asked them not to." His words stun me, but he continues: "My mom's final request was that you not see her like that... all she said was that she didn't want to take you away from the life you loved. That it was easier that way. And you remember how insistent my mom could be."

Despite all the words I have learned in my life, all the sentences constructed, it seems now I can't think of a single one to say to understand *why* Marjorie would want me to stay gone, even if I had been busy, so Charlie continues.

"She declined significantly four more times after that summer, each time losing the ability to do something else. It's weird the way the disease works, there's no rhyme or reason to the way it takes over and breaks you down. The doctors gave us a rough timeline when she was first diagnosed, based on the progression of the disease when we found it, so we knew we were living on borrowed time."

Finally, Charlie settles into crossing his legs, his hands in his lap as he finishes his story: "By Christmas, she was on hospice, and come spring she was gone. She actually made it a month and a half longer than predicted."

"She always was a fighter, wasn't she?"

He nods. "She was."

Charlie squeezes my hand when he sees me staring at the headstone.

"Don't feel guilty, Harper. She passed peacefully on a concoction of sleep and medication, surrounded by her friends and family, knowing my dad had come back to us and we were going to be okay."

I bite my lip in concentration, wishing I had been one of the people to surround her.

"There was one thing that always helped her get through the tough days though," he says.

"What?"

"Your books."

He says this like it's a logical answer, but I can't help but stare at him incredulously as I reply, "My books?! My books are one of the most depressing things anyone can possibly read!"

A small laugh escapes him as he smiles.

"Yeah, but they were *you*. Morbid, depressing, and lacking happy endings, they were still your voice and your words. It was our way of having you with us."

I can't believe it.

"So that's why you read all my books?" I ask.

He nods again. "Yeah, Mom was pretty insistent on me reading them to her, and when she passed, I kept it up. I like having a direct outlet to my family, whether they know it or not."

It's all beginning to make sense now. All the weird side-stepping and beating around the bush in conversations, the reading of my books, the anger from my mom about never coming home; it all makes sense.

What doesn't make sense is why Charlie would show me this now.

"Why didn't anyone tell me, Charlie? Why was I the last person to know?"

"Like I told you: Mom's orders," he shrugs, "None of us understood it. We begged and pleaded to call you, and I should have. I should have done it anyway, just so you could say goodbye the way we were able to. But I don't know... she was so insistent; how could we not listen to her final request: "No telling Harper till she comes home"?"

It's not the answer I want, not even close, and it leaves me with more questions than actual answers, but it's what I get for now. And it's maybe what I'll get for always.

Charlie takes my silence as permission to continue, "I know there's bad in the world because I've seen it. But I've seen the good, too. You can't appreciate one without the other, and I just felt like you forgot." His eyes search mine like they're looking for forgiveness for all he's said.

"You deserved to know this; I just hadn't planned on telling you today. I would have gone about it differently, cushioned things a little more, but this just seemed like the right time," he concludes.

I nod my head in understanding.

"How can you believe in happy endings still, after all that?" I ask when I've mustered up enough courage to get the words out.

"Because of my mom's smile. Because of my sisters' resilience. Because of my dad's sobriety. Because despite every way we fell apart, we still ended up together, and sure, we are a little more broken than when we started, but I wouldn't change it for the world."

So simple, and yet so profound.

Charlie continues, "Everyone kept saying 'the Lord has a plan for this' once mom got sick. I don't know if that's entirely true - if it was the Lord's will my mom died early of a terminal illness. Or at least, I'm not sure *why* that would be His plan. I just think the Lord takes a mess the devil makes and creates something beautiful with it. Or maybe, it was a part of His plan all along, because He knows so much more than we ever will. His goodness is greater than the evil in the world. He will always triumph over the brokenness and help us heal, and Mom made sure we knew that when she walked out her life with such grace and peace."

He looks so much wiser than his years, his eyes now fixed on a point in the distance.

"It may have been the Lord's plan for my mom to be a testament to living your life well because you aren't promised tomorrow, but it has never been His plan for defeated, suffering, and broken to become a place we stay."

We are broken, but we are still beautiful.

I see flashes in my mind of sermons telling me the same message: no matter how broken we may seem; the Lord still does something with our brokenness.

I just always believed I was too broken for that to be my story.

"I want to write a happy ending."

The confession is coming out of my mouth before I realize it, and I wonder if more tears will follow.

"You what?"

"I want to write a happy ending and I don't know how."

There it is. The words I've been dying to say, lifting some of the weight off my chest.
A crack in my ever-constant armor, like removing my helmet or laying down a sword.

Charlie looks exceptionally confused, positioning himself on the ground so he can face me. "What do you mean?"

I sigh before crossing my legs beneath me.

"You're right. I'm supposed to be here writing a new book, and I can't. I can't write another *sad* ending, not when the world is so full of it. Your mom deserved a happy ending Charlie, *you* deserve a happy ending. My agent expects another "classic Harper heartbreak", but I don't think I can do it. So, I want to write a happy ending, I have to try. I just don't know how."

"I'm going to help you."

An arched eyebrow is my response.

"Seriously, I'm going to show you the world is full of happy endings, and you're going to help me plan this wedding."

He says it with conviction, fully resolute: fully Charlie.

There's a spark igniting in his eyes, just like they would before a game in high school. I imagine Aiden is here starting a chant, and I want to join in the battle cry.

"Okay."

It's not quite a battle cry, or even a cheer, but it's me: fully Harper.

I will no longer stand on the sidelines, I'm going to try and be the cheerleader I looked down upon in high school, for everyone I've failed along the way.

And Charlie is going to help me do it.

4

I don't know how long we stay in the cemetery, Charlie and I, telling stories about his mom and the years I missed, but I know that when the sun goes down, he gives me his hand and guides me out of the darkness.

I run a finger along the bend of his hand as he opens the car door for me, and I realize how comforting his callouses are. He gives me a small smile and a quick squeeze before shutting my door.

We ride in silence to my house, and I don't even bother asking about my car when we pull into the driveway. I can stop by tomorrow and get it, or the next day, or the next, because it seems my stay in Pinecrest is going to be exactly as long as I was planning for it to be.

I wave goodbye to Charlie and try to ease my way into the house, but it's no use: Sleet has already bounded out of his bed to me, greeting me with a soft whine.

I clamp my hand over his muzzle, hoping to stop an impending bark, but I give up when I recognize the sound of my mom's rocker by the fire. Red begins to creep over my face as she continues rocking in silence.

I feel like a child who has been caught sneaking out, and I begin to wonder if there's a chance the stairs block a view of my body when my mother begins to speak.

"Sally called me today. Said you had quite a scene at the bakery," the tone of my mother's voice is inscrutable as she pushes back and forth in her chair.

Rock, rock, rock.

"Um, yeah, I guess so. I apologized to her - don't worry."

Rock, rock, rock.

She rests her teacup on a plate and the fireplace crackles.

"Harper... are we really going to do this again?" She asks me, sounding weary before anything has truly begun.

In the amber glow of the fire, the flames cast dancing shadows along the wall, sending me back to a time before things fell apart:

I am home for Thanksgiving break during my sophomore year of college, and to put it plainly - it had been a hard semester.

I don't tell my family this though.

In fact, I haven't said much of anything the entire time I've been here.

What is there to say that won't disappoint my parents?

With Aiden showing out, getting into every law school he applied to, while still remaining the perfect son who manages to visit home as often as possible, I feel like the greatest letdown possible: the child simply trying to pass her creative writing courses who hasn't been home until this break. The child making choices that her parents would consider less than desirable.

My parents were skeptical enough about letting me major in English, but now I've taken it a step further and started to flounder.

How much do my parents really need to know?

What can they truly do to make it better?

I'll be fine. I'll figure it out. There's no need to worry them or let them try and convince me to come home or switch majors.

I can do this. I will do this.

For every ounce of me that has been broken apart by these courses, I know they have to be doing something.
They have to be making me a better writer.
They have to be getting me closer to my goal, right?
That's why we do this: artists suffer for their art. That's what all my friends say at least.
And my parents won't understand that.

"Harper, what is going on?" My mother asks me one night, sitting in her rocker.

I had asked to stay home from the library today to work on my writing instead of helping her set up for the upcoming events at the library – something that once upon a time, would have been an out-of-character choice.

"I don't know what you're talking about," I tell her.

She purses her lips, trying to maintain composure despite not believing me.

"You stayed in all day writing – that's not usual for you."

"You don't know what's usual for me anymore," I quip back.

I'm not sure whether or not I mean for my tone to sound so disrespectful, but my mother looks shocked.

"Excuse me? There is no need to take that tone with me, young lady," my mother's brows furrow in concern, which is potentially more infuriating than had she just gotten mad at me.

"Harper, if something is going on in New York then we can talk about it – you don't have to stay there if you don't want to – you know that."

"I know that you've been trying to get me to quit pursuing my dream since I told you I wanted to be a writer," I reply gruffly, standing up from the couch and staring down at my mother.

She laughs, "That's very funny, now are you ready to talk about what's going on? You're not acting like yourself, and your father and I are just concerned."

Concerned.

I think that's the word that makes something in me snap.

Because no matter how well-intentioned my mother's "concern" is, all it feels like is another person telling me that I can't do this.

Another person telling me I'm not good enough.

And after nearly two years of bottling up the hurt that rejection has built in me, her words uncork it.

"Well maybe try being less concerned about me from now on if it's such a burden to you!"

Standing, my mom tries her best to remain composed, convinced that this is just me avoiding some deeper issue.

Some issue that is none of her business to know.

What does she know about art or what it takes to be an artist?

"Harper, I am going to give you the chance to apologize, sit back down, and have a civilized conversation about why you're acting this way, or you can go to your room."

I feel a fire lit inside me in the most destructive way possible. I want to burn this house to the ground; I want to turn this whole town to ash to get this hurting out.

But instead, I tell my mother, "Why don't I just go back to New York and make everyone's life a whole lot easier? You all seemed to have much more peaceful lives before I came back."

She scoffs, "It certainly was more peaceful before you decided to pick up this attitude, but I know it's because there's something you're not telling me."

"So, what if I am? Since when is it your business to know everything I do."

I feel like an animal backed into a corner – the only thing I can do is bite.

I can see my mother slowly coming unraveled, as she tells me, "As your mother AND the one that pays your tuition, it actually is my business to know when there's something wrong with my daughter."

I pause trying to think through my words, trying to figure out what I can say that will get her to leave me alone; to stop pressing me to talk about what I'd rather keep inside.

"You know what the great thing about New York is?" *I spit at her.*

"What?" *She says, crossing her arms, as if she thinks we are going to make progress.*

"You weren't there."

She looks as if I slapped her.

"Oh really? Well, if you love your independence so much, why don't you have it? If you don't get this attitude back in check come morning, you will not see another dime of that tuition money and we will move your butt back home, or you can pay for school yourself."

There's no way she can mean that.

I wanted her to stop trying to fix me, not cut me off.

And maybe on another night I'd stop and apologize. I'd confess what darkness I've seen and felt in the last two years.

Maybe on another night, I'd actually ask *her to move me home.*

But not tonight.

Not when I know that if I ever want to be known for my work I have to push **harder.**

"I don't need to wait till tomorrow. I'm going back to New York now."

Despite the evident surprise on her face, she tells me: "Then do it."

She says it like it's a challenge, like she thinks I'll still change my mind.

But the minute this conversation started, something deep within me knew: I don't care what I have to do – I will succeed. I've given too much of myself to not make this work.

"Fine then, I will."

She doesn't stop me when I pack my things and leave early the next morning. I don't think she realized how serious I was, but now she's determined to let my stunt run its course.

My dad simply hugs me goodbye and asks that I text him once I've crossed the state lines.

The shock doesn't wear off till I'm sitting in my dorm that night. And when it does, I cry like the child I am: I am free. Finally, after all my dreams.

I can find a way to succeed.

But I am also terribly alone.

Returning to the present, I step further into the living room.

I was a brat that night.

I was also hurting, and alone, and desperate to be anywhere else.

I know all of those things now, though not much has changed.

Deep down, I think that night split something between me and my mother.

It was a small fight, in the grand scheme of time and fights that have been fought, but it was also the same kind of small as a tectonic plate: you don't notice it till their movements have caused damage that's significant, irreversible, and shaken the very foundation you're built upon.

We didn't speak to each other the same after that conversation – neither of us willing to be the one to address what my mother knew I would never want to talk about.

So, I cut all my ties to this town for good – friends and family alike.

I accrued some debt paying for school myself, and shortly after got my book deal that paid for the rest of it, and I didn't think of

Pinecrest or its people hardly ever again until that wedding invitation came.

And as for my mother and I, we just pressed forward into the gradually unraveling relationship we have now.

Swallowing hard, I look at my mother, all these years later, in her same spot: glasses resting on the bridge of her nose, covered up with a knit blanket, staring into the fire.

An image of a deathly ill Marjorie floods my mind, and I see my mother sitting beside her through it all.

The chair moves backward and forward, snapping me out of my trance.

"I don't know what you're talking about," I meek out, finally answering her question. At this point, I don't even believe myself.

The rocking stops.

Planting her feet on the ground, my mother stands up, falling just a little short of eye level with me.

"Are we really going to have this conversation again, where you act like nothing is wrong, when we both know something is?"

"Like I told you before, *nothing* is wrong," I say with some finality, trying to avoid this topic the same way I did several years ago.

"Yes, it is! Something is wrong – because you're not the daughter I knew for eighteen years!" She practically shouts, like she's held her tongue for as long as possible. "Unless you became a new person when you moved to New York, then something happened, and I don't know why you won't let us help you."

"Because I don't need your help! I never have!" I shout back.

If she wants a screaming match, then believe me, I have plenty of anger to unleash.

"So, what? You mean to tell me you're the happiest you've ever been in the last ten years? That everything is great?"

"No!" I cry desperately, "Everything is not alright, because Marjorie is *dead*, and no one told me!" I feel the tears welling up in my eyes as my voice breaks on the last word.

"Charlie told you..." My mother whispers, processing this new information.

"*Yes*, he told me. My question is, why didn't *you*?" I practically spit back.

"Because you were *gone*! Because you were gone, and you never wanted to come back, and all I wanted was for you to have what made you happy!" She shouts, and I hear my dad stir in the room down the hall.

I now see that my message all those years ago finally got across – striking its target exactly as I intended.

I wonder now if I would take it all back.

"I never wanted to come back because you didn't love the person I became," I spat. "I couldn't be successful here."

"That's a lie and you know it! All I ever wanted was to support you and cheer for you, but you left, and you changed. *That's* what's so maddening! We could have made this work in some way, but you're not *you* anymore," she sounds exasperated - like it is taking all the energy from her to tell me just how far I've gone.

"No Mom, this *is* me. I started a new life because the one I had here was suffocating me. I never came back because I *outgrew* this place."

"You've made that fact abundantly clear! You never call, never visit – like we were something you could just discard and shed like a second skin! I just don't understand where we went wrong."

I throw my hands in the air, taking out all my exhaustion, and grief, and hurt on her.

"Because I didn't need to be fixed and that's all you tried to do to me!"

I'm panting and out of breath from yelling – how can I de-escalate things now? When so much has been said.

Because I love my mom, and I'm tired, and I should stop, but it's too late.

"I didn't come back because every time I did, I was reminded of everything in my way; I was reminded of a mother who tells lies because it's too hard to tell her daughter that her friend is *dead,* and I saw nothing but evidence for why I needed to leave this town behind."

My mother looks gutted. I know I'm speaking from a place of hurt, and betrayal, and confusion, but I'm too tired to care.

Every bit of pain I've held back for years can no longer be contained – as if Marjorie's death was my way of hitting a max capacity of pain.

"You don't mean that... you can't believe that."

"You haven't given me a reason to think otherwise." My voice is nearly inaudible, and tears have spilled out of my eyes again.

My dad walks into the living room.

"Ladies, everything okay?"

No Dad, it's not. Because I've just said unspeakable things to my mother because I'm hurting, and I don't know how to take them back.

I'm sorry won't patch up everything I've just unleashed, and I feel a pit forming in my stomach at the knowledge.

"I'm going to bed," I say.

I can't meet my mother's eyes as I turn and ascend the stairs, fully knowing, in some sick and ironic way, this at least hasn't changed: a decade later I'm still storming away to my room.

As I lay on my bed, I can hear my mother's quiet cries beneath me.

I imagine my father holding her, drying her tears, wondering how his daughter got to be so broken.

I wonder the same thing.

My mom and I didn't always fight. In fact, we rarely did.

Tense, hormone-induced spats? Absolutely.

Screaming matches and lashing out just to hurt each other? Never.

I play back over what I said to Charlie in the cemetery: our bargain.

We always had bets going as children; he, Aiden, and I were what most would consider "competitive", and this is just another one.

I can write a happy ending, I can help him plan this wedding, I can *win*.

Maybe that would change things between my mother and I - prove to her I'm not as much of a miserable wretch as I've shown her I am.

Can things this broken be fixed? Can I be fixed?

My phone vibrates in my pocket, and I pull it out: an email from my agent, a voicemail from my landlord, a tag from a post on Twitter promoting my last book, a short novel of wedding details, and a folder of pictures of potential bridesmaid dresses from Rose, and most recently: a text from Charlie.

I smile at the foreign name on my screen.

The last time I got instant messages from Charlie Grant was when we still had our iPods in high school. I open the message.

C: *Healing "Heart-breaker" Harper and Charlie's Epic Plan to Win the Dynamic Duo's Latest Bet:*

Of course, he gave it a title, I roll my eyes and read on.

C: Should you choose to accept your mission and are not the total wimp you were in high school, meet me at 1200 hours at the Grant residence.

C: In the event of failure, your poor excuse of a vehicle, shall not be returned to you. Good luck, Agent Marshall.

I hold my phone to my chest where I still feel the hurt from the fight, and the ache of my loss, and I wonder if Charlie Grant is capable of fixing up more than just cars.

5

The Grant residence is towards the center of town, tucked into the cul-de-sac of a little neighborhood that can best be described as "charming".

I use the morning walk to run over plot lines in my head, admiring the fresh layer of powder coating the town. Based on the rate the cold front is moving in, I know we are sure to have heavy snow before Christmas.

I wonder if I'll even be here long enough to see it...

Characters float through my head, as I round a corner and I think maybe I've come up with something, until I remember it was the plot of *All the Broken Things,* which I published three years ago. Shoving my hands deeper into my pockets, I heave out an aggressive sigh.

My mom was gone this morning before I even woke up - left for the library.

I wonder if I'm allowed to stop by after I visit with Charlie; if me magically materializing there for the first time since I moved away will help make amends in some way, but I know deep down it won't.

"Give her space" my father advised me this morning when I glumly fixed myself a cup of coffee in the kitchen. Despite his advice, I could feel the rift between us: a reminder he will always take her side in the end, and I'm in no condition to be on the hunt for allies.

Aiden calls me when Charlie's house is in my line of sight.

"What did you do?"

"Good morning to you too, Mama's boy."

I can almost feel the eye roll from Aiden I know radiates across the phone line.

"Not the time for sarcasm Harper, what did you do to our parents?" I use my silence to adjust my coat, pulling it tighter around my body. "Hello?" He says impatiently.

"Hey, yeah I'm here," I shouldn't be ill with my brother for being mad at me, but I do wish someone had even considered taking my side.

I remember the days when Aiden might have come and comforted me after a fight like last night – serving as a mediator for my mother and me. But I suppose I can't expect much when I've been little more than a voice on the other end of the phone, and an occasional cup of coffee, to my brother lately.

"I only confronted her about the fact that no one felt the need to tell me about Marjorie passing away."

My response is met with silence.

"Harper…."

"You don't have to give me the same excuses Mom did, Charlie already tried explaining things to me -"

"Charlie?" He questions, cutting me off.

"Yeah?" I reply, hostility edging its way into my voice.

"Charlie explained things to you?" Aiden stammers, "He felt comfortable enough to talk about things with you?"

"Yes, and he did a mighty fine job at it. Something any of you could have done before him," I tell him.

"I'm just surprised he was willing to open up to you."

Why is everyone so surprised Charlie just shared the truth with me?

"Aiden!' I vocalize my frustration, 'Can everyone stop being so surprised he told me, and start addressing the fact none of you did? I've seen you so many times since it happened, and you never even hinted at something being wrong! So now, I am trying to talk to my *brother* – not a lawyer who is going to judge me and give me carefully calculated answers."

He's quiet for a moment before saying, "It's not my job to *judge* – just to present evidence and cross-examine."

"Seriously, if you don't turn off the work-brain, I am going to strangle you through this phone," I tell him.

This is exhausting – if I wanted to spend my morning being lectured, then I would have just stayed home instead of answering the phone.

"That's what I'm trying to tell you! We're all so surprised because Charlie doesn't talk about these things often – it's big that he shared it all with you."

Oh.

"Still..." I tell him, finding my voice, "The point is: I had a right to be mad. That's important stuff no one told me about, or even considered telling me."

"I'm sorry."

My brother's apology shocks me so much I have to physically stop a few yards away from Charlie's driveway. I can already see my car sitting near the mailbox: Charlie must have driven it home from work.

"I'm sorry no one told you," he says. "We should have, Marjorie was your friend too."

"Thank you." My voice comes out quiet.

I won't sing my brother's praises for finally addressing the elephant in the room and apologizing for not telling me about anything that happened to my family in the last year, but I suppose that means I also should be thankful he's no longer on my case about my relationship with our parents.

"So, what are you up to today?" He asks me, trying to maneuver the conversation to a more casual topic.

"I'm actually at the Grant's house," I tell him, staring up at the house before me.

Aiden's deep laughter rings through the phone. It's familiar and comforting – serious one moment: the fearless older brother; laughing the next – eager to change the subject and lighten the mood.

"What on earth for? Not getting enough time with Charlie while Rose has you two wedding planning together?" Even though he can't see, I shrug my shoulders.

"I don't know… he's agreed to -' my voice falls short as I realize admitting to my deal with Charlie would require admitting I'm here to work, which wouldn't improve my current standing with the family (Aiden has always been quite the tattle-tell). 'He agreed to do some wedding planning things today, you know flower arrangements, bridal shopping, all the things…"

I never was a good liar.

"Wait, what is Charlie bridal shopping for –"

"Got to go, love you, bye!" I rush out, not giving Aiden a chance to investigate further, before hanging up the phone.

It's perfect timing because Charlie has now come out from around the side of the house.

He wears a heavy flannel jacket and old work jeans with his boots (boots so worn out I'm fairly certain he had them in high school), and his eyes are bright in the cold. Our breaths begin to mingle as we walk closer to each other.

"Good morning Turkey Chaser!" He exclaims cheerfully. I roll my eyes.

"Really? We're sticking with Turkey Chaser?" His smile broadens at my displeasure.

"Oh absolutely, partially because I love how much you hate it, and never plan on letting you live that down. And then partially because Heartbreaker must be reserved for special occasions."

"Of course, like cryptic and terribly dorky late-night texts," I joke.

He lets out a small laugh thinking about the message he sent me last night.

"I thought you might enjoy a late-night duty-call from Charlie Grant, probably been wanting that since we were in middle school," he waggles his eyebrows at his play on words, evoking a solid punch in the arm from me.

"Hey, watch it city slicker," he says with a laugh. "I'm not one of your doting coffee-shop-crushes you can just beat up on whenever you like. I am your tour guide to happily ever after, and I demand respect!"

More eye rolls and play fighting breaks any tension that might have been residual from yesterday's breakdown, and I wonder if Charlie and I have always been this close - this comfortable with one another.

He welcomes me into his parent's house before I can think twice, and it's in their living room that I'm greeted by two strangers I think I knew in a former life.

Aria and Beckett were little girls when I left town, but now they've blossomed into young women. It's a sucker punch similar to seeing the way my parents have aged or hearing about Marjorie: it's a reminder I left everything behind, and life didn't wait for me to come back.

"Hey, girls! Say hi to Harper," Charlie instructs them.

Neither girl bothers to smile at me, surveying me with wide, wary eyes, but it's Aria (the youngest) who breaks the silence.

"Hey."

I smile, trying to connect the teenagers before me with the little girls they once were.

Both girls have the chestnut brown hair of their father, but all of the Grant children have Marjorie's watery blue eyes.

It's their best feature, next to the constellations of freckles scattered across their faces, and I try to ignore the tightening in my chest when I realize just how much Beckett looks like Marjorie.

"How have you been?" I ask, trying for conversation.

"Fine," Aria says again.

Beckett won't stop surveying me with the precision, skepticism, and disgust of a scientist uncovering a new disease. Aria simply looks scared.

Charlie is the one to break the growing awkwardness that has taken up residence in the room.

"Well, I just came in to grab my gloves… if you need us, we'll be over at my place," he tells them. I watch Charlie grab his gloves from the kitchen and usher me back outside.

The cold bites at my face as I try harder to shield my neck and chin with my jacket's stiff collar.

"They've changed so much…" I mutter out.

Charlie tries to hide his feelings with a smile.

"Yeah, a few years will do that…"

I nod, letting the crunching of our boots in the snow fill the quiet.

"Have they always been so quiet?" I ask.

Charlie doesn't answer me at first, and I wonder if he didn't hear me, but his body tells me otherwise.

His shoulders shake like Atlas carrying the weight of the world as he releases a long-held breath, and I wonder how much more has happened that no one has told me.

Charlie offered me honesty, but at the end of the day, I'm still a stranger. I'm still the girl no one knows the full truth about, the one who skipped town without a second thought, and I wonder if Charlie senses that. If it's a wedge keeping him from sharing the rest of the past with me.

"Mom dying was hard on all of us, but especially for the girls. They were so little... being a teenage girl, turning into a woman... it's hard without another woman to guide you."

He loosens another sigh before continuing, "And don't get me wrong, your mom has been great. She takes the girls shopping, and taught Dad how to do their hair, and the whole town really rallied around us when Mom passed away, but still. They know they're missing something the rest of the world seems to have."

There he goes: Charlie Grant proving me wrong once again. Opening himself up to the world in a way I'm not sure I'll ever be capable of.

"Bex is especially tough to figure out. I think starting high school has been a lot harder than she wants to admit. So, don't take it personally if she doesn't talk your ear off - she doesn't talk much these days anyways," he explains.

I imagine if I were in their place.

Even though my mom and I fight from time to time, she's always been there for me. For her to just *cease* being there is almost too much to bear.

"You've been quiet yourself this morning," Charlie prompts, "what's going on?"

I shake my head. My problems seem astronomically smaller when compared to his.

"Me and mom just had a bit of a spat last night is all."

He nods his head, thinking over a response. "What about?"

"Nothing." Another head shake. "Just how long it's been since I've been home."

"Makes sense."

Nothing else.

My head turns at his short response. "Makes sense? That's all you have to say? No great words of wisdom to impart?"

He shrugs his shoulders, marching on into the cold.

"You're the writer, remember?" The frankness of his comment stings me, but I dismiss it as frostbite as we finally approach the little guest cottage in the field behind the Grant's house.

Charlie tells me that he moved into the guest house once he came home, wanting the independence he had gotten used to when living by himself but needing to be close to his family.

He didn't leave after his mom passed because he knew his dad appreciated having him on standby for the girls, and he liked knowing he was only a short walk away if they needed him.

The cottage was an off-limit zone to us growing up, as it was actually a functioning guest house at the time, all white with its clean linens and fluffy duvet. That didn't stop us all from sneaking over from time to time during dinners to get away from the house.

I remember finding the boys here one night playing cards and drinking root beer (they let me stay in exchange for my secrecy and a pack of Swedish Fish, but I wasn't allowed to play with them – only watch).

As he welcomes me into his home, I look for the little ways it might have changed since those nights.

There's pictures and diplomas on the walls in place of the abstract canvases Marjorie used to hang up, but all the little quote signs still hang exactly where she put them when they moved in.

Each adage is filled with more cheese than the last, but completely and totally "Marjorie".

"So, what do you have planned for me today? I would like to get my car back eventually." I can feel the tension between us dissipating as Charlie remembers the reason I'm here in the first place.

"You remember what this place represents right?" He asks me.

I nod, "Yes, our childhood, cheating at card games, and a profound love of red gummy candy."

"First of all, I wasn't cheating – that was Aiden," he says defending himself. "Second of all, I hope you brought some candy, because that is still the entry fee."

Rolling my eyes, I quip back, "Had I known there'd be a price of entry, I would have reconsidered my options."

Charlie gives me a dry laugh in response.

"Well, I might let you slide this one time since it is a special occasion and whatnot…" He gives me a devious grin and I note the sparkle of mystery in his eyes, telling me he knows something I don't.

"What special occasion?"

I run through pacts, birthdays, and anniversaries wondering if I somehow managed to forget something important.

Charlie makes a big flourish with his arms, gesturing towards the windows and doors, enjoying this experience all too much.

"I'll have you know that last night was the first snow of the year!"

"It snowed a week ago," I remind him. He dashes away my thoughts with his hands as if they are cobwebs.

"But this is the first snow you're in town to witness, so it's the only one that matters."

I give him a glimpse of a genuine smile – one of the few I've had since I got into town.

"And what does one do for the first official snow of the year? Or, at least, for the one that matters?" Charlie's devilish grin is back as he looks me up and down.

"You brought warm clothes, right?"

* * * *

A quick change later into a thicker jacket, hat, and gloves borrowed from Charlie, I'm ankle-deep in snow, wondering how I ended up agreeing to spend time with a full-grown child.

"Come on Harper, you've got to help me build Olaf!"

I look around to see Charlie trying his best to start a snowman and almost bust out laughing at the sight.

"I don't see you trying!" He counters, "Remember, we are having *fun!*"

"Yeah, yeah, yeah, I'll get on that." Rolling my eyes, I decide the best course of action is to appease him, especially if I ever want to get back home to my writing.

When was the last time I built a snow man? Freshman year? Sophomore year?

When high school started, we typically either found a hill to snowboard and sled down, or I was in *Written Comfort* with a coffee and a book, sometimes even the library working.

Then when college rolled around, there was plenty of snow in Central Park, but no one seemed to have the time.

Why would you in New York? Building snowmen is for children.

"Excuse me, earth to Harper, I don't see you having the time of your life." Charlie is beside me now, half of his snowman already complete.

"I'm working on it. You know, envisioning it in my mind. Be the art and whatnot."

"Mm, yeah, you do that... I realized I left the carrots and coal in the cottage, so I'm going to get them. I want at least a base constructed when I get back here."

"Sure thing, Sergeant." I salute him as he walks away laughing.

He can't really *mean coal, can he?*

I try to start the snowman's base by forming a little snowball and rolling it in the powder at my feet, but as I roll it, it dissolves, falling apart in my hands.

I try again with the same result, except this time the snow sticks to my gloves, seeping in and chilling my hands.

I let out a grunt, my frustration growing.

It's just a stupid snowman. A literal child could do it.

I can hear Charlie coming up behind me when he asks, "Having a hard time there, Heartbreaker?"

"It's fine. I've got it."

I abandon the ball-rolling method and take to simply pilling snow together, forming an awkward mountain. When I try to smooth it out to be more round though, it crumbles like all my other attempts.

"You know I can help you if you need it?" He offers.

"I don't need help building a snowman, Charlie."

"Okay, if you say so..." He backs away slowly like I'm a rabid animal, and I begin to think I might be one.

Shoving the snow down with my hands I release another frustrated scream. Charlie quirks up an eyebrow but says nothing.

Another ball, rolling, rolling, crumbling.

I think about how easy it used to be to do this.

Another pile, forming, forming, toppling.

Charlie is almost done with his, putting the finishing touches on now.

Standing up, I brush the snow stuck to my gloves off on my jacket, before bending down to form another ball.

This time, I can't even get the snow to take shape, squeezing it into smithereens.

"This is stupid! This is childish! And I'm over it!" I throw my sock cap to the ground, storming back towards the cottage.

Tears of embarrassment burn my eyes as I blink them away – what kind of fool can't build a snowman?! How dead *is* my inner child? And why does this realization make me so unbearably *sad*?

"Hey, Harper wait up!"

I ignore Charlie's voice, marching onward to the warmth, wondering why I agreed to this in the first place.

"Harper, stop!"

His voice gets caught up in the wind, and I pretend I never heard him in the first place.

"Harper, I said *wait*."

He's beside me now. Red-faced and slightly out of breath from running in the cold, but beside me regardless. "What are you doing?"

"This is stupid Charlie," I throw my arms up gesturing to the winter wonderland around us. "We aren't kids anymore, and I shouldn't have agreed to this in the first place. You win, I'm sorry for wasting your time."

Confusion is clear on his face, but I think he will let me go and save me from confronting these shameful feelings, but as I begin to turn away, he grabs my arm, turning me back around.

"Harper, it's not that big of a deal. I wanted you to do this because I thought it would be fun, and yes, it *is* childish, but that's the point. The first step to holding on to a happily ever after is tapping into your inner child you have locked in some scary closet with Edgar Allen Poe and that creepy clown from *IT*."

"It's actually more like that cupboard under the stairs from *Harry Potter*," I say defensively.

"Of course, it is," he mumbles into his hands as he facepalms. "You said you wanted to change right? Look on the bright side and write a happy ending?"

I silently nod my head yes.

"Well, this is the first step: calm down, Harper. This is building a *snowman*, it's not rocket science, and it is far from perfect. Even Frosty had un-proportionally placed buttons and Olaf was lopsided. Snowmen are *founded* on the concept of imperfection, just like happy endings."

Charlie Grant you poet.

"And I made a promise to you," he continues, "I'm going to help you. Now pick your hat back up, and let's build a snowman, you freak."

He messes up my hair like the big brother he is, before heading back to the pile of snow I once called a snowman.

"Okay, so you had the right idea with starting with the snowball, do it again," he tells me.

I roll my eyes while gathering the snow into my hands, squeezing it to form a compacted ball, but as I squeeze, the snow begins to fall apart again.

"You're trying too hard; you have to be gentle with it. Here, like this," Charlie wraps his big hands around mine and gently presses them into the snow. A shiver races down my spine that I dismiss as the cold.

Slowly, we form a perfectly round ball of snow.

"Good, now roll it on the ground to make it bigger."

I do as he says, going slowly this time, picking up more snow with each roll.

When I've finally managed to form a passable base, I look back at Charlie for approval where he grins, giving me a thumbs up. "That's my girl, now let's build this snowman."

* * *

"Romeo and Juliet."

"Absolutely not."

"Why not?!"

"Harper, we are not naming our snowmen after the two most tragic lovers in literature," Charlie tells me.

"But it fits perfectly! They are fated to fall apart.... Literally." Finally cracking up at myself, I lose it as Charlie rolls his eyes, looking to the heavens for help with the heathen I have been. "At least I didn't suggest Jack and Rose! They *literally* freeze to death!"

"You've got to be kidding me," Charlie says, seriously measuring me with a sideways glance, deeply disturbed by my sick sense of humor, which only makes me laugh harder.

I survey our snowmen: a man and a woman, properly dressed for the winter with dark coal eyes and carrot noses, smiles reaching to where their cheeks would be.

I can't help but smile a little harder at their stick hands intertwined.

"I just think if you didn't want your snow lovers named after fictional characters with tragic endings, then you should have picked a different partner to construct them with." I shrug simply, refusing to budge. Charlie finally looks down at me, all smiles and ruddy cheeks, lips chapped from the cold.

Somehow, still annoyingly perfect.

"You're not letting go of this one, are you?" He asks.

I shake my head no.

"Fine then, Romeo, here's your Juliet. I hope you enjoy each other for a little bit longer than your namesakes got to." I clap my hands in celebration releasing a little squeal of joy.

"You are *way* too happy about this," Charlie says shaking his head at me.

"I am a perfectly reasonable amount of happy, thank you very much," I say.

"Mhm, right...." He looks me up and down, his arms crossed behind his back taking me in.

Suddenly, I feel self-conscious of my snotty nose and messed up ponytail as he looks at me with those transparent eyes.

"Maybe you won't be able to gloat so much after this," he starts, and before I even have time to realize what he's saying a snowball is being launched in my direction. Forgetting any feelings of insecurity, I dodge the ball of ice with determination.

"When did you even have time to do that?!" I exclaim.

"Doesn't matter!" Charlie shouts before ducking behind our Romeo to launch another snowball at me.

I run a few yards away to collect myself, gathering up my own ball to launch back at him. It misses him by several feet.

"Is that the best you can do?" He yells at me from across the yard.

I try again getting a little closer, only for it to be returned by a ball hitting me square in the shoulder. Ice slips past my collar and runs down my shirt, eliciting a scream.

"I'm sorry, I'm not an ex-D1 athlete, unlike some people!" He laughs loudly and I use the distraction to launch one at his unguarded face. It nails him in the forehead, and he stumbles back, processing my accuracy. Stunned at my luck, all we can do is laugh as we watch a red circle form on his forehead.

This means war.

Back and forth we go, for what could be minutes or hours, exchanging snowballs.

When we are too exhausted to keep score, we collapse on the ground breathing hard beneath our heavy winter coats.

I fall down beside Charlie, who watches thoughtfully as our breaths mingle in the air above us.

Neither one of us speaks for some time, simply letting snowflakes collect on our eyelashes.

"Thank you for today, Charlie," I say genuinely, meaning it. "I haven't had that much fun in a while".

"Of course," he smiles at me sweetly, "it's what friends are for."

He looks back at the sky after contemplating something.

"If you thought today was fun, just wait till you see what else I have in store. Do you think you can handle it?" He asks me.

For once, it's not a challenge, so much as a simple question: his inadvertent way of making sure I still want this.

"If the rest of what you have planned is like today, then yeah, I think I can…" I confess quietly.

Romeo and Juliet watch over us: children in bodies older than they feel, letting the cold creep into our bones, where something much warmer is starting to spread.

6

The next morning, my cup of coffee and inspirational journaling is interrupted by a phone call from Rose. A frantic voice greets me on the line, "Harper? Harper are you there?"

I sit up straighter in my seat as I answer, "Yes Rose, what's going on?"

"Oh, Harper it's ruined! It's all ruined!" She exclaims.

"What are you talking about? What's ruined?"

"My Japanese stewartias!"

I try to think of a way to not sound rude, while letting her know I have absolutely no idea what she's so upset about.

"Is that a certain type of shoe?" My guess is only met by a cry of anguish.

"No! No, a Japanese Stewartia is a *tree*! A beautiful, sort of birch tree, and we were going to have dozens of them at the reception! We were going to hang fairy lights all over them and use them to light the reception area, and it was going to be beautiful!"

I think Rose is almost on the verge of tears when I venture to ask what happened to the trees.

"The nursery just called to tell me they had a horrible battle with the frost this year and lost too many trees!"

"Oh," I say quietly.

"Not just oh, but oh no!" I hear the tremble in her words. "What am I going to do without any decorations or lighting for the reception?!" This time a small sob does escape, and I remember Rose was brought up with an affluent family that didn't just chop down a Christmas tree from the neighbors' plot of woods.

Mustering up as much bridesmaid bravery as I can find within myself, I try to calm her down.

"I'll find something Rose, don't worry."

She is most definitely worried, and I most definitely don't know what the *something* is that I am going to find, but I have a feeling I know someone who would know just the right thing.

"Are you sure?" She asks, taking deep breaths to calm herself.

"Yes, I can handle this! You just worry about getting yourself ready for your big day and getting here. I told you I could take care of the rest."

I hear a sniffle through the phone and then, "Okay..."

Breathing a small sigh of relief, I rejoice at having avoided a complete and total meltdown from Bridezilla.

"Are you going to be okay?" I ask, imagining her nodding on the other end as she quietly says yes. "Alright, well then I have to let you go now, so I can get back to something I'm working on, but it was good talking to you. I can't wait for you and Aiden to be back in town."

After coaxing her off the phone and hanging up, I immediately text Charlie.

H: Wedding Woes: the Japanese Stewartias have died and we need to find new decorations/lighting for the reception ASAP. Any ideas?

Charlie is quick to respond, as I see the little typing bubble pop up, moments after sending my message.

C: My condolences? But yeah, don't worry! I have something in mind, so I'll take care of it.

I smile at his assurance.

Of course, Mr. Happily Ever After has it all under control – why would I be surprised?

It's nice being able to rely on him because I know none of these problems surprise or scare him. I suppose growing up with sisters will do that to you.

Refreshed by the surprisingly pleasant nature of depending on someone, especially when that someone is Charlie, I prepare to return to writing, but before turning off my phone, I see the little bubble pop up again.

C: How's the writing going? Did Romeo and Juliet inspire you yesterday?

H: If by "inspire" you mean "feel compelled to find some poison or a dagger"? Then, yes.

C: Wow. That was dark.

I wish I was kidding, but my "inspirational time" by the window in my bedroom has done nothing to further the writing process, and despite Charlie's best efforts, yesterday's activity did nothing to create any new ideas.

H: I'm sorry, I'm just stressed about this deadline. It's kind of a big deal, and this writer's block stuff is bad news.

H: Puts me in a dark place when I can't find some poor, innocent character's life to mess up.

C: A real writer's paradise. And you mentioned ... but you really have nothing?

H: *Nothing, nada, zilch, zelch, zero, none, nope, not one.*

Charlie LOLs at my rambling before calling me.

"Don't you have a job you're supposed to be doing or something?" I say when I pick up the phone.

"You know, I could be saying the same thing to you."

"Yeah, well I'm an excellent multi-tasker," I quip back. He laughs at me before speaking.

"Oh yeah, SO excellent you can do absolutely nothing AND talk at the same time! A true genius is among us – my apologies."

"Aren't you supposed to be helping me?" I whine, "Because sarcastic comments from the peanut gallery are doing nothing to move this process along."

"Alright, alright, it looks like another car is pulling in any way. So, I have got to go, quit harassing me at work anyway!" I can hear his laughter and feel his teasing through the phone as he hangs up, leaving me alone in the silence once more.

It's *fun* being friends with Charlie.

I realize that now, appreciating it more so than when I was younger, and he was just *there*.

We had never been that close of friends before - not the way he and Aiden were.

Charlie and I were more like familiar strangers: knowing each other, but not really; always together, but never talking.

I was never going to be his first call, or choice to hang out with, but he'd happily give me a ride home from school or stay for a family dinner.

Being one of the captors of each other's attention is something new for us.

But thinking about Charlie isn't what I'm supposed to be doing right now - writing the next great American novel is.

I look down at my journal where random words and phrases are scribbled out.

Fragments of fruitless ideas: crow, cow, corn, turkey, snowplow, cars, corruption.

All useless ramblings of a failing mind that is supposed to be creative.

I try writing without thinking, to see if my subconscious will produce anything miraculous in the same way the self-help ladies tell you to do on Pinterest:

An influential man has two sons, one of which is illegitimate. The half-brothers hate each other but must come together to keep from tearing apart their basketball team and the girls they love. The uncle is in love with the mother.

One mother is a struggling alcoholic and drug addict.

I stop myself looking down at what I've just written before screaming into my hands: this is the plot for *One Tree Hill*.

I lean back in my chair, looking at my childhood bedroom. Back in New York, I would always draw inspiration from my surroundings.

Simply glancing outside the apartment window to the city below me used to be enough:

A tourist never once looking up from their phone was good enough to inspire a commentary on society and the digital age, it could create a whole world in which people had lost their humanity to a screen.

A businessman shouting to his colleagues, carrying himself high and mighty compared to the homeless man laid out on the street, was actually a shark, devouring its prey. Always hunting, always removing the weakest link till they were invincible, only to have justice served in the end.

I used to be big on poetic justice.

I could look at the deeply broken world around me, and I could cast judgment on whomever I wanted to with a swoop of a pen, or a stroke of a key.

It was easy to be a voice for the weak when you felt that way yourself.

But now I am just tired.

Tired of the brokenness, and always being the one to have to fix things, because the problem with poetic justice is it's rarely happy.

That's what people get wrong about their "happy endings" - they are never happy, because that's not the way life works.

I hadn't been lying to Charlie when I told him the dog didn't come back, and the people don't get better, and the broken is never healed. Because the world is just screwed up, and no one wants to deal with the reality of what "fixed" looks like.

They want to believe a kiss can reverse the stroke of midnight, but Cinderella never gets the glass slipper.

No, she keeps working to earn the income that pays for the leaking roof over her head and feeds her children who will never know their father.

I saw Cinderellas every day on the way to class in college, I knew many of them personally.

And despite Charlie's unique situation, not everyone has a Pinecrest community to lean on. Most people just have the ugly stepmother and stepsisters.

Dejected, I convince myself a cup of tea is what I need to continue writing.

Carefully, I make my way down the stairs, hoping not to disturb a sleeping Sleet, which is ultimately useless because the dog smells failure from a mile away, and I've just walked into the living room.

So, the lovable furball follows me into the kitchen where I come face to face with my mother.

She looks me up and down, taking in my messy hair and sweats I most definitely went to bed in and watches the dog lie down in the corner of the kitchen.

We still aren't on speaking terms after our fight, and I still don't know how to fix things.

That's why I do what I've always done and simply stow away in my room till the storm passes, while I pray maybe another cup of caffeine and some fictional characters will solve my problems. But has that ever really worked before?

Now come to think of it, all that ever did was prolong the problem, avoiding the inevitable…

"One lump of sugar or two?" My mother asks, setting down the kettle of tea she's already made and getting out the jar of sugar cubes.

I look at the two cups and wonder if somehow this is a miraculous healing from God.

"What? Unlike some people, I still remember how my daughter likes her tea when she's been writing."

The hurt in her tone reminds me of the fact that this wound is far from healed, and she has most definitely figured out I'm here to work, not play.

Softening her voice, she says, "Contrary to popular belief, I am still your mother, and I can still sense when you're working away in your room… the screaming clued me in as well."

"Sorry, I didn't want you to know I came home to work."

"Why not? You've made it abundantly clear where your priorities lie," she says, matter of factly.

After dropping two sugar cubes into my cup, my mother spins around and returns to tidying the kitchen as if nothing happened.

"How's the library?" I ask.

"It's fine," she tells me.

I nod, letting some silence pass, since you know, I love the awkward tension so much.

I almost consider using now as an opportunity to stow away to my room, but that would leave me alone with my notebook and a dozen missed emails from my agent which is possibly more terrifying than my current state.

"Is the library still doing the 12 Books of Christmas?" I try.

I actually see my mom perk up at my question: the 12 Books of Christmas is a twice-weekly event the library hosts, where for two nights each week, for the six weeks leading up to Christmas, a new book is featured, and a different activity is done, in correspondence with a book.

They do *A Christmas Carol* and hot cocoa, have local artists come in and present their work – ranging from poets to painters, and novelists, or show a holiday movie that is based on a book.

"They are. The next event is on Friday if you and Charlie want to come..." She quirks up a suggestive eyebrow that I balk at.

"And why on earth would Charlie and I be there *together*? Or my attendance be dependent on him?" She shrugs harmlessly.

"Because you're friends and friends hang out together... unless there's something else going on you want to talk about?" I can't help but laugh.

"There is absolutely nothing going on between us, aside from wedding planning... for Aiden and Rose!" I clarify for good measure.

"And that's why you were over at the Grant's place yesterday? Wedding planning?"

"How did you know about that?!" I exclaim.

She laughs in the knowing way mothers do when they have the upper hand.

"Bex came by the library yesterday evening. She helps me the way you used to," she explains.

I swallow hard at the memory of being my mother's constant companion in the library.

How old was I when that changed? 15? 16?

Old enough to know it wasn't "cool" to hang out with my mom in the library anymore, which was right around the time the teen angst started to set in, which ultimately drove me from this place years later.

"What's she like now? I mean... what are they all like now?" I say cautiously, wanting to tread lightly in conversations with my mother.

"A lot changes when you're gone for so long..." My mother's eyes soften, but her lips remain a firm line.

Why can't I just cry into your arms like I used to when I was little?

Why does there have to be this striking line dividing us, like we are fighting on opposite ends of a losing war?

I want to scream it and shout it and go back to the way things used to be. But my mother is stubborn and so am I, and I still refuse to give her answers to her questions – regardless of whether or not they stem from a place of concern.

I know that sharing will only make me feel ashamed.

"Yeah, the girls looked a lot older when I was at the house," I say.

Turning away from me to fiddle with a towel, or to simply look away from my gaze, my mother speaks to the wall.

"Aria and Beckett are both in ballet now..." she begins, "they'll perform in the town's *Nutcracker* performance Christmas Eve. They're quieter than when they were younger, but they're both just like Charlie. Aria has his sweet, sensitive side. Beckett has his passionate and determined side. Beckett obviously took after Marjorie in the looks department, but they all have her eyes."

I remember thinking the same thing.

She continues, "They are smart *and* quirky, and miss their mother dearly, but they love the friends they have. Even the ones that left..." I try to ignore the tears welling up in my eyes. "Bex has a hard time trusting people... she doesn't want to open up to people again only for them to leave, or something to happen, so she clings closest to Charlie most of all."

I don't blame her; he seems like a good person to cling to.

"Charlie is good like that - I'm sure he's been a huge help with raising the girls," I offer. My mother nods in agreement.

"Yes, he has, but you're seeing that for yourself, aren't you?" She pauses a moment, weighing something in her mind, "What is really going on with you and Charlie, Harper?"

"Nothing', I insist again, 'he's helping me break through my writer's block or something... rediscover my inner child, fix the broken mess I am... It's nothing," I wave away her questioning with my hand.

She doesn't press, and I'm thankful, because there's no way to tell her the true catalyst for the desperation to fix all my broken bits, was being whole enough for her.

I think our conversation is over, my cup of tea drained, and her cleaning done, and I prepare myself to put back on the armor everyone in this house has shielded themselves with since I came back, but before I can reach for my metaphorical helmet, my mother speaks:

"You were never broken sweetheart."

A chink in the armor begins to grow.

"Thanks mom."

7

My earliest memory of the 12 Books of Christmas was probably when I was around four years old. It was Christmas Eve, and they were reading *The Night Before Christmas* to the children, serving cider to the adults, and the kids were having cocoa with as many marshmallows in it as they wished.

Now of course, my parents had been reading this book to me since I was born, but this time it was different.

I was allowed to sit with the big kids in the reading room, and when the lights were dimmed and the paper snowflakes hung from the ceiling, it was almost like being back home in the living room by the fire.

Christmas Eve is supposed to be a magical time in Pinecrest, with the local ballet school putting on their production of *The Nutcracker*, followed by all the children in town going to the library for the last night of the celebration.

Little girls in their ballet costumes, and boys in their pajama pants, crowd together to hear my mother read them a story.

Even though different librarians have read it through the years, I always thought my mom did the best job.

It was the first time I truly fell in love with a story, and it's what made me want to write my own. It was the bond my mother and I shared over our love of books that kept me coming back every year and even led to me working in the library for a brief time.

That's why I know, regardless of how I left things, I must call an honorary truce for the fourth night of the 12 Books.

I called Charlie that morning to let him know I would be attending, unsure whether I was seeking his moral support or suggesting this be one of our challenges. Regardless of our motivation, he is by my side with a stupid grin plastered on his face as we walk into the town library.

As the glass doors slide open, I'm greeted by a strange sense of nostalgia.

Everything is more modern in the most out-of-place way, because "high-tech" is something Pinecrest is not.

The old dial-up computers with their large blocky keyboards have been replaced by sleek new desktops, the walls have been painted brighter colors of white and gray, replacing the dingy yellow walls that used to surround us, and the books all have a sense of being newer, with their brightly colored spines lining the shelves.

I find solace in the corner of the library that is clearly older, with leather and cloth-bound books lining the old oak shelves of my youth, but catch my jaw dropping at the technology center where there's a small cart of electronics for rent.

It's like watching the old and the new exist simultaneously.

Processing the new additions to the library, I allow Charlie to guide me deeper into the building towards the back.

I grow more comfortable as we walk, the features of the library aging the further we get from the entrance.

It's like being walked through history, making it apparent the only thing that has been truly updated is the entrance and foyer of the building.

By the time we reach the very back of the library where the 12 Books of Christmas is held, I feel as though my world has returned to normal: the chairs are old and dilapidated in the most comforting way, the shelves are a dark wood, the books are all gently loved, and the lights overhead are just a touch dimmer than the rest.

My mother's handiwork shows all around us where fake snow lines the shelves, twinkling lights wrap around tables, and snowflakes hang from the ceiling.

It's only been a few weeks since Thanksgiving, and a larger part of me is giddy at the idea of seeing how much more extreme she can get for Christmas Eve than I care to admit (this is the one place I allow myself to partially coexist with holiday cheer).

Before joining the crowd, I run over to a very familiar bookshelf in the far corner.

The wood grain is soft to the touch, and I move old volumes out of the way to clear off the shelf: there, etched into the wood, are mine, Aiden's, and Charlie's initials.

We carved them there in middle school when we got bored one afternoon.

I remember being so horrified when Aiden whipped out his pocketknife, but equally as giddy when they cut out the clean lines of the "H" in "Harper".

Unexpectedly excited, I look to Charlie: "It's still here after all this time!" I exclaim.

"You've missed this, haven't you?" Charlie's grin is one of self-knowing satisfaction as if he's won some kind of prize.

Rolling my eyes, I tell him the truth.

"Who me? Miss the gaudy bauble and bustle of the holiday season in Pinecrest? The ridiculous nostalgia of my childhood? Maybe just a little…"

His smile broadens before encouraging me to find seats near the front before it gets too crowded.

I make my way towards the first row of chairs that have been set out for the audience, since the guest reader hasn't arrived yet.

It's always a surprise who the guest artist will be: we've had everyone from big names to small, and since I still haven't seen my mother, it must be someone impressive she wants to keep a secret.

I shift with nervous excitement in my seat as the room fills with people, the anticipation building.

Finally, my mother exits from her office, carrying a large stack of books, catching the eyes of everyone in the nearly packed audience.

My heart picks up a beat when my father follows behind her carrying a sign…. a sign that looks vaguely familiar….

Before I can jump to bolt, Charlie puts his arm around my shoulder, stroking sympathetically as if I am a nervous child or a cat, he wants to prevent from running away.

I jerk away from his touch because this *cannot* be what I think it is.

I feel ambushed: my mother won't meet my eyes, but she grins at the audience as she sets the stack of books down on the podium, taps the microphone to see if it's on, and begins speaking.

By the time her voice is resonating throughout the room, my dad has already set up the poster on the small stage, where I can unmistakably see my face: a collage of a high school Harper very much so still an aspiring writer and member of the Pinecrest community, and the Harper I was a few years ago when my career took off, still full of fire and drive to conquer the world.

I don't think I recognize either of those girls anymore, even though they have my eyes; my hair; my face.

Zit covered or a beaming smile, they are Harper Marshall, even if I can't remember how.

"Tonight, I am very pleased to announce the guest reader of the evening is our very own local author, and my daughter, Harper Marshall. She has come all the way from New York to spend the holidays with us!"

I think I'm going to be sick as my mother gestures for me to stand and come up to the podium.

"You can do this Heartbreaker, consider it a part of our deal," a wink from Charlie and a quick squeeze of the hand and I know this isn't really my choice.

None of this has been... but it *could* be.

I could choose to be brave... and Charlie kind of makes me want to be.

I look into his eyes for reassurance, all too aware of the dozens of eyes now staring at me, waiting for me to move.

"It's just like building snowmen: you have to start small, and let the ball build itself," Charlie offers sympathetically.

I nod, unsure of whether that truly applies to reading my most depressing works of fiction to the entire town I fled, but too nervous to truly dig into the logic.

"Harper Marshall, everyone," my mother says one last time with a flourish of her hands before leaving the stage the opposite way of me, giving me room to walk up the few small steps on shaky legs.

The knots in my stomach twist tighter as I wipe my wet palms on my pants legs, silently wishing I had dressed a little nicer before I remember where I am; then I remind myself that Pinecrest doesn't care what I wear to a book reading - they never have.

Surveying the audience, as I adjust my mic, I see the audience is largely made up of adults.

Good.

Children don't need to have nightmares about my stories.

Noting the bottle of bourbon someone has set out next to the milk and cookies, I realize this was *meant* to be an adult reading night.

Everyone was in on it except me, and Charlie's obscenely bright male-model smile tells me he knew from the beginning.

I make a mental note to kick him for this later.

"Hello everyone, thank you for having me." My voice reverberates around the room sounding unfamiliar and strange. "Tonight, I will be reading from..."

I shuffle through the stack of my books laid out before me, trying to find the mildest one, when I see a sticky note stuck to the cover of my second novel.

It had always been one of my best pieces of work, still full of the excitement of being a breakout writer, without all the blunders of my first novel.

The sticky note reads *Marjorie's Favorite* in my mother's scrawling script, and I feel a different kind of pain at those words.

Holding up the title, I announce the book I'll be reading, and dive in before I can second guess myself.

I don't take my eyes away from the book as I read the first few pages, too afraid to see what the world thinks of me.

Book tours were always my least favorite thing about releasing a new novel, so I tried to keep them down to a bare minimum, but as I reach the end of the first chapter someone in the audience sneezes, and my head automatically jerks up.

My gaze is met by a sea full of faces that seem vaguely familiar in the same way people at family reunions always do when you haven't seen them in a long time, and the most shocking part is they are all staring back at me with hope, love, and genuine *interest*.

They *like* my book.

This is enough to spur me on and convince me to add more inflection to my reading – to savor finally doing the thing a 16-year-old version of myself used to fantasize about.

The Harpers on the poster would be proud.

When I reach the end of chapter two, the crowd is begging for more and clapping, and with a nod of approval from my mom (who might be wiping tears out of her eyes), another tray of cookies is brought out and another round of drinks is served.

We go on for at least half the book, but I know it's time to end once we reach the climax.

Jaws drop and tears are shed as the main character's love interest dies, and the audience is left to wonder what will happen next? What can be the driving force without love?

But they will have to check out the book to find out.

As I slam the book closed with a dramatic flourish, the audience erupts to their feet applauding.

Regardless of whether it's the alcohol or the words I've read off the page, I don't care what got them to their feet, all I know is some part of me has made an audience of people move… and that's a good feeling.

* * * *

Charlie gently presses his hand to my back as he guides me out of the library, helping me weave through the crowd.

My body buzzes from the attention, and my cheeks have begun to hurt I've smiled so much.

After the reading, everyone wanted to catch up and hear about how the writing was going since the book I had read had been such a hit (which almost sent me into a panic attack). A few people even asked me to sign their copies of my novels, but the attention was growing to be a bit much, and sensing this, Charlie made up some excuse about needing to get home to the girls.

Once we are outside though, he reassures me: his dad is watching them for the night.

"I didn't want anything to take me away from this," he explains.

I nod my head in response, taking deep breaths of the cold air around us before spinning around in a childish glee.

Even though the dead middle of winter is still weeks away, the air has taken a turn for bitter, and after being in a small, heated room, it feels magical.

"Want to walk?" Charlie asks, offering me his hand as we set off for the sidewalk leading to town instead of his truck. I take it, commenting on how pretty the evening is, with stars twinkling brilliantly overhead despite the chill.

"You can't get stars like this in New York," I tell him.

"I'm sure, seems a little too cramped for my liking," Charlie confesses.

"No, not really," I insist. "I think you would actually like New York a lot more than you think," I urge.

"Most people are really friendly because they were once tourists and new to the city, so they are always offering directions and tips on what restaurants to check out, and the city has this magical balance of old and new all at the same time,' I continue, 'Like you can walk down one strip and see a Captain Jack Sparrow cosplay standing in front of a juice bar, but then walk another block and see the location of an early 1900's French Opium den that was probably ran by Al Capone."

He nods as if this has him sold. "Of course, and those are the main selling points for a city quite literally defined for its arts and culture: opium and Jack Sparrow."

I throw my hands up as if he's cracked the code.

"Yes! You get it! Prioritizing like a real New Yorker," I tell him.

He nods satisfied with my compliment as I laugh, delirious from the frosty air.

"Well... maybe I will have to come visit it sometime. Only for the trendy juice bars though, I've really put my French-opium-den days behind me," he tells me with a wink.

When my heart thumps a little harder, I remember that is the wink that won over the hearts of Pinecrest High School.

I listen to our boots crunching in the snow before adding, "Yeah, you'll need to come visit me sometime."

Charlie looks over at me partially surprised, so I clarify, "You know, since we're friends now," I add, as if there will ever be a reason for Charlie to come to New York, simply to visit me.

He glances away, and I'm suddenly very aware of just how cold my hands are without his around them, so I shove them deeper into my coat pockets as we turn onto Main Street.

Downtown is dead this time of night, but everything stays lit up for those out in the evenings.

It feels like one of the safest places in the world with nothing but the warm glow of Christmas lights keeping it lit.

"Were we not friends before?" I turn to Charlie as he asks his question, but he remains focused ahead on something in the distance.

Why is that the one detail he picked up on out of everything I said?

"What?"

"You said '*now* that we are friends', haven't we always been friends?" My face heats at his question, and I suddenly regret my choice of words.

"Oh, I mean, yeah, technically, I guess. Sorry, my bad."

Charlie still won't look at me, but I notice the way his hands shift in his pockets – his whole body tense.

"It's okay if you didn't consider us friends until now Harper, I just didn't realize that was the case. I thought we've always been pretty close," he says dismissively.

I let out a deep sigh. "That's not exactly what I meant."

"Then what did you mean?" Charlie presses. He's not angry, he's just sad.

I didn't know I had so much power over Charlie, let alone what the question of our friendship would do to him.

He's finally looking at me, as we approach the park, and I swear the look in his eyes could shatter me.

It's not far from puppy-dog eyes, but there's a hint of something broken that makes me swallow hard. Something that makes me want to wrap Charlie in my arms and never let go, something that makes me want to take away all the doubt and hurt this world has caused him.

"I think we have always been friends, sort of...' I start, 'Or at least we were familiar strangers, but I've never felt like you were truly *my* friend, you were always Aiden's."

I pause before continuing, "Everything you two did, you did together, and I always felt like I was just third-wheeling. You two were these glorious planets rotating through the Heavens, and I was simply a star sitting in your galaxy. Or maybe a ring rotating around you."

My laugh is dry, so I take a deep breath and try to clarify what I mean.

"It used to feel like I was in your orbit, but I was nothing special, nothing worth looking at - I was simply there. And lately, you've made me feel like something a little brighter,' bashfully I admit 'it's nice having Charlie Grant's undivided attention."

Saying those words out loud, that I've thought so many times, feels liberating and honest, and I'm glad I said them, but Charlie's silence is unsettling.

It makes me wonder if I've said too much.

We've stopped walking now, and I'm watching our breath puff out in clouds between us. I look to Charlie for some form of answer, but he simply stares at me for a long time before pulling me into a hug.

Letting the sudden warmth spread through my body, I squeeze him back. I can feel the muscles in his back contract at my touch, and I breathe in the smell of his aftershave, all cedar, and snow, and motor oil.

I ignore the way that everywhere he touches along my back burns, like a fire has been lit within me in the most delightful way, and instead go back to wondering why he is hugging me in the first place, and why it feels so *good*.

Without looking at me Charlie whispers, "I always thought you were my whole sky, Harper: all the stars, guiding me and Aiden home."

He speaks into my hair, gently stroking my back, and I remind myself this is nothing more than friendly.

Nothing more than one friend comforting another, but then he adds: "You're my brightest star, Harper - always have been, always will be".

Silently, I say a prayer of thanks that he's not looking at me right now because if he was he might see the tears welling up into my eyes; or the way my brow is raised in confusion; or how my face is glowing pink.

And then, he might realize all those things don't matter because deep down, that's the nicest thing anyone has ever said to me.

* * *

After our moment of... whatever that was, Charlie and I go to the park in the middle of the town square.

Dusting the thin layer of snow off the seat of a swing, I plop down and begin pushing myself back and forth.

Charlie makes a spectacle of running through an obstacle course like a child, sentimental and serious sides all forgotten, while I count how many seconds it takes him to do it.

When he reaches an attempt he is pleased with, he slides down the slide one last time before situating himself in the swing beside me.

"I miss swinging," I remark to no one in particular.

"It is one of the most pure and simple joys in life," Charlie agrees.

Our swing chains squeak with the weight of our adult bodies.

"I think all of life's problems can be answered on a swing set," Charlie tells me.

"Oh yeah?" I ask.

"Yeah," he says with a nod.

"Why is that?"

"Because, up high, the air sucked out of your lungs, your stomach dropping to your feet – it makes life seem a lot less serious and a lot more fun. It makes answering the hard stuff easier," Charlie explains.

"I suppose so," I concede, "they were always my favorite on the playground in elementary school."

"And why was that?" Charlie asks, his smile growing.

I glance at him and shake my head because he already knows, "Because they made me feel free."

"Point proven," he declares.

"Not to mention, it was by far the best place to get new gossip," I add, making a point to avoid his eyes, looking at the starry sky above me.

"Oh yeah?" Charlie says with a laugh, "And what juicy gossip was a nine-year-old Harper partaking in?"

I pump my legs harder, swinging back and forth, letting my toes drag in the snow to slow down, before I kick off again. "Well, obviously everyone had to talk about the time you kissed Cindy Bartow behind the trees near the pond," I tease him.

"That was because Aiden dared me to!" Charlie proclaims, trying to defend himself.

"That's not what Cindy said," I point out, my eyes drawing to the side to watch Charlie's reaction.

He rolls his eyes at me before pushing off the ground himself, his swing tempo mirroring mine.

"I'm sure that's not what Cindy said, but it *is* the truth," he reiterates.

"Mhmm... if that was the truth then why did everyone see you going double-dutch with her the next day?" I ask.

"How do you remember this stuff?!" Charlie asks incredulously. "And what does "go double-dutch" even mean?"

"You don't know what it means to swing double-dutch?!" I nearly fall off my swing I'm so shocked.

He shakes his head at my raised brows.

"It means, you swing in-sync with your crush to let everyone know you're together, and if you did it long enough, it meant you'd be together forever," I explain.

"Girls are absolutely ridiculous," Charlie laughs.

"We were nine – ridiculous is what we did best!" I return.

Dismissing my argument with a bewildered look on his face, Charlie watches our swings go back and forth before saying, "Hey, Harper."

"Hey, Charlie?"

"Did you notice something?" he asks. I don't need to look at him to hear the satisfaction in his voice, but I glance towards him anyways: we're swinging in sync.

"Does this mean you have to marry me now?" He asks, waggling his eyebrows.

"Does this mean you're proposing to me?" I try to say it jokingly, but I can already feel my face flushing. I silently pray Charlie can't see well in the dark.

"Maybe," he hedges.

"Maybe?"

He laughs at his own coyness.

"Personally,' I tell him, 'I would prefer a clear and distinct proposal, with a ring when it's official."

"Oh, would you?" Charlie retorts with raised brows.

"I would," I pause before adding, "with doves, near water, and a singing mariachi band."

"Mariachi band? I definitely pegged you for more of a string quartet kind of girl," he says skeptically.

"You know, that would definitely be better, but could they still wear sombreros?" I plea, potentially enjoying this bit a little too much.

"I mean, this is your proposal, officially, I think they can wear whatever you want," Charlie concedes, shrugging his shoulders

"Alright then: a string quartet, wearing sombreros, riverside, with doves, at sunset."

"At sunset?! Now you're just being demanding," Charlie says incredulously, swinging his legs in a wide arc that sends him soaring.

"Love demands greatness," I tell him, flinging my arms out to the side with a dramatic flourish.

"I'm sure it does,"

Charlie says, his smile so broad I'd think he's close to his face cracking in two, as our laughter dies down.

I feel a delayed flush of mortification as the park grows silent.

A sombrero-wearing string quartet? What was I saying??

Why did Charlie bring out only the most horrifying and dorky side of my personality?

I mentally make a vow to try and prove to him I'm not a complete and total weirdo before I return to New York.

We swing in a tandem silence for a moment longer before it begins to grate on me.

While I'm not incapable of enjoying silence, something about Charlie makes me want to spill every thought from my head, and I feel safe to ask the things I'd normally hold inside, so I ask the question I've been wondering all evening: "Charlie, did you know I'd be the guest reader at the library tonight?"

A soft laugh and then, "yes".

"Why?"

He looks puzzled at my question. "Why did I know?"

I shake my head no.

"Why did you all do it? I haven't released a book in a year, currently have writer's block, and am at an impasse with my mother who *runs* the library, and you knew all this. So, why do it? I could have just walked out of there and ruined everything, then what?"

"But you didn't."

I laugh at his evasiveness. "That wasn't what I asked."

He shrugs his shoulders before digging his heels through the snow.

"Did you enjoy it?"

I chew my lip before answering, knowing my ability to withhold any amount of truth from Charlie Grant is near impossible.

"Yeah... I did," I admit.

"Then that's why." He says it with definitive finality, making me think he won't say anything else, so I press.

"What?"

"You enjoyed it," He says shrugging his shoulders, "I know you did because I saw the way your face lit up, and the bourbon cannot solely be blamed for that; and I know everyone else loved it because I was a part of the audience; and those things are reason enough to do something like that."

I cock my head to the side wanting more, and Charlie releases a somewhat uncomfortable sigh before continuing.

His words come out in a rush, as if it will somehow make them easier to say, and I wonder how the same man who can spit straight poetry on our walk here has regressed to struggling with his words.

Finally, he utters out, "You are always talking about how your work doesn't make people happy and isn't worthy of praise, so I wanted you to see there are whole audiences of people in your very own hometown who love your work."

Charlie swallows hard before continuing passionately, "I wasn't kidding when I said my mom was super into reading your books; she was *so* into them that she convinced every person she talked to, to read your books as well. And you know what? They loved them!"

I'm dumbstruck, but he presses on, "I know you want to write a happy ending, Harper, but I needed you to see you and your writing matters no matter what genre it's in. I needed you to see people love you, happy ending or not, and the only thing that matters is if you can love yourself and your story in the same way."

A million feelings wash over me at his words: conviction and surprise and a warm fuzzy sensation similar to adoration.

The glass of bourbon and exhaustion make the edges of my brain fuzzy, but my heart is thrashing wildly in my chest like it wants to break free and say words I've yet to articulate in my mind. And for that reason, the only thing I can manage is a thank you.

"Of course, I meant it," he says with a determined head nod.

I know you did. I know you've meant every word you've said tonight.

Looking at Charlie, all bright-eyed and blushing from his sudden confession, I wonder how he and I were never this comfortable before.

How did years of tragedy and distance bring us closer together?

Switching gears, Charlie asks me what I meant earlier by "familiar strangers".

"I like the wording, it sounds nice, but I feel like its meaning isn't," he says.

I laugh at his statement.

"I just meant we aren't strangers – we are very familiar with one another, but we don't really *know* each other in the way friends do. Like I know all about your family life and the surface things I saw of you in school, but I don't really know *you*."

I shuffle my feet in the snow, avoiding his eyes as I confess what I've been feeling more and more with each passing day I spend with him.

"I don't know what Charlie Grant is like when he's by himself, and I certainly don't know who the man sitting next to me is. I knew the elementary Charlie who was goofy, and awkward, and liked to play in the mud with my brother, and kiss girls behind trees because he was dared to; I knew the high school Charlie, who was golden boy extraordinaire, teacher's pet, and all-around all-star; but mechanic Charlie who is borderline a single dad is still a mystery."

A mystery I want to unravel... I think to myself.

He nods his head, processing this.

"I guess you're right. It's funny, I could say the same thing about you, you know. I know all the ways to get on your nerves, the way you bite your lip when you're concentrating on a piece of writing, the fact that you like to sit in the back of movie theaters because it makes you nauseous, and that you made all A's in high school, but I don't know your favorite color."

I smile at that – at the fact that he didn't think I was completely crazy.

"It's the little things, isn't it?" I offer.

He nods in agreement, "Yeah, it is."

Silently we swing back and forth, not daring to look at one another – our swings periodically pierce the silence with a squeak.

"It's purple by the way," I say off-handedly.

He looks confused for a moment.

"You didn't know what my favorite color was - it's purple. But like, the really light, sort of lavender purple you see in the wildflowers in spring or the sunsets when they're particularly lovely."

I think I might melt in the warmth of Charlie's smile.

"Good to know. Mine is green, like dark forest green, when all the trees mix together, and it gets all murky."

I like that fact; I had no idea.

"Favorite food?" I ask.

"Lasagna," he replies without pause.

"That was such a quick answer, are you sure?"

"Yes, a lasagna with slightly crisp, burnt edges so you have a little crunch. And multiple types of cheese are preferable - my turn," Charlie says, ready to move on to the next question.

I bust out laughing at his seriousness.

"How do you take your coffee?" He asks me.

"In a mug? Uh, I don't know, it depends on the place."

Charlie shakes his head in disgust before saying, "That's not an answer: if you have to drink coffee one way for the rest of your life, how would you drink it?"

I think it over for a moment before answering.

"Drip coffee with vanilla oat milk creamer – the creamier the better."

"Noo, of course you would!" Charlie cries.

"What?!"

"You're one of those people who really just has a big cup of sugar milk with a splash of coffee in it, aren't you!"

"Not *completely*, I just like for it to be sweet and taste like vanilla!"

"Do not lie to me, Harper Marshall, I know the truth. You are no real coffee drinker, and it saddens me to find this out. Not to mention – oat milk creamer is terrible for you!" He groans before hanging his head in shame (which is a similar reaction to the one I get from any coffee snob who judges me when I order in a New York café).

It's not my fault coffee is so bitter!

"Let me guess, you like yours black?" I ask.

"Yes!"

"No!" I make gagging noises for added effect. "Why would you do such a thing?!"

"Because it's better for you, it tastes good, and it doesn't taint the pure name of coffee with processed creamers and milk."

"Wow, I had no idea you had such strong feelings about coffee creamers."

He shrugs as if this is unavoidable, "Well, I do."

We both erupt into laughter. It shatters the silent night that has settled over the sleeping town, oblivious to this new game we've created.

I go for another big swing during our momentary silence and Charlie watches. When I look back, he's smiling.

"I like this getting-to-know-you stuff, it's a nice change from the heavy."

I couldn't agree more.

"You're kind of fun to know, Charlie Grant," I confess, he visibly puffs up at my words before I chide him, "Don't go and get a big head about it."

I shove him playfully, but when he swings back towards me, he grabs my chains, planting himself directly in front of me, my body between his legs.

"I could say the same for you, Harper Marshall," our voices are barely above a whisper now, and for some reason, the way he's saying my name is tying my stomach in nervous knots. Like going up on a roller coaster, I know eventually something will drop.

"So, what do you have planned for me next, Charlie? I think I'm starting to actually like this game," he fights a smile when I say his name, glancing quickly to my lips and back up - something telling me he likes this just as much as I do.

"How do you feel about infiltrating a super top-secret organization, whose practices border on cultlike Ms. Marshall?"

"Well, I must ask Mr. Grant, is it baseball moms? Debra's blood cult?"

He shakes his head no to both of my guesses, his smile growing.

"What could it possibly be?" I ask.

In response, he brings a finger to his lips in a hush-hush manner before whispering:

"Do you like gingerbread?"

8

Making gingerbread is an art, or at least it is to the Ginger Community, who I found out, are in fact, real people.

Charlie discovered them one day after dropping off the girls at their dance class.

Apparently, in the building next to the town's only dance company, a group called the "Ginger Heads" rents the space as a place to practice for an annual baking competition in Asheville, North Carolina. It is there that people come from all over the world to attempt to make the most elaborate gingerbread house. The house gets judged on creativity and structure and must be entirely edible.

I have never been so simultaneously horrified and mesmerized by something in my entire life.

"So, they are supposed to just let us join in on their literal training session today?" I ask.

Charlie rubs his hands together excitedly as we approach the building. There is a wolfish gleam in his eyes, bordering on frightening.

"This feels like a very bad idea," I attempt as we get closer to the door.

"Listen, you're not breaking my heart this time, we *are* going to make some gingerbread today," Charlie scolds me.

I want to be my usual self and say no, turn around, and walk away from this ridiculous idea that we are going to bake cookies with real professionals, but I remind myself I'm not doing that anymore. I am actually *trying*.

And besides, I still have an impending deadline, and may at least get inspiration for a cookbook out of this.

When we open the doors to the rental space, the smell of spices consumes me in an almost choking manner.

After I manage to claw my way out of the seasonally scented fog, I notice the medical precision of the organization system set up in the building (it rivals Waffle House, which is an admirable comparison to have).

Six baking tables are set up in two rows of three around the room, and mixers line a shelf near the back wall. I see an industrial oven in the corner and wonder if it's always been there, or if they moved it in simply for the season.

An involuntary shudder races through me, when four, nearly identical, red-headed bakers look our way in sync, as if they are clones.

Charlie smiles broadly at them, previously only having waved through the window before today, but they do not return the gesture.

"Who are you?" One demands.

"Back up?" Charlie tries, his grin faltering now with less confidence.

The Ginger Heads grunt in unison, signaling to gather together to confer. They bend their identical red-heads together and murmur but are suddenly stopped when our attention is brought to the back of the room.

A stout woman with a large head of red and gray curls enters wearing a chef's uniform, somehow balancing a baker's hat atop her head. She is clearly in charge, with her stoic expression and full cheeks. The wrinkles around her eyes indicate she is much older than the rest of the bakers, despite *also* having an uncanny resemblance to them.

"Charlie!" She breaks into a grin and waddles over at a surprisingly quick pace to hug him tightly. Charlie seems just as thrown off as I am, because he glances my way for some kind of clarity, as if I will know who this woman is and why she knows his name. "I'm George, we talked on the phone!"

"Yes! Hi, how are you?" Charlie, polite as always, catches up with George for a few minutes, as if they've known each other their whole lives.

Eventually, I gather that George is the mother of the other four bakers (hence their resemblance) and they have been entering the gingerbread competition for 10 years now.

They've never won before, but this year they intend to.

Normally, their days consist of perfecting shapes, flavor, and color, but today they are allowing us to help.

George, short for Georgia, proves to be as sweet as the peaches she was raised around and her children Al (Alabama), Tina (Tennessee), Wyatt (Wyoming), and Ida (Idaho) are quite the opposite (I remind myself to ask Charlie later what on earth he thinks her husband's name is, and if this is where his theory about the slightly a cultic tendency stemmed from).

We are assigned one of the back tables, directed to a mixer, and given two spare aprons, before George gives us our assignment.

While I do feel as if I've returned to my high school home economics class, I can't help but feel Charlie's infectious energy waving off and on to me. It makes me want to do something, or create, or simply live.

It's a good feeling to have coating you.

I survey the blueprints before us (yes, legitimate blueprints), and see we have been directed to build the village for the gingerbread… creation.

Even looking at the blueprints, I'm still unsure what it is, and quite frankly, I'm too afraid to ask.

Charlie and I set to work, trying to carefully follow George's directions, as she commands this metaphorical ship from the front of the kitchen.

We stifle our whispers and laughs as the bakers respond to her commands each time with a resounding "YES CHEF!".

"Charlie, you have *definitely* helped us get initiated into some kind of cult."

"Ah yes, the Satan cookies are the best."

"Do you think the final ingredient is a drop of blood or reciting some weird chant?"

"Absolutely, but I draw the line when a goat gets brought in here."

"Do you think her husband knows she's running a child labor camp? Or maybe he's a part of it?"

"He was actually the sixth table, but he refused to say," another round of "YES CHEF!" cuts us off, but this time Charlie joins in, screaming it at the top of his lungs.

I have to stop myself from crying so the Ginger Heads don't notice just how terrified I am of their "family bonding". But I feel it, something like true happiness welling up inside of me: a willingness to simply laugh and not care that I haven't felt since, well… the last time I was in Pinecrest.

A feeling that is easier when I'm beside Charlie.

"On your right!"

A ginger baker brushes past me with a tray and almost takes my head off because I was too deep in thought to notice, but Charlie pulls me out of the way before I can be hit.

He crushes me close to his chest and I suddenly feel warmth radiating through me.

I feel his heartbeat, behind me, thrashing wildly into my back, and his arm still gripping me tightly. Leaning my head into his chest, I look up and see him smiling down at me.

"Hi chef," I say, and I feel something, warm and thick, like syrup, spread through me as his lips tug into a smile above my head.

When did he get so tall?

And have his eyes always been so sparkly of a blue?

It makes my knees go weak, and for a split second, I wonder what would happen if he wasn't still holding me so close before I remind myself that this is *Charlie*.

Not someone you get weak in the knees about, but a *friend*, and I don't have too many of those right now.

A shout of, "On your left" breaks us apart and we return to the task at hand, obviously further behind than the other bakers.

I make a mental note to avoid this precise thing for the rest of the day because I am supposed to be baking gingerbread, not wondering what cologne Charlie wears that I am finding so very intoxicating.

We try to work in unison, going back and forth from one side of the table to the other, adding ingredients to our mixing bowl, but each time we seem to misjudge each other's distance, and our effort to avoid touching turns into a constant running into one another.

I step on his toes, literally, and he bumps my shoulder.

I try to dodge him by going left, but he doesn't go right, and suddenly we are crashing into one another.

He tries to step around me, but then I'm turning, so we end up face to face pressed against the counter.

It's truly a brawl the WWE would be amazed to witness.

I know my face is a million shades of red, but Charlie seems unfazed by it, which makes this feeling significantly worse.

I *refuse* to be "one of those girls" I knew in high school, who drooled over Charlie Grant simply because he was somehow attractive AND a nice person.

Because he is my friend, and after last night we agreed we weren't doing the heavy.

We are finally something more than familiar strangers, and my sudden infatuation with counting the exact number of freckles he has scattered along his all too, infuriatingly perfect face, will not mess this up.

But then I look over at him, rolling out our finally finished dough with a soft smile playing on his lips, and I see the flour streaked across his forehead.

"Um, Charlie, you have a little something on your face," I say, trying to gesture with my fingers without touching him, which only seems to confuse him more.

"What? Where?" He tries to wipe at random spots on his face, which makes it significantly worse because his hands are *covered* in flour... and now his face is, too.

I roll my eyes laughing. "You have only made this so much worse."

He shrugs his shoulders unfazed by this.

"Maybe I like having flour on my face, ever think of that?"

"Mhm," I nod with pursed lips. "I'm sure you do."

His lips begin to break into a smile when he says, "You should really try it sometime. I hear it's going to be all the rage in fashion this year," and then it's on.

Flour is smeared across my face, so I fling icing in response with the spoon I'm using to stir. He throws some flour from the bag he's using, and I scream with glee. I take some spices and add them to the mix of white now coating both of us, and he smears some icing across my cheek. I go to wipe more flour down his apron, but he grabs my face with his hands and gives me war paint in the form of flour. However, instead of breaking apart like we've done so many times before, we stand at a draw in battle, gazing into each other's eyes.

I'm suddenly extremely aware of how full his flour-dusted lips are, and how it feels like my heart is in my throat, making it so I'm unable to speak.

And he's smiling down at me with that stupid Charlie Grant smile that's melted hearts, and mine will not be one of them.

It won't.

Not just on principle, but because he's my brother's best friend, and because I am not the girl who gets the happy ending, because there is definitely no such thing as happily ever after.

It doesn't matter what I think or feel though, because George is clearing her throat beside us, and we are being brought back to the reality where we have just destroyed the very pristine baking station of the Ginger Heads, who are watching us with so much venom in their eyes I can almost taste it.

Except for George, who simply looks amused.

"Sorry to interrupt, but I think the cookies may be ready to put in the oven".

She's right, they are, all the little ginger people lined up on parchment paper, beside the makings of their house.

Charlie dutifully returns to the task as if nothing just almost happened between us, which *nothing* did happen, and he puts them in the oven.

One of the twins, either Al or Ida, aggressively twists a timer for the proper baking time, while I sheepishly begin cleaning up our station. I don't even bother cleaning myself off because I know if I look half as messy as Charlie, then there is flour in places I may never find.

"Gosh Turkey Chaser, you've got to be more careful next time," Charlie winks at me before picking up a rag himself and beginning to clean.

* * * *

"Mhmm," satisfied moans fill the room as we all collectively breathe in the scent of freshly baked gingerbread.

I have to say, while the blueprints may have been a tad intense for my liking, they proved useful as Charlie and I watched the team dutifully piece their construction together.

Everything fit together somewhat flawlessly, and I was filled with a sudden flush of pride at being a part of something so seamless. The Ginger Heads let us know we were allowed to pipe some icing onto one of the roofs since this wasn't the final house they were submitting for the competition and merely a practice round.

I opt for the blue icing and Charlie picks up the green bag, and we carefully write our names on the cookies. Charlie starts up a chant in my name, as he prompts me to sprinkle edible glitter over "Harper" before the icing dries, and I oblige, if only so he will stop yelling.

I can't help but laugh at the look of sheer exhaustion on the baker's faces as we finish decorating, and I know they have regretted every moment of allowing us to be here.

George is the only one who seems to have potentially enjoyed this experience, telling us she is "thrilled with the change of pace".

I wonder if by "change of pace" she means "absolute chaos".

If so, then we were definitely what she was looking for.

"Well, any time you need an extra set of hands, we've got you covered," Charlie says as he slings his arm around my shoulders like a good-natured older brother, and I know this is what the world being restored to its natural order looks like.

Charlie doesn't remove his arm from me as he leads me out of the building, and I try to imagine what a sight we are: all covered head to toe in icing and powder, smelling of freshly baked cookies.

It's a vision that makes me smile.

"Do you think they'll ever let us enter their building again?" I ask Charlie once we are outside.

He laughs shaking his head, running a hand through his hair, causing a flurry of flour to fall.

"For sure, we were clearly a much-needed addition to their team." I laugh at his remark.

"Oh yeah, if they ever need some professional mess makers, we've got them covered."

"Definitely." Charlie digs his toe into the ground, dragging it back and forth through the snow. He looks like he has something on his mind.

"What's up?" I ask. He jerks his head up, startled.

"Nothing, just thinking."

I nod my head confused by the sudden attitude change.

"What are you thinking about?" I prompt, not willing to let him sit in his thoughts alone.

"It's really nothing, it's just the last time I was with someone baking gingerbread, it was Mom a few Christmases ago."

I nod my head in understanding. Suddenly, the thought crosses my mind that maybe these activities aren't just for me to heal.

"I think she would have really admired your baking skills today," I tell him gently, resisting the urge to pat his arm and make my feelings more confused with excess touching. Oblivious to my internal attempts at refraining from creating an awkward situation, he smiles at my comment.

"You think so? You weren't half bad yourself." He gently shoves me, in a far less awkward motion than I would have, had I done anything, and it makes me blush more than I will ever want to admit.

Breaking our silence, a reminder pops up on my phone: WRITING TIME!

I thought by setting alarms for designated writing times, I could force myself to write something – so far, it has done nothing other than remind me that I'm not doing my job.

"Do you need to go?" Charlie asks me.

"Yeah, probably... besides it's not like we can really do a whole ton else looking like this," I say with a laugh gesturing at the mess we are.

"Oh yeah, you're probably right..."

I can tell that even if I'm right, neither one of us really wants to leave, and the thought fills me with more mixed emotions than it should.

"I did have one question for you," he asks. I look up in response, seeing a light rose color spreading over Charlie's face.

"Yeah?"

"Would you mind helping me find a gift for the girls? Like not just one in the store, I want to go through some of mom's old things to find something of hers to give them, but I want help from a woman who knew her to make sure it's something they'd like."

Of course, it's about his mom and the girls.

Of course, he would be so thoughtful as to want a gift so sentimental for them.

"Absolutely, but are you sure you want me to help?"

He breathes a sigh of relief before saying, "Yes, definitely, there's no one I'd rather have beside me."

Uh oh.

Not the weird squishy feeling.

I ignore it, I smile, and I push it down into the deep dark depths of my soul where it cannot, *should not,* resurface, and I tell Charlie just how willing I am to help him out as *friends* do.

"Anything for you Charlie, you know that."

9

I'm still laughing when I walk into the house, having caught a glimpse of myself in the windowpane of the door.

I look like a *mess*.

When I open the door, my dad is sitting in his chair by the fire reading a book. His eyebrows quirk up at the sight of me, "You look like you had fun today?" It's more of a question than a statement, and I can't help but laugh as I try and explain.

"Yeah... Charlie got us roped in to helping this group of bakers in town called the Ginger Heads? I don't know, something about helping me "channel my inner child"."

I'm not afraid to confess to my dad what we were doing – he's always been a safe space.

"You've been spending a lot of time with Charlie lately, haven't you?" He says with a suggestive eyebrow. I groan.

"Come on Dad, not you too. You know Charlie and I are just friends, *and* Aiden and Rose asked us to work together for the wedding. We're merely catching up after the last few years." I will keep reiterating that point till everyone, including myself, believes it.

My dad simply nods, looking down at his book, before glancing at the clock in the corner and asking, "What are you up to?"

"Aside from looking like the leftovers of a children's birthday party? Not much, maybe a little writing, why?"

"I was just about to take the dog for a walk, what do you say you get cleaned up and come with me."

"Sure!" I exclaim. It's an odd time of day to randomly decide to go for a walk, but since my dad retired early, he might have adopted this habit.

Besides, anything is better than more fruitless writing attempts.

"Give me a few minutes, and we can go."

* * * *

The cold nips at my face as I rub my hands together, trying to keep the chill at bay.

Unlike me, Sleet relishes the chill, tugging on the leash, attempting to frolic in the snow.

"How've you been kiddo?" My dad asks after several minutes of quietly taking in the view on our walk.

Pinecrest has always been peaceful at all times of day - something I might even hesitantly admit can be kind of nice compared to the constant barrage of noise I've grown accustomed to - it is almost soothing.

"Good, how about you?" I ask. He shrugs in response.

"I'm good, enjoying the time to slow down and really savor life. You and your brother are growing up so fast."

My dad appears wistful as he surveys the wintery world around him, thinking back on the walks we'd take as kids through our neighborhood.

"I know. Aiden getting married – seems so surreal."

"Mhm," he agrees softly, "and what about you kid? Any guys I need to be fighting off? I could break out the shotgun if you really wanted me to?" I can't help but laugh as I roll my eyes.

"Certainly, no need for that," my dad is still smiling at his own joke as I continue, "I don't think I've been on a date since my senior year of college."

"Good," he nods his head, "let's keep it that way."

I appreciate his joking, rather than vocalizing the concern of me being a spinster the way I think my mom would. My dad looks me over, trying to read my face as I drag my feet through the snow. "So long as you're okay with that?"

"I don't seem to have much of a say in the matter, do I?" I offer.

He shrugs, "You have as much say as you believe you have in every manner. Or at least a much younger Harper seemed to think so."

Hm... I had never thought of it that way.

"Besides," he continues, "I certainly think Mr. Charlie Grant would give you a say."

"Gross!" I gag as my dad winks his eye and busts out laughing, hoping he can't decipher the blush on my cheeks or the secret thoughts I had earlier today, "My dad is officially no longer allowed to give me dating advice. It's too weird!" This only makes him laugh harder, doubling over, nearly dropping the dog leash.

"Fine! Fine!" He concedes, face red from laughing at my abject horror at feelings I could maybe, MAYBE, consider partially true, "change in subject: how are you and your mom?" I hesitate, thinking over how to respond.

My dad loves me, profoundly, but he's notorious for taking mom's side, and anything I say can and will be held against me in a Marshall court; he and Aiden have both always been that way: alarmingly honest, if not brutal, even when you didn't want them to be.

"I mean, not great? I would like to be able to be in the same room as my mom without fear of detonating a bomb. But it's been that way for a while, so what's new?"

"Do you want it to stay that way?"

I try to read my father's expression, to see if this is really his way of serving as some kind of undercover spy for my mom, attempting to will me into breaking down first.

I can't see anything but transparency on his face.

"No... but I don't feel like I have much of a choice there either," I confess. "She wants me to be the same person that I was at 16, and I'm not that kid anymore – and I don't want to be a project for her to fix."

"That's not it at all," my dad says, the shock evident in his voice. "Your mother has never wanted to "fix you" – and she has always encouraged you and Aiden to grow in whatever direction the Lord wants you to – she just didn't want to completely *lose* her relationship with either of you in the process."

He shrugs, "All any of us have ever wanted from you Harper, is to let us in – to spread your wings and fly but remember that there was a nest you flew from."

My dad and I talk about books, and ex-boyfriends, and work, but never things like this.

"It's always seemed like that's what she's wanted though – always pushing me to open up and talk about whatever it is she thinks is wrong with me –"

He cuts me off, "Would talking through the last couple of years really be such a bad thing?"

I try to think about the Harper that I am now – not the one that was freshly wounded eight years ago. I think about all the hurt I've felt and kept inside, that I tried so hard to cover up so I wouldn't be a burden to anyone. Would it be such a bad thing to talk about it now?

The voice in my head immediately says *yes*, but I find it hard to open my mouth and speak, so my dad continues.

"Did you ever consider that maybe we could work through whatever you were experiencing together?" I didn't. "Your mom and I try really hard to read you kids' minds, Harper. But we can't be *in* them. We can't help you unless you tell us."

My face suddenly feels hot, as if my father knows so much more than I've ever really told them. And it's a feeling that makes me want to cry, which I am just about tired of doing.

"Thanks, Dad; I'll keep that in mind," we've paused to let Sleet sniff the neighbor's mailbox. My father watches me with concerned eyes.

"We love you Harper, your mom and I both. And you two will work things out... eventually."

I smile, tears pricking at my eyes.

"I know it Dad, I love you, too." He nods, satisfied.

My dad has always known when to stop pressing.

"So, tell me more about this gingerbread baking – I'm incredibly disappointed in you and Charlie for not knowing to bring some home!" I laugh, settling back into my skin, thankful for the subject change.

"It was insane, they all were named after states..." and so I launch into the story of the Ginger Heads.

* * * *

We keep walking and talking for a long time – talking about books, and movies, and the city.

It feels good.

It's been too long since I've caught up with my dad.

When I was younger, we would go on these daddy-daughter dates: I would put on a dress, and he would get me flowers, and we'd drive into the nearest city, and I'd feel like the luckiest girl in the world.

I was lucky – to have a dad who made it so abundantly clear he loved me.

I think it was those trips with my dad that made me fall in love with the city – made me want to move to New York.

As I got older, and simply eating at a semi-nice restaurant was not enough to satisfy me, Dad would find secondhand bookstores or unique coffee shops for us to go to.

He understood me: Mom and I shared the library; me and Dad shared adventure.

We would talk, and strategize my move, and I realize now I never should have cut him out. I should have still called him the way I do Aiden.

Maybe if I hadn't stopped talking to my dad, I wouldn't feel as alone as I do now.

He tells me about the retired life, and how it's much better than being a real estate agent, and how much he can't wait for Aiden to get married so he can have grandkids to spoil. We also talk about sports (I can't participate much in the conversation, but it makes him happy).

Eventually, our hands go numb and we make our way back to the house. As we approach the door, my phone pings.

C: What do you think about church on Sunday?

The text surprises me so much that I wonder if Charlie texted the wrong number.

"What's wrong?" My dad asks.

"Nothing," I shrug, "Charlie is just inviting me to church?"

"You should go," my dad insists, "unless you're chicken?" I glower at him.

If there's one thing my dad knows from our many outings together, it's that "chicken" is something I refuse to be called.

Or at least it was when I was eight.

"Are you serious? Chicken? That will not work on me anymore."

"Baaack, baack, baack," my dad proceeds to make chicken noises. I roll my eyes.

Maybe, if time with my dad is something I missed deeply without realizing it, the church is too.

I highly doubt it – but *maybe*.

Besides, it's impossibly hard to say no to Charlie.

"Okay, maybe I will."

"That's my girl," my dad says with a wink before walking in the door. "I missed you." He says it like it's an afterthought as he closes the door, but I know he means it.

"I missed you too Dad."

10

On Sunday morning, I begrudgingly go to church.
Someone looking in on this situation, might pause to ask why: did the big bad villain of the quintessential 2000's movie, suddenly have a spiritual awakening? Is this choice of my own free will?

No, not exactly.

There's just a few tiny complications: a certain blue-eyed golden retriever of a human being is rather persistent, my ego can be ignited by the same insults that spur on eight-year olds, and I am all too willing to be game for nearly everything that golden retriever suggests.

Saying yes to Charlie is becoming easier than I ever thought possible, and I'm not sure how to feel about it. He makes me want to do things I never thought I'd try again. Be someone I didn't think it was possible for me to be.

Saying yes to Charlie gives me hope.

That's why I find myself standing in the church parking lot, my mother staring me down somewhat questioningly, and Charlie looking all too satisfied.

My dad gives me an encouraging smile as I tug down my sweater dress even further, overly self-conscious as to whether or not my dress is too short.

I haven't worn a "church dress" in years - most days it's sweaters and jeans or business casual for a press event. That unique balance of dressy and casual every woman in Pinecrest seems to have created, evades me, the same way it always did growing up when I felt stuffy and uncomfortable in my floral dresses and ankle-length skirts.

I had to scour Pinterest for ages to find something even resembling the outfit I am now wearing.

"You know they're not as strict as they used to be about what people wear," Charlie leans down and whispers to me. I jerk up at him glaring, irritated he recognized my discomfort.

I thought I was doing a better job at pretending.

"I don't care what they think," I tell him defiantly, trying to cover up another tug at my dress.

"Right, that's why you wore a sweater dress you owned in high school and clearly haven't worn since senior year," he chides.

I shoot him another hateful glance.

"You don't know the ins and outs of my wardrobe. For all you know, I could have brought this with me from New York."

Charlie skeptically nods his head, "Sure, we can go with that, but seriously, the church isn't like what it used to be. There's still a few stuffy old ladies, but the new pastor really turned things around."

I take the chance to glance around me, as we climb the church steps and enter the building, and I realize Charlie might be right: instead of full-on suits and ties, the men mostly wear jeans and button-downs. The women are dressed similarly: flowy house dresses, long pleated skirts, some even wear jeans! It's a revolutionary concept I didn't think would ever grace the doors of one of Pinecrest's few churches, but it's an idea I can get behind.

When we enter the sanctuary to find our seats, I note that even though the pews we sit in haven't changed, the entire atmosphere of the room has.

The church of my childhood was stuffy, pale, brightly lit, and well... old.

Sundays were filled with opening our hymnal books while the choir sang and hearing an old man preach about the fires of hell. It was more condemning than compelling, but it did propel me, Charlie, and Aiden down to the altar at least once in our lives to repent of our sins.

Church as a child was simply a way of life, like a social club, but it was never a choice.

It was stiff-backed seats, judgmental eyes, and parents talking for much too long after service. And it usually included me falling asleep at least once during a prayer.

This church before me now though, seems much more like a community.

A welcome desk at the doors of the sanctuary offers brochures on counseling and flyers for the latest events in town, and a smiling greeter offers me a program.

Shocked, I take it, clutching the paper booklet in my sweating palms.

I didn't realize how nervous coming back here would make me, but when my eyes land on the clustered group of old women towards the front of the church, who always seemed to have something to say about how I was so unlike my brother, I remember why.

They're older now, but I'm sure their gossip is still just as nasty.

Charlie ushers me into a row of seats towards the back of the church, counting out enough for his dad and sisters who were following behind us.

The old women follow us with their eyes, taking in my sweater dress that is probably tighter than they'd like, and I assume they're deliberating just how unacceptable it is for me to be here with Charlie.

More likely than not, they are too busy condemning me for the sins they're sure I incurred while I was in New York to even judge my outfit.

"Fix your face," Charlie instructs me, snapping me out of my internalized monologue… and panic.

"Excuse me?" I gasp, taken aback. "You fix your face!"

Charlie laughs at my shock.

"Calm down, I'm only joking… a little. You look like you're about to get in a fight with the senior women's Sunday school class."

"Well, it's because they still haven't learned to mind their own business," I say defensively. "I can feel their judgment from across the room."

"What?!" Charlie seems genuinely surprised by this observation.

"Yeah, they've been looking over here this entire time, and they keep talking amongst themselves in their little gossip circle. They're no different than when I left!"

Charlie cranes his neck to appraise the situation before getting up without a word and marching towards them. My stomach drops to my feet as I watch him walk towards the group with an air of both righteousness and determination.

It is the most terrifying thing ever.

He greets them with his most charming mayoral smile, and I wonder if he is simply using this as an opportunity to campaign. But then he begins gesturing my way, and I hear the words "Harper" and "home" getting tossed around.

I feel my face turning a shade of red that best resembles a beet and begin to count all the number of ways I might need to kill Charlie Grant when this is over.

Aiden has other friends, what will being short one best man do?

But then, something happens; Charlie's smile contorts into a firm line, and the women stop laughing; they stop chattering altogether as Charlie says the words "Christ-like" and "neighborly".

No longer am *I* the one red with embarrassment, but rather these women, as their golden boy reminds them just what makes him so very golden: you don't tolerate people getting made fun of, and definitely not in the House of the Lord.

When Charlie walks back over to me, a little flustered but not at all ashamed, I feel a warmth begin to spread through me. Something almost giddy, and ridiculously proud to be sitting next to the man beside me.

"Sorry about that," he says.

"Don't be sorry at all... thank you. They've been tossing my name around since high school."

He shakes his head, "No one should be treated like that, certainly not you. I'm very sorry Harper."

There's sincerity in Charlie's eyes, unlike anything I've ever seen. It's a reminder of the incredible friend he is.

"You know you didn't have to do all that for me... I don't want you ruining your mayoral campaign or any of the arranged marriages they might have set up for you."

Charlie suppresses a smirk and laughs, "Oh, trust me, they're not the kind of people I want helping me get ahead, and they're most definitely *not* the kind of women I want as my in-laws."

And then, he does the dumbest thing possible: he winks at me.

Charlie Grant *winks* at *me*. In *church* of all places!

The somersaults my stomach then does, must solely be dismissed as a delayed by-product of my anxiety, because I refuse to acknowledge the flush rising to my cheeks again.

"So, uh, they have programs now?" I try to change the subject, holding up the now crumpled paper program in my hand.

"Yeah! That was a new thing they started a few years ago, thought it would be a good way to engage with the community."

In an attempt to distract myself from the all-consuming headiness that is Charlie Grant, I intensely survey the program, flipping the pages over and reading every line, taking in every word on the announcements page: Wednesday night activities, a men's cookout, toy drive, soup kitchen.

I smile, fondly remembering the church's soup kitchen we used to help out at as kids.

"What else is new around here?" I ask.

Charlie chews his lip thinking, glancing around the room.

"Well, obviously new paint job," he mentions, pointing to the walls that are a softer gray now, which couples nicely with the dimmed lights around the room, growing dimmer as the countdown clock for service gets lower.

"The song lyrics are now on screens instead of books," he continues. I see the hymn books are gone, which does a funny thing to my heart.

I've never been the best singer, and I considered the songbooks incredibly archaic, but I always liked the stories within the hymns; written in a time when people were still careful to pull from the Bible when writing a song, and it was epic tales being told instead of just words about the "goodness of God".

"And the pastor is new, obviously," Charlie nods back towards the doors we came in, where the pastor now greets people.

He's middle-aged with salt and pepper hair receding from his brow, but he seems like a kind man - always shaking people's hands, asking them how they are.

I like him.

As the lights finally reach their lowest point, and the clock hits zero, the doors to the sanctuary close and the last people dwindle in.

The band goes on stage, which is solely made up of a young couple holding microphones and guitars (very different than the choir robes I remember), and they begin to strum a few chords. I watch the words appear on the screen and recognize none of them (like I said, it's been a while), but before the singing begins, the pastor comes by and squeezes Charlie on the shoulder.

"Hey Charlie, how are you?" He says with a smile. Charlie returns the grin, and they do one of those man hugs that I've never fully understood, where they clasp each other on the shoulder, and sort of hug, but also not really.

"I'm good, how are you?" Charlie asks him, once they've broken from their bro-hug.

"Great! Excited and blessed to be here this morning," he tells him before noticing me hiding behind Charlie's large form, "Charlie you dog, where are your manners? You didn't introduce me to your friend. Nice to meet you, I'm Mark Richards," I take his hand, shaking it.

"Hi, Harper Marshall, it's a pleasure meeting you."

"Harper... as in Andrew and Mary's daughter?" He asks me before I nod hesitantly.

"Yep, that's the one." I wait for what comes next: "the famous writer", "the city slicker", the "absentee child".

"I have heard some wonderful things about you! I'm blessed that you chose to be here this morning." He smiles again before giving Charlie a nod and walking to the front.

That's it?

I'm surprisingly relieved.

Whatever it is he's heard about me, all it's left is "wonderful things", and as generic as that is, it feels like a blank slate.

Like a chance to make a first impression for myself without a title attached to it.

"Told you everyone isn't judgmental and rude here," Charlie says with a pleased smirk.

I don't deny it.

Suddenly, a crack of light spreads from the closed door, spitting out Charlie's family in a flurry of chaos. Aria quickly slides into the seat beside Charlie, where he wraps his arm around her. "Hey kiddo, what took you so long?"

"Bex took *forever* to get out the door."

"No, I didn't!" Beckett argues with her sister, both girls looking a little disheveled.

"Yeah, you did!"

"No!" The girls begin to argue as Charlie's dad sits down looking downright exhausted.

"Girls stop arguing. What matters is you're here now," I notice it's Charlie who uses a soft, but stern voice to correct the girls and get them in line, not his father, and it makes me wonder just how much parenting Charlie has had to do in the last few years.

Charlie doesn't seem to object to the task though, squeezing Bex on the shoulder once the girls settle down and sharing a soft smile with his father who nods his head with appreciation.

It's a very realistic moment as a family, one Charlie handled with grace and poise.

And it also makes my stomach do more of those stupid somersaults like it's preparing for the summer Olympics.

I choose to focus on the music taking place instead, reading the words off the screen, and attempting to hum along. Charlie's off-key, but passionate voice sings along beside me, and when I glance his way, he has his eyes closed and his hands raised: he's worshipping. I can't help but watch, and pray it doesn't seem like I'm gawking, as Charlie goes through every song that way.

An energy seems to emanate off of him, of power and warmth, a genuine love for the object of his affections – a genuine love for God and His spirit.

It moves me in a way I haven't felt in a very long time.

I try it myself, briefly, just to see if I can experience it too: the energy, or maybe see some image behind my closed eyes that would make this feel more real, and less like I'm singing to simply a name, but I don't feel the spirit moving around me the way I can feel it coming off of Charlie. It feels like something is lacking in me... not lacking... more like *longing*. Gnawing for something just out of reach... I'm just not sure what.

The yearning feeling persists throughout the rest of the songs, and I try to piece together what it could be. It feels like when you've forgotten a word you've known your whole life, and it's just on the edge of your tongue waiting to be realized – except the word never comes to me.

Nice to see I have writer's block in my spiritual life as well.

When the music ends, Mark takes the stage and preaches about the peace of God.

He says it surpasses all understanding and meets us in our darkest moments, just like when Paul was in prison and still yearning to share the Gospel: he was comforted by the spirit of Christ and filled with a fervent desire to continue sharing the Word in every way he knew how. Mark tells us, whether we are imprisoned literally like Paul, or simply imprisoned by the chains of life like anxiety, depression, financial burdens, or sickness – we can still feel God's peace in prison.

It makes me feel funny in a way I'm not quite sure how to describe.

It makes me contemplate asking Charlie if he wrote the sermon notes for Mark.

"So, Mr. Happily Ever After, what was the point of today?" I whisper to Charlie.

"Shh," he whispers back.

"Come on, tell me," I plead. I hear someone sneeze, and then my own mother shushes me from a row up. I roll my eyes before taking out a pen from my purse and writing on the edge of my paper: **what is the point??**

You clearly haven't been listening to the sermon, Charlie writes back.

Yes, I have! Goodness, peace, joy despite our circumstances – but you had no way of knowing what he'd preach on! So, what was your reason?

Charlie contemplates a moment, or perhaps pauses to listen to the sermon, before responding to the little message thread I've created.

You can't know the joy of a happy ending till you know the joy of the happiest ending of all time.

For a moment, I'm stunned. I didn't expect Charlie to get all preachy on me, let alone take any of this so seriously.

What's that supposed to mean? I write back, seeking some confirmation for what I think he's trying to say.

Salvation.

That one word seems so simple when it's written on the corner of a page. The reality of it is a lot more complex, and complex isn't something I really want to do anymore. But it causes a shift within me. Suddenly, I am acutely aware of the fact that Charlie deeply desires I pay attention to this message, and it makes me want to crawl out of my skin.

Because it means Charlie doesn't just care about me like a brother or a friend, it means he cares about my *soul*. And that thought is almost too much to bear.

I shift in my seat, no longer knowing how to sit comfortably. What I want, is to get up and walk out of this church that suddenly seems too dark and too small, but seeing as there is a whole pew of people blocking my way to the door, I try to settle in. To readjust and dismiss the severity of this moment. Charlie notices.

Grabbing my pen, he begins to scribble down the side of the program before handing it back to me and squeezing my knee with a reassuring smile:

Ecclesiastes 3:1-11

Since he doesn't write anything else, I take out my phone and Google the verse reference. After pulling it up on a Bible site, I read:

> *"To everything, there is a season, and a time to every purpose under the heaven: A time to be born, and a time to die; A time to plant, and a time to pluck up which is planted;*
> *A time to kill, and a time to heal; A time to break down, and a time to build up; A time to weep, and a time to laugh;*
> *A time to mourn, and a time to dance; A time to cast away stones, and a time to gather stones together; A time to embrace, and a time to refrain from embracing; A time to get, and a time to lose; A time to keep, and a time to cast away;*
> *A time to rend, and a time to sew; A time to keep silent, and a time to speak;*
> *A time to love, and a time to hate; A time of war, and a time of peace. What profit hath he that worketh in wherein he labored?*
> *I have seen the travail, which God hath given to the sons of men to be exercised in it. He hath made everything beautiful in his time: also, he hath set the*
> *world in their heart, so that no man can find out the work that God makes from the beginning to the end."*
> *– Ecclesiastes 3:1-11*

A sudden peace settles over me as I read the words. They feel like permission, as if they are saying "Take your time, this is your journey to take" which is just as daunting as it is comforting.

It feels like Charlie believes in the journey I'm taking, almost as if he's looked at the mess I am and said "You seem worth the wait" … as a friend of course.

And deep down, I know it could be the Lord saying the same thing.

* * * *

When service is over, we all file out of the church and onto the front lawn, where everyone stands mingling, walking to their cars, and making plans for lunch.

"So, did you like church?" Charlie asks me as we approach our cars.

I pause, turning around to look at the church and the people standing outside of it.

"Mm... a little, but I'm still not really sure it's for me."

There's no point in sugar-coating things with Charlie, I have nothing to lose, especially when it comes to church – I'll be out of here in a few weeks and back to the safety of my apartment, and coffee shops that have no judgmental older women who claim to be "servants of the Lord" while they talk about people behind their backs.

Charlie doesn't seem to accept my answer, shaking his head he gestures at the group of women, "That's not the church I'm talking about." He directs my attention to the other side of the entrance where Mark stands tending to his congregation; I see a young family as well, with their little kid sharing the crackers he was given in Sunday school with another child.

Charlie speaks again, "That's the church I'm talking about. *Big C* church, that cares about people's eternity and knows it's not just enough to say you know the Lord, but realize you have to walk it out as well."

I watch for a moment longer, as a small group of teenagers gathered, animatedly discussing the sermon, and an old couple hobbles to their car hand in hand.

Finally, I look at Charlie.

"That's a church I could maybe get behind."

11

After Sunday, two days of borderline radio silence from Charlie pass before I get worried.

I wonder if my skepticism and behavior in church upset him. It's not like Charlie and I *have* to spend every day together. However, it has become somewhat of a thing; a routine if you will: I wake up, have a tense and awkward breakfast with my mother (who is still only speaking in fragments to me), pretend to write some, briefly catch up with my father about sports teams I only know so much about and the books we've both been reading, and then I go out with Charlie. But ever since things started to get tense between us, in the all too comfortable, "care about your soul" kind of way, the only text I've received has been: "Sorry, busy with work".

I've gotten no nicknames, no missions, no happy-ending-inspiring activities, and it worries me.

Maybe he has read my mind somehow and knows I am starting to feel treacherous, terrible things, and saved me the trouble of sorting through those feelings by removing himself entirely.

Maybe he's waiting on me to drastically turn my life around before allowing me into his any further.

I relegate myself to checking off wedding activities on my own: I approve the flowers, I pay for the cake, and I even set up a consultation to get fitted for my bridesmaid dress. I talk to Rose and

Aiden and evade emails from my publisher because writing is the one thing I haven't done.

I allow myself to imagine that Charlie would be proud of me for facing my fears of wedding-themed activities and grinning my way through them while tampering down the hurt I feel at the reality that he *still* hasn't mentioned going through Marjorie's things; maybe he was only saying it on a whim.

And, despite my best efforts, deep down beneath all of it, I can't help but hate the way everything is just so *boring* without him.

It makes me wonder if he's found someone else to spend his time with, and then I hate myself for even wondering such a thing.

Why would it matter if he had found someone else to help him with finding gifts for his sisters or doing minor tasks for his friend's wedding?

It's not like I mean anything to him.

It's not like there's any way for me to know if that night in the park is permanently imprinted on his brain as well, or if there was some secret message coded between our notes passed in church; no way to know if I am simply alone in these thoughts.

Trying to discern what any of it means is a pointless and agonizing task best avoided altogether.

Another agonizing task I've been avoiding is writing. This is unfortunate because there is no avoiding the reality that I have to write *something* - I'm a writer, albeit not a great one at this point, but a writer, nonetheless.

So, I keep sitting down in the kitchen determined to create.

* * * *

An hour and a half after sitting down, I'm still staring at a blank screen.

"You should get out of here," my mother suggests, standing in the doorway of the kitchen.

I turn around in my chair, indignant, "Listen, I know you and I aren't exactly on the best of terms right now but –" She cuts me off continuing:

"I meant, how you used to in high school; unless you were up in your room writing, you would always go to a coffee shop or something to work – it helped you clear your head."

"Oh," I say quietly. "Sorry. That might be a good idea."

She shrugs her shoulders, fully entering the kitchen to begin fixing lunch.

"It's alright. I've come to accept that you and I just aren't on the same page right now. I can't read you the way I once could, and I upset you by pressing, but you're an adult now. If you'd rather keep your life private, then you're entitled to that, and I'll just accept that I'm the person you only see around the holidays sometimes. And I'll keep learning to be okay with that."

Even though my mother's voice is reserved, every word she says sends a knife-like pain through my heart *because it's not true*. Because I miss my mom. And I want to tell her the truth.

I want to uncork the last nine years and try and make sense of everything I've felt and seen that has left me so hopeless, and I want to apologize and have her hug me like she used to when I was a kid – but I can't.

I want her to confess why she never told me all these things about Marjorie or came to visit me herself. And I want to tell her about this weird feeling in my gut I just can't seem to shake since going to church. I want to ask her if she knows what this word is that I can't seem to bring myself to fully realize.

I want answers and explanations, and to rip open these wounds I've so delicately tried to avoid touching and cut out all the scar tissue.

I want healing to happen. But I don't even know where to start.

I try to make the words come out, but they don't, and it makes me want to scream.

I've made attempts to pinpoint when it was that I lost the ability to make sense of my feelings, and every time it shuts me down. Like a self-defense mechanism that has been set up by my subconscious, stopping me from going too far; back to what hurt me, and so I stop.

My sophomore year of college, I had a roommate who majored in psychology.

She believed the world was one big traumatic event waiting to happen, and I remember her telling me that "the human brain can only take so much"; you can only get hurt so many times before your brain stops healing; only process so many stimuli before you short-circuit, like a computer that's overheated.

So, in response to this psychological "overheating", a lot of people who undergo exceptionally stressful events go into this catatonic state: their brains are overheated, or the pain is too great – it's like they've cut off an emotional limb, and rather than bleeding out or risking dying from the pain, their brains just... stop.

The world doesn't feel real, and no matter how hard they try, they can't push through to address the pain till they're ready.

They have to wait until the bleeding has slowed, and they're somewhere safe, to acknowledge all the pain that they've experienced.

Sometimes, I wonder if my brain has done this.

But despite this wondering, I don't push it.

I've never needed to overcome the hurdle that is my brain or think about what those four years in college brought out in me. Why would I try to acknowledge the gaping wound, when I've managed to survive for so long?

So, I let my mother keep believing I don't need her anymore because that's better than the alternative: asking for her help. Because she shouldn't have to fix me. She can't.

"You didn't do anything wrong,' is all I can manage to say, 'I still love you."

My mom's smile is not entirely convinced.

"I'm always going to love you too," she says sincerely.

I know it's as far as we are going to get with the conversation, so I take my mother's advice, pack my things up, and leave.

* * * *

I walk through town to get to *Written Comfort* which was always my go-to writing place as a teenager, but I stop short when I pass the mechanic's shop.

The gray pick-up truck seems to mock me from the parking lot: he's here.

I shouldn't stop and see if Charlie is there; I shouldn't because if he wanted to see me then he would reach out.

But I've never been good at doing what I should…

* * * *

Debra greets me with a twinkle in her eye. "Harper! It's good to see you!"

If the word "jolly" were turned into a human being, I think it would look a lot like Debra.

"How have you been dear?" She asks. I smile at her because she deserves that.

"I'm good, how are you?"

"I am just wonderful! Thank you for asking!" She beams back.

I glance around the office for any sign of Charlie. As I do so, Debra notices the two cups of coffee and the sandwich I'm holding, not to mention the way I'm distractedly glancing around the office.

"Can I help you with something?" She offers.

I breathe a sigh of relief that she's not making me sit through more small talk.

"Yeah, actually, I was wondering if Charlie was here?"

Another thrilled smile.

"Yes, he's just down in the garage, would you like for me to call him up?"

I shake my head no, "Would it be alright for me to go down and see him?"

Debra bites her lips nervously, "We're not really supposed to let civilians in the garage… safety and whatnot."

"Oh, I promise I'll be careful," I offer quickly. She looks around as if someone is going to bust us for sharing this little secret.

"If you promise to be careful, I don't see why such a *close friend* of Mr. Grant's can't go down for just a minute." She winks, and the action alone thrills me so much I could almost hug her.

Instead, I leave her with a "thank you" and open the door to the garage.

As soon as I descend the garage steps, I realize this means I have to *see* Charlie AND try to come up with a logical explanation for why I stopped by his workplace unannounced.

Lost in thought while stepping around the various machines and tools, I try to find him, stopping short when I actually do.

My stomach immediately ties in knots, and I feel my mouth go slack looking for words.

Charlie is hunched over the hood of a truck working, and the afternoon light is pouring in the windows of the shops illuminating him.

I'm limited to his profile from my angle, but from where I stand, he seems to glow.

A golden light emanates from his hair, skin, and brow where sweat has collected in an all too perfect way. Even the oil smudged on his face looks like it belongs there.

90's Christian rock music blasts from an old radio in the corner, and a machine whirs in the depths of the shop, but it doesn't matter because Charlie is *dancing*: swaying his hips and nodding his head in a rhythmic way that makes me want to laugh and smile and beg him to stop and keep going, all at once.

I'm suddenly aware of how hot it is in the shop, and how good Charlie looks when he concentrates, and his hair is stuck up in a fabulously messy way, making him look like he's in high school again.

He's the Charlie I remember, but not, all at the same time – past and present coexisting in a startling way that makes me wish I hadn't come and interrupted something that now seems so intimate.

I think if I leave now, I can make it back to my house, maybe even make it back to New York, before he is any the wiser, but as I turn to leave, I trip on a cable and knock several boxes to the ground.

Charlie looks up startled but soon breaks into a grin when he realizes it's me, causing my concerns to melt away. Because it's *Charlie*, and he's never been someone I should fear.

"Harper? Hey, what's up?"

Shyly, I walk towards the car he's working on.

"Nothing much, I just hadn't heard from you for a little while, so I thought I'd stop by... bring you some lunch or something." I hand him the sandwich and coffee (that I almost spilled) which he takes gingerly, thanking me for the surprise.

"Sorry, I would have cleaned up if I had known I'd be having company," he says with a laugh, gesturing to his filthy mechanic jumpsuit.

Despite the joke, it takes an alarming amount of self-control for me to not say something deeply horrifying like "I'm glad you didn't" or "I think I like you dirty" because it's such an un-Harper thing to say. Then again, he is in a very un-Charlie-like state right now.

"It's alright, I was just stopping by on my way to *Written Comfort*."

He quirks an eyebrow noting the coffee I've handed him with the café's label.

"Okay, so maybe I wanted to run one by after I got there."

He doesn't seem entirely convinced.

"So maybe, I'm actually just procrastinating on writing and thought it would be nice to check on you since I haven't seen you in a few days, and I was starting to miss your stupid face, and I wanted to make sure the Ginger Heads hadn't come back to get you and hold you for ransom in exchange for us agreeing to never reveal the intense baking secrets we learned during our time with them."

At that he smiles, because he knows it's the truth.

"Well, I'm still here in one piece, and if it makes you feel any better, I missed your stupid face as well," he winks at me, pulling up two boxes for us to use as makeshift chairs while he eats his lunch.

"And sorry I've been sort of MIA this week," he says unwrapping the parchment paper covering his sandwich, "With the temperature dropping, engines are starting to freeze up and cars are falling apart left and right. I've been swamped with work and just let things get away from me."

I reassure him things are totally fine, and the world has not ended in his absence. And I silently reassure myself at the confirmation that I didn't push him away Sunday.

We are *okay*. We are still us. And his text was genuinely his way of letting me know he was busy.

"How's wedding prep going without me?" He asks, biting into his chicken parm (a favorite of the boys back in high school – I should know, I was the one charged with picking up their order regularly).

I shrug my shoulders in response, looking away from his lips that I was staring at a *little* too hard.

"It's been bearable... I scheduled a fitting for us tomorrow. Or at least, it's a dress fitting for me, and you can get any suit alterations done if you want?"

He thanks me for thinking of him and lets me know he'll be there since he's supposed to pick up his suit this week anyway.

"How's the writing going?" He asks.

Normally, when someone asks me that, it feels like their attempt at a polite intrusion – like they don't genuinely *care*, they just want to make sure I'm not writing about THEM; but when Charlie asks me that, I know it comes from a place of genuine curiosity.

"It's not really," I tell him. "I keep trying and it's just so hard to focus. None of my old tricks seem to be working, and I just keep getting distracted. Some days it's like I'm so uninspired my own *brain* is trying to run away from me."

I release a heavy sigh before confessing, "My mom was the one who actually suggested getting out of the house to write, so I tried the café, but it was too quiet. I *hate* being alone with my thoughts – it lets me think too much."

He nods in understanding, and I appreciate the sympathetic look on his face.

"Maybe try doing something that isn't one of your old tricks?" He offers.

"Like what?"

"Like writing in a mechanic's shop for the day?" His lips quirk up in a half smile of hesitation as he makes the offer, and I glance around the building.

"Are you serious?"

"I am… is that a good or a bad thing?" Charlie asks, his eyes darting nervously around my face, trying to discern my reaction.

I laugh at the apparent fear in his voice.

"A *great* thing! I'd really appreciate hiding somewhere that keeps the whole town from trying to read over my shoulder or ask me how New York is. Besides, if all else fails, I'm at least here with you."

And I swear, the smile he gives me makes my heart flutter a whole heck of a lot more than it should.

* * * *

Charlie and I work remarkably well together.

We both hate silence, and the noises of the shop remind me a lot of the streets of New York, outside my apartment building.

From my position in an old lawn chair in the corner of the shop, I keep him entertained and attempt to lighten the mood when he gets frustrated with a car part, and he keeps me on track when I ever so apparently am trying to chase a rabbit trail.

It doesn't hurt when I look up from my computer screen and find myself staring at a golden Charlie, dancing or singing off-key, staring in intense concentration at a job.

He works smoothly, with deft precision, in a way I find reminiscent of a surgeon.

Some jobs are easier than others, and some are near impossible, but he finds a way to help someone regardless.

At one point, he tells me he likes working on cars because they remind him some things in life can be fixed, even when everything else feels out of control.

"Ah you, ever the optimist," I tease before he scolds me into returning to my own happy ending. Shockingly, at some point, between the coffee and the company, I begin to write.

It's nothing remarkable, it will need revisions for sure, but it's *something*, and as I write, I realize the feeling of my fingers gliding over the keys was something I missed.

I don't know if it's a happy ending I'm working towards, but it is something about a golden boy believing he can save the world...

* * * *

"How'd you get involved with the whole mechanic gig anyways?" I ask Charlie when we reach a quiet pause while working.

He leans against the front of the car he's been working on, palming a wrench thoughtfully.

"Remember those shop classes they'd make all the guys take in high school?" He asks me.

"Yeah?"

"Well," he admits, "I took them just for the easy A at first – I kept thinking, 'How hard could working on cars and building stuff be?' But then I started the class, and it was nothing like what I expected."

"How so?" I ask. A small smirk lifts the corner of his lips into a smile, almost bashful as he reflects on feelings from a lifetime ago.

"I had to work for it."

I tilt my head to the side, hoping he'll keep going.

He does. "Everything in my life had always come so *easy* to me: sports, grades, girls – I never had something truly challenge me – not the way that class did. And I *loved* it. I loved not immediately knowing what to do and having something that took thought, energy, and sweat and didn't involve a ball. I liked how it was practical and quiet and no one expected anything from me."

He smiles wistfully, "Cars were this machine I could take apart – inside and out and put back together. Their pieces have to go together perfectly, like a puzzle, and they either run right or they don't. People aren't so easy."

I'm surprised by most of what Charlie says, I had thought everything had been easy for him. He made it *look* easy. And I don't remember him mentioning a love for cars growing up either – but then again, I suppose there was a lot I didn't know about the Charlie Grant from my youth.

"But you said you studied business in college – why not engineering or technical school?"

He shrugs, setting the wrench on the edge of the car before leaning his back against the hood.

"I still loved baseball *more* – when looking at something to do for the rest of your life, picking the thing that comes naturally just makes more sense to an eighteen-year-old. But then when mom got sick, I couldn't just sit there and do *nothing*, especially after I stopped taking classes, so I thought I'd get a job."

I swallow hard at the vision of a scared Charlie in his early twenties, wanting desperately to find some way to help his family.

"I picked up a couple of hours here, saved up my money, learned more on the job than I think a technical school could have ever taught me, and in a way, it kind of saved me."

He explains, "It gave me something to look forward to every day, and it helped people when I felt like there was nothing else I could do. Like I said: people are hard – cars have solutions." I nod along. "I probably sound like some control freak, I'm sorry."

Charlie runs a greasy hand through his hair, smearing some oil across his face, sheening from sweat.

"No, you're not crazy at all. In fact, it's the sanest thing I've ever heard."

Charlie perks up, eyes guarded; he looks like the boy I remember him being, soft blonde hair falling across his face. "It's the reason I write," I confess.

"Really?" He crosses his arms skeptically.

"Really." I can't believe I'm telling him this, "I started writing because it was the one thing that made me feel in control. I could exact justice on whoever I saw fit, however I saw fit. I could make people do things that made far more sense than their actual actions, say the words no one else wanted to say. I could be the realist no one wanted to hear – I fell in love with writing, because when you're lost in your own little worlds, anything you want to be real *is* reality."

I pause, releasing a nervous breath, "I had control when I felt powerless – to stay, to leave, to make things happen. Writing made my world make sense."

When I look up from my lap, where I've ever so bashfully been staring while I made my confession, I see Charlie smiling at me.

"So, the Heartbreaker breaks hearts because it gives her a sense of control?"

"Yes, she does," I confirm.

He nods, letting our truths sit in the air.

"We're just a couple of control freaks, aren't we?" Charlie asks. I laugh a little in response.

"Maybe, or maybe we're just human. And humans like trying to have control," I offer.

Charlie ponders this for a minute.

"Want to lose control for once?" He asks. There's a mischievous look in his eyes.

"And ruin the gray hairs I'm trying to give myself before thirty?" My laugh comes out strained and a little nervous.

"No, I think you want to lose control with me," he winks. My insides are a flurry of feeling like a bottle of soda being shaken up.

"What did you have in mind?" I ask cautiously.

"Come with me," he extends a grease-covered hand, hoisting me up from where I sit.

Carefully, I set my laptop down in my chair and follow him to the back of the shop.

I can't see much out of the ordinary: just walls of tools and trash, and an old rusty car that looks beyond saving.

"What are we doing?" I ask. Charlie looks at me over his shoulder.

"*We*," he picks up an old baseball bat he has tucked into the corner, "are going to *break*," he gestures to the car, "that."

"No, we aren't!" I gasp.

"Why not?!" He protests.

"Because! You're Mr. Fix It – which is the *exact opposite* of destroying a car."

"You are *so* right, and also so *very wrong*, Ms. Turkey Chaser – because this car is here with the *intention* of destruction."

I roll my eyes before telling him, "That makes zero sense."

"It makes all the sense in the world," he counters. "Ricky from the scrap yard called me one day to see if I could get any usable parts off of it, and when I couldn't, he suggested I take some stress out on it anyways, since he'd do nothing but crush it. So here we are – seeking our cathartic release. It'll inspire you – I *promise*."

"What a very bold promise," I tease.

"Come on... you know you want to. It's like when people get their best ideas out on walks – you just need to relieve some tension."

This is beginning to sound like less and less of a terrible idea...

"Okay... but don't you think we need protection of some kind?"

"Of course, I'm already on it." He tosses me a pair of protective goggles, similar to what we'd wear in biology labs in high school, along with the bat.

"So, I just," hoisting the bat over my head, "go like this?" I make a downward swinging motion towards the already dented hood of the car.

"Yep, exactly like that."

"Okay," I nod, "I can do this."

I can do this, I can do this, I can do this.

I begin to swing down and – "I can't do this!"

Charlie rolls his eyes and lets out an exasperated breath.

"Fine then, I guess you just need somebody to show you how it's done."

Taking the bat from my hands, he brings it down on the car with a resounding clang, like a car wreck.

I flinch, but my shoulders relax when I see the smile on his face.

He whacks it again, taking out a headlight, that skirts across the garage floor. I raise a questioning eyebrow, but he shakes his head. "Make a mess, I'll clean it up when I'm done."

Okay... *I can do this.*

"My turn," I declare. He hands me the bat as I roll my shoulders back, loosening up.

"That's my girl," he says, absent-mindedly. I ignore the blush rapidly spreading across my face and swing the bat into the car – for once not thinking about everything going on in my life.

The shock vibrates up my arms, but with it, I feel a jolt of excitement and a release of a fraction of the tension I carry in my body.

"That was fun," I whisper, in awe of the catharsis of destruction.

Charlie's eyes are bright looking at my wild grin.

"I thought you'd like it – now have at it," he winks, and at his permission, I go to work on the car.

I dent in the hood, and the fender, and bust out the other light. A squeal of glee comes out of me when I use the end of the bat to finish busting out the window, and Charlie gives me an approving cheer.

Who would have thought? Charlie Grant: good guy extraordinaire and vandalism enthusiast.

We keep taking turns beating the car, till there's little to no car left, and as we return to our respective positions with our hearts racing, sweat trickling down our backs, I feel more alive than I've felt in ages. And lighter. Like I had released some of the stress I'd been holding.

He was right.

"Hey Charlie," I call to him as he begins to turn around and go back to work, "thank you for being a control freak. I think the world is a better place because of it."

He smiles, equally relaxed and ready to return to work.

"Of course, Harper, thank you for losing control with me."

"Any time," I wink, before he turns to face the car with a laugh.

* * * *

By the time the sun is setting, and Charlie is closing up for the day, we are both coated in a light sheen of sweat, and my fingers have begun to ache.

After our exercise in losing control, I managed four pages.

It's no novel, not even close, but I will take what I can get for the first time in months and count today as a small victory.

Charlie holds the door for me on our way out, and I realize now just how cold it's begun to get. At this rate, a white Christmas is bound to happen, and my inner child does a little jig at the thought.

"I really liked having you around today Harper, thank you."

"Of course! Thanks for giving me somewhere to hide out. I think you and I work pretty well together; don't you think?" I could be imagining it, but I swear I think I see Charlie blush.

"I definitely think so," he replies, glancing around at the town square and locking the door behind him.

When we hover outside the door, Charlie twisting the lock in place, I think about the reason I even came here in the first place. After the great time we had, I told myself I wouldn't bring it up, but I can't stop the words from spilling out of my mouth (which now that I think about it, my self-control around Charlie Grant is essentially non-existent).

"Hey, I just wanted to say I'm sorry for Sunday," I stammer out awkwardly. "If I was rude or awkward or anything…"

Charlie looks shocked, attempting to cut me off from bumbling through an apology:

"Harper, there's nothing to be sorry for. I meant what I wrote: whatever the Lord is doing in your life will be in His timing when *you're* ready. I just really felt like I couldn't keep taking you to do all of these activities synonymous with happy endings, and not share with you what I think is the happiest thing we can experience in this life. I want a happy ending for you Harper… in all its forms."

"Oh…"

I don't really know what else to say when someone is so transparently tender and careful with me.

"Thank you," I tell him softly.

"Of course. So, don't apologize for anything, okay?" He says firmly.

"Okay," I return.

He nods, satisfied. Thinking our business here is done, I turn to walk home, but it's Charlie's turn to stop me:

"Hey, I was wondering if you wanted to have dinner tomorrow? Like at the house?" He pauses for a moment, and my stomach pinches with nerves… he's not asking me out, *is he?*

He continues, "I was thinking you could come over after the dress fitting and we could look for the girls' gift, and I thought you may like to just stay for dinner as well."

Something mildly akin to disappointment races through me before I shrug it off, positive it's just exhaustion after a long day.

While I've been analyzing Charlie's question in my head, he's shuffled somewhat awkwardly, taking his hands in and out of his pockets, like he's not quite sure what to do with them.

I now realize I *like* watching Charlie Grant squirm – it's fun to be on the receiving end of it, rather than being the one to constantly feel like they're unsure of what to do next.

"I would love to, but the girls aren't going to mind, are they?"

"No," he reassures me, "they'll be thrilled to have another girl around." And while I'm not entirely sure that's true, they're his sisters, so there's no point in arguing with him.

"Great! I'll see you tomorrow?" He asks me, that ever-present excitement and hope filling his eyes, each time we make a new plan.

I smile back with a yes before turning again and walking home, only pausing to watch Charlie load up his truck and head home.

He offered to give me a ride, but I said no, opting for a walk through the snow instead.

I already know I'm much too excited to be spending time with Charlie again, and extended time in a confined space with him is the last thing I need.

So, like a mantra, I repeat my new goal to myself on the way home, hoping the cold will freeze it into my brain somehow before tomorrow arrives:

I am not going to fall for Charlie Grant.

I am not falling for Charlie Grant.

There will be absolutely no falling for Charlie Grant, because above all other things, he shouldn't fall in love with me.

12

Aiden's call is the first thing I hear when I wake up at six in the morning.

"Who died?" I answer.

"No one, why?" He says. I can hear a taxi whizzing by in the background.

"Because I'm trying to understand why you would call me at this hour."

I swear I can *hear* him checking his watch.

"First of all,' he says, 'six o'clock isn't early, and I'm on my way to the gym."

I forgot about my darling brother's early-bird tendencies.

"Second of all, what did you do to my best friend?" He asks. I sit up straighter at his words.

"What do you mean?" He pauses to sip on what I'm sure is his daily green juice (he's routinely tried to send me some via mail).

"Why are you having dinner with Charlie's family? You haven't done that since sophomore year."

Wiping the sleep from my eyes, I try to decipher Aiden's tone. It doesn't seem angry, more or less concerned, and deeply, deeply confused. Then again, aren't we all?

"Because I am helping him go through Marjorie's things to find a gift for the girls, and he offered to let me stay for dinner after," I explain.

"Oh," he replies quietly.

I'm awake now, and more than a little irritable from being woken up. He may be used to waking up early, but I am not, nor do I appreciate the tone with which I've been awoken.

"Why does it matter?" I press, irritation seeping through my voice.

"Maybe because you and Charlie have never been friends before, and now you're hanging out all the time-"

"At the request of our mother and *your* fiancé, who has dumped planning a wedding on me at the last minute. Charlie is just helping!" I refrain from telling him the deal made between me and Charlie because that seems too private, too... personal for some reason.

I now notice the other end of the phone line has gone quiet. "Aiden, are you there?" I ask.

"Don't hurt each other, okay?"

It's not a command, but a gentle plea. I shift uncomfortably in my bed; thankful Aiden can't see me fidget right now.

"I don't know what you mean," I reply coyly.

Aiden loosens a deep breath, and I visualize his thick brows knit together in concern: the way they always get when he's concentrating hard.

"Yeah, you do Harper. I know my best friend and sister well enough, to know you already know exactly what that means."

I hate that he's right.

I hate that he doesn't even know the whole truth about me, that he hasn't been here in weeks... and he is right.

"Okay then," my voice is soft, and I hate the defeat laced through my words, "I'll be careful."

As if by magic, Aiden's normal, happy-go-lucky voice is back, chipper through the phone, despite moments ago speaking words into existence that have left my heart feeling heavy and gross, like it's done something wrong.

"I know you will. At the gym, got to go, love you, bye!" Then he's gone, and I'm left alone with myself and my thoughts.

* * * *

Around noon, I meet Charlie outside the doors of the dress shop, and it might be the first time he doesn't look completely psyched out of his mind to do something - fitting my mood properly.

"What's wrong? Don't love hanging around bridal boutiques?" I try to tease. He shakes his head, his mouth pursed in a firm line.

"No, not exactly. Makes me all itchy and bored, takes me right back to shopping with my mom when I was a kid."

What a guy thing to say, I think, rolling my eyes.

While I am not particularly thrilled either (after my conversation this morning with Aiden) and have come to the realization that this will require I lose my usual ensemble of a sweater and jeans, I will grin and bear it for Rose, who has been non-stop texting me wedding details from the moment Aiden gave her my number.

If it wasn't the Japanese stewartias, it was an idea on how to arrange the tables for the dinner after the service, or a cute pair of earrings to compliment my dress, or an update on one of the bridesmaids who has bailed out.

At this point, I'm not entirely sure she doesn't just have a bridal party of one.

Rose is not so extreme that I would call her a "Bridezilla", but I'd be lying if I said the constant reassurance she requires wasn't just a little exhausting.

I've begun to find great humor in imagining what life looks like for Aiden and Rose, as her type-A, perfectionist habits seem more and more juxtaposed to my brother's nonchalant, "live life to the fullest" mentality.

Then again, we all know what they say about opposites attracting.

This thought leaves me with the comforting knowledge that she will be around for quite some time; meaning, the least I can do for her is hopefully prevent an aneurysm from taking place before the wedding, by trying on this dress and sending her a picture proving it fits.

* * * *

Anna, a girl I knew in high school, now runs the shop in place of her mother, and she uses now, as I try to zip up the dress, as an opportunity to fill me in on the last nine years of her life.

She apparently has two kids now and married a guy in our math class who I don't remember.

Good for her I think, trying not to visibly flinch or frown as she drones on about a domestic life that will never be mine.

It's not like those things matter to me anyway, I say to no one but myself, as some form of mild self-assurance.

"All done," she declares with a flourish of her hands.

A ball of fear begins forming in my gut as I look down at the mermaid-styled dress coated in burgundy sequins, trailing down before me – so unlike anything I've worn before.

"Wow, you look great Harper," Anna says with a sweet smile, "I'm glad you and one of those bridesmaids were the same size, otherwise we would have had to order another." Then, she seems to whisper out of the side of her mouth, as if we are sharing some secret, "I'm not entirely sure it'd be here in time".

With that in mind, I suck in a deeper breath, making sure it fits, and allow myself to be ushered out of the dressing room and into the foyer where mirrors line the walls.

Charlie sits in a chair, staring at his phone, looking rather bored when we walk in, but as I step up onto the pedestal, bringing my dress into full view, he sits up a little straighter.

I ignore this, reminding myself of our reality.

"You clean up nice," he stammers out.

I hear Anna snicker beside me before turning to look in a mirror, seeing what everyone else sees, and I'm so shocked my mouth literally falls open.

The rich color of the sequins turns my olive skin into a golden tan, and my dark eyes appear richer in color.

I can't help but like the way my chest is accentuated by the deep V-neck of the dress, and how the A-line figure hugs my body just right.

It makes me wonder if I ever truly thought of myself as beautiful until this moment, and as Charlie tells me I "really do look good", I realize *no, no I didn't*.

I make a mental note to thank Rose for choosing such a lovely dress, as I swish back and forth in the mirror.

I, Harper Marshall, *like the swishing*.

"So, you really think it looks good?" I look to Charlie for confirmation, who is watching me with an unrecognizable look in his eyes. Something hidden, beneath the general shock of seeing me in a dress at a time other than junior prom, almost resembles desire as he whispers the word *amazing*.

It sends a shiver down my spine that I despise, and brush aside in favor of more time in the mirror.

"I definitely think this dress is the right fit Harper, I'll set it aside for you and send you the invoice," Anna tells me from behind the register, breaking the spell the sparkles have over me.

"Oh, yes, yeah that'll work. Thank you," I tell her, avoiding Charlie's eyes as I walk back carefully into the dressing room, making sure I don't trip on the small train the dress has.

I don't want to see his facial expressions anymore; to know what he really thinks of how I look, because it's not the real me, and it's not right.

It's a dolled-up version with a lot more glitter, but it's not me.

Besides, I don't think I can handle much more of those savage eyes, wanting and warm from his position in the chair.

It's an unfamiliar look I've never seen on Charlie, and the unknowingness of it all frightens me just as much as the truth behind it does.

I run my hands down my sides once behind the dressing room curtain with Anna, unafraid to enjoy the sensation of the sequins beneath my fingers in the sole company of another girl who knows just how good it feels to pretend to be a princess.

"It's fun isn't it?" Anna whispers to me with a secretive smile, "feels good to wear that much glitter at once".

It's not a question – it's a statement she already knows the answer to.

Shyly, I smile, and much to my horror, bust out laughing.

"Gosh, it just feels so *different*, you know. Like I can *be* anyone, which is stupid because it's just a dress, but it's so *so* pretty..." I ramble, overcome with this new sensation.

I don't remember the last time I described something as "pretty" as a grown woman, with this much enthusiasm, but this dress definitely fits the bill. Easing my nerves, Anna laughs with me.

"I know exactly what you're feeling," she affirms before setting to work undoing the zipper.

When the dress is halfway unzipped, she asks, "Do you not get to dress up a ton for book tours and stuff? I always imagined life in New York like all those shows you see. Seems so glamorous..."

I shake my head as I step out of the dress, making room for her to hang it up.

"Not really at all no. I'm sure there *is* a glamorous side to New York, but I haven't seen it; I'm usually in sweats or a sweater hiding behind my laptop in my shoebox apartment."

It's supposed to be a joke, but Anna doesn't laugh, and I realize it does actually sound a little sad.

"Not that I'm not more comfortable that way – I am! I just don't really go out to a ton of places that justify needing to dress up," I continue. This doesn't make things any better. In fact, Anna is now looking at me with a justifiable amount of pity in her eyes.

Wow. I've lived in New York for nine years and haven't remotely attempted to experience truly *living* there.

Those were the things I tried to avoid in the name of work.

Everything I've done has always been in the name of work...

"Well, if it makes you feel any better, being at home with two kids under five doesn't leave a ton of room for dressing up and going out, so you want to know what I do instead?"

"What?" I ask her, pulling my cable knit sweater over my head, almost fully dressed.

Anna pauses before answering, looking around to make sure no one is listening, once again.

I'm beginning to wonder if she knows something about dress shops I don't...

"I like to try on the wedding dresses when we get a new shipment," she finally whispers.

I can't help but laugh because it's truly genius.

Why go to a store and spend money, when you *literally* own one?

"That's amazing, when was the last shipment in?" She smiles, pleased I like her idea.

"Today actually…" Anna is looking at me with a twinkle in her eye, and I know she can't truly be willing to offer this to me. "Would you like to try one on?" She says joyfully.

Like to? Maybe.

Should I? No, definitely not.

Because I am not getting married any time soon, or quite possibly ever, because that would mean admitting to some small part of myself that happy endings are real and possible for people like me.

"Oh, come on, please?!" She whines, "If only to save me the trouble of trying it on myself?"

"You just told me you liked trying them on!" I say incredulously.

"But I like seeing *other people* try them on more! I like seeing women feel beautiful, and there is *nothing* like a wedding dress to make you feel all those things!" She exclaims.

I look around the dressing room desperately seeking some kind of excuse.

"Aren't you going to get in trouble? What if someone walks in?"

She shrugs like this is the most minuscule problem in the world.

"There aren't any appointments set for today, I've caught up on all the alterations that need to be made, and if someone walks in then we will just tell them you and Charlie are getting married and you are a customer, which isn't a total lie." Under her breath she adds, "It's not like anyone would be surprised with the way he's looking at you". I don't ask her what she means by that, because I think it would make my face redden more than it already has.

"Please Harper, you'd be helping me out," she finally says.

I glance at the time on my phone and see that our appointment hasn't taken nearly as long as it was supposed to, leaving a whole lot of downtime for Charlie and me.

"You know you want to…" She says, waggling her eyebrows.

She's right.

I do want to, and isn't a part of looking on the bright side seizing the moment?

I tell myself this will make Charlie proud, and hesitantly agree, before being drug off to a sea of glitter, white, and taffeta.

****

Twisting my hair into a low bun, I admire the gown before me.

After the sequins, I wanted to go for something simple, something more Harper, but Anna has somehow managed to maneuver me into a princess gown.

With my bust wrapped in a cream-colored fabric, the dress is strapless. Crisp, clean white fabric continues down to the bottom of the gown, where crinoline puffs it out. Small flecks of silver glitter trail down the body of the gown, looking like fallen snow, or stardust, and a few properly placed diamonds make me look like I've stepped down from the winter sky.

The sight causes a warmth to spread through me: slow and sure, confident and quiet; I feel like a woman standing before the mirror, instead of a little girl playing dress up like I thought I would.

It takes several silent moments to pass before Anna and I dare say anything, and even then, all we can manage is "wow".

It doesn't require any prompting for me to slowly make my way into the foyer, because unlike the first dress, I *want* to see more.

At first, I let my vanity run wild, truly taking it all in.

I beam, grinning ear to ear, swaying in the soft light of the foyer, surrounded by sparkling images of myself. And then, after I've taken a moment for myself, I look for Anna to thank her for this special moment, only to find she dismissed herself silently.

I brace myself, for Charlie's boredom or teasing, but when I turn to face him, my heart stops.

If our eyes were capable of speaking the way tongues do, I think Charlie Grant's eyes would be writing sonnets.

Or maybe they would be chastising him for showing such emotion.

Perhaps, they would be saying nothing at all, at a loss for words.

As he stands and walks towards me, my

heart begins to hammer, racing a million miles a minute, reminding me I am alive; my heart didn't stop, even if my breathing did.

I am alive, and I am here. And so is Charlie.

Tears have turned his blue eyes into radiant pools, and a soft smile plays at his lips.

Beneath all of it, there is a pain.

A pain I can't place, that rips my racing heart in two.

When Charlie stands before me, I try to speak, but I realize tears have collected in my eyes as well.

I wipe them away quickly, sniffling, saying with a smile, "What's wrong?"

To consider myself a writer, Charlie Grant renders me speechless. Incapable of articulation. His presence rips all my words away, leaving me with nothing but raw feelings.

Feelings I'd rather spend the rest of my life covering up, than offering them to him exposed and trembling with fear.

He's still smiling, unaware of the turmoil rolling within me, but it doesn't reach his eyes, and that action alone makes me want to throw every mantra, lie, and word from Aiden out the window, so I can truly understand what I'm feeling right *now*.

"Nothing," he offers bashfully, taking my hand and squeezing it twice. "Just thinking."

I swallow hard. Gosh, *why do I want to cry so badly?*

"What are you thinking about?" I manage to stammer out without breaking down, and Charlie pauses.

My hand is still in his, and he's gently stroking my knuckles with his thumb, making each stroke feel like a lick of some unfathomable fire, and his stupid smile is still there alongside the tears.

He swallows hard before speaking, truly thinking over his words.

"I'm thinking about," he says, his voice barely louder than a whisper, "how truly, *profoundly*, beautiful, my best friend's little sister looks in a wedding dress. And how I don't know if I should be saying those words out loud, or if it's even alright for me to feel the way I do…"

My heart stops again, and I want to say something, I do, to tell him I don't care what the cost is, I want him to say all those things and more out loud, but instead, Charlie squeezes my hand with finality before turning around and walking out the doors of the shop to wait outside.

I stumble in a daze back to the dressing room where Anna waits, trying to convince myself the last minute was a dream.

A strange, beautiful, heart-wrenching, glitter-induced dream.

But my heart is still racing, and I can still feel the fire racing up my arms in place of Charlie's touch.

It was real.

* * *

The Grant's attic is exactly what I imagine the attic of a widower and his three children would look like: a solid four inches of dust and an insurmountable number of cobwebs.

I reach for the overhanging chain to turn on the single lightbulb that illuminates the attic. Once I do, everything is washed in a warm, yellow light.

I force myself to lock eyes with Charlie as I look behind me to avoid inhaling the blanket of dust falling from a rafter.

He averts his gaze to a box at our feet labeled *"Charlie Sports Trophies"*.

It's not at all what we are looking for, but it's something to look at that isn't me.

I don't think I entirely blame him.

The ride to his house had been eerily silent as if our moment in the dress shop had violated some unspoken treaty I was supposed to know about, and my attempts at small talk had done nothing to diminish the mounting tension.

All I gained from the experience was that: the girls are going to be brought home from ballet by a friend, his dad is making dinner, and he has no idea what we are looking for, forcing me to return to the task at hand, moving one dusty box after another, trying to find something to capture the essence of Marjorie Grant.

"Mom wasn't all that into material things, but I still want it to be something personal, so it's just hard…" Charlie finally comments after a few minutes of searching.

I pull an old dress out of a box labeled "give away" that will never leave this attic.

"Do you think they'd like some kind of dress of hers?" I offer. He shrugs.

"Maybe... it would just have to be something they actually cared about, that could be adjusted to fit them. Mom wasn't exactly their size." I nod in understanding: my mother and Marjorie both shared the belief the memories one could make and the action of enjoying life, was far more important than the trend of calorie counting.

I sift through some more boxes, finding old necklaces and rings, making a mental note. I find a pile of his dad's old shirts and baby clothes from the girls. Towards the back of the attic, I see a stack of books protruding from a cardboard box.

The light hardly reaches to this dark corner, but the dust coating them implies they haven't been here long.

I note the sharpie writing on the box that is undeniably Charlie's: *Mom's Books.*

I fold the flaps of the box down and begin sorting through the titles: Whitman and *Little House on the Prairie*, a collection of a series I remember her reading with the ladies' book club in the library when we were younger, and a few old self-help novels on how to raise children right.

I pretend to not see the titles related to ALS treatments and natural remedies, but no matter how hard I try, I can't ignore the covers I know all too well: my books at the bottom of the box.

I pull them out, feeling my heart simultaneously swell and shatter at the sight of the annotated pages. Yellow for lines she thought were funny, pink for quotes she loved, and little notes written in the margins in a blue pen. Her cursive script litters the inside covers of my paperbacks, but she used sticky notes in the hardcovers. All of the inscriptions detailing the praise she would have given me for each book.

"Find anything?" Charlie asks, walking up behind me, casting a shadow over myself and the box. When I turn to him with quivering hands, his face falls.

"She's really gone, isn't she?" I stammer out.

I thought I could do this. I really thought I could, but the pieces of her are everywhere, and there's no way for me to put them together and bring her back.

Charlie doesn't answer my question, but he does gently take the book from my hands and wrap me in a hug.

"I'm sorry Charlie, I really believed I could do this, but it's just… a lot."

He nods with understanding, stroking a hand down my hair, reaching the small of my back, and it's nice. I didn't even realize I was crying till I saw the wet spots on his shirt.

"We all went and saw a grief counselor after it all happened. I don't think I ever told you that," he says softly.

I shake my head no – he had never told me.

"Yeah, I don't know," he continues with a head shake, "it was weird, and she always spoke in this voice that was soft, and supposed to be soothing, but it just felt fake. She didn't know the way we were hurting. Our whole world had just been flipped completely upside down." He's staring off into the distance as if watching the memories play out before him, a film of all the things he's tried to forget. "She did tell me about the stages of grief though: denial, anger, bargaining, depression, and acceptance."

"Did it help? Knowing those things?" I ask, my voice muffled by his shirt that I haven't stopped pressing my cheek into, finding safety in his strength.

"It did actually," his voice sounds surprised, like he doesn't want to admit it. "It made me feel less crazy knowing what I was feeling wasn't coming from nowhere. Like I was supposed to be feeling those things, and it was okay. To go through all the steps, and sometimes go back to them, and even get stuck in some longer than others."

Neither one of us says anything for a beat before he continues, "All that to say, you're not crazy or broken. You're just healing, and you can take as long as you need to do so, and I'll never force you to do something you don't want to do or aren't ready for."

"Thank you," I whisper into his chest.

I'm surprised that I find him so warm and comforting in this dark corner of the past, but I realize I'm glad that if I have to bear my brokenness to anybody, it's him.

"We can keep looking for something for the girls," I declare.

He loosens the hug and lets his hands fall to my waist, looking down at me as if he is trying to read my expression.

I wonder if maybe he believes he can read my mind in the same way I want to be able to read his.

"Are you sure?" He asks cautiously.

The protective edge in his voice is not lost on me, as if he thinks he can protect me from myself – from making a decision that will hurt me more.

"Yes," I say with some finality, "I can do this. *We* can do this."

He nods, his lips pressed in a firm line. His brow is creased in concentration, and I have to resist the urge to smooth it out with my fingers.

It makes me wonder if he will simply overrule my decision - as if I am merely agreeing out of a great act of self-sacrifice.

"Okay, if you say so."

He trusts me. Better than that, he trusts me to know myself and my needs.

He always seems to.

With a final nod of silent agreement, we set back to work: we go through box after box, some making us cry more than others, and we let ourselves feel it all.

When the burden gets too heavy to bear alone, we hold one another, unashamedly letting our tears fall, showing them to no one but each other.

Sometimes we let each other feel things alone.

I know there are certain things Charlie feels as a son, that no matter how desperately I'd like to sympathize, I'll never understand.

Those moments are for him.

In turn, he lets me mourn my friend.

Occasionally, I voice the guilt I feel that I'm not sure will ever fade.

I wish there was something I could have done, if only come home to see her, instead of neglecting how precious and short life can be.

Charlie lets me vent, standing across the attic giving me both the physical and emotional space to do so, and each time he responds as best as he can.

Sometimes that means silence, but other times it is words of comfort.

He doesn't dismiss my past or brush away my actions we both know are wrong, but he reminds me humans are flawed by design, and I now understand just how fragile life truly is.

It makes me feel heard in a way I didn't even know I needed, and it makes me think about my own mother. About how she and I still aren't really speaking, and it reminds me of just how urgently I should make things right because every day isn't promised.

Talking to Charlie makes me feel as if I have been stripped of my past, of everything that's really held me back, leaving me vulnerable and raw - naked before him. And he takes it all in stride.

And I'm not scared of it. It makes me feel safe.

Like the cagey feeling in my chest can settle.

I don't have to hide from him, I realize, as he fixes me with his watery blue eyes across the attic.

In the filtered light from the lone window, I think maybe, Charlie Grant might see me better than I've ever seen myself.

Like he's somehow uncovered the darkness that lays within and not shied away; instead, he's stayed.

When we stumble upon a gift for the girls, we both feel lighter than when we started, whether we could ever admit it out loud or not.

With pink eyes and runny noses, I hold up an unfinished quilt.

Pulling it out of a box labeled with the date from four years ago, I recognize Marjorie's handwriting.

"I never knew this was up here," Charlie tells me.

As we take out the items, I feel like we are being transported back to the past: inside the tub are the patches to finish the quilt, the quilt itself, a sewing kit, a stack of letters, some old VHS tapes, and a stack of polaroids. At the bottom of the tub lies a note; Charlie picks it up with steady hands and reads with a trembling voice:

To Whoever Finds This Box,

This is my last gift to you.

I know soon, I won't be able to finish this quilt any longer, nor will I be able to write, and I felt like it was only fair I got some say in what I leave behind in this world.

To whoever finds this, I ask you to finish my quilt and give it to my family.

Tell them to remember my hugs every time they wrap themselves in it.

I also ask you to distribute these letters to their proper readers. I tried to cover all the majors I knew I wouldn't get to be there for, but I'm sure I will have somehow missed at least one, and whichever one that is, tell my family I love them.

I have always loved them, and even if I don't want to leave them, I am at peace.

I am going to be with my Heavenly Father whom I've always loved more than this earth anyway, and He is going to take care of everyone I will leave behind.

I have no regrets from this life, and I want whoever reads this to feel the same way.

You only get one life, and it is a short one, filled with millions of plot twists like this disease, but every story still matters.

My boy understands this. He sees the silver lining to every rain cloud, and I hope that never changes...

All my love, to everyone, always,

-Marjorie Grant

The note is short, but it is perfect.

It is Marjorie in every shape, way, form, and fashion.

Who needs to find a gift, when she left one herself?

Tears streak Charlie's face, but he smiles as we flip through the Polaroids. Each one is a memory from either her or her children's childhood.

I see a young Marjorie, smiling, madly in love with the man in the photo: Charlie's father. A young Beckett sits butt naked in a pile of stuffed animals - we get a good laugh out of it.

I'm the first one to pick up the stacks of letters.

Within it, there is a stack addressed to Charlie, one to Aria, a stack to Beckett, and one to their father, all labeled with specific holidays or occasions like "wedding day", "high school graduation", and "birth of a child". There are others though, less specific, like "when you need a smile", "when you've met the one", and "words of wisdom".

My smile broadens as I hand the stack to Charlie, who sifts through the stack intently.

"Harper, did you see these at the bottom?"

I didn't.

He shows me more letters I had brushed past: "final words" to my mother, "life advice" for Aiden, and there, at the bottom of the stack, is a yellowing envelope that simply says my name.

No directions or details, only *Harper Marshall* in scrawling cursive.

Now is not the time, I know that. Marjorie knows that too. Which is why I gingerly take the envelope from Charlie and set it aside for when I will read those words, because I know then, and only then, will I be ready... whenever that day is.

Somewhere, within the house, Charlie's father calls us to dinner.

With a satisfied excitement, we carry the tub down the ladder, knowing this is just another step towards healing: another chance at happily ever after.

13

I haven't had dinner with the Grant family in almost a decade. The last time I did was before the winter formal in the tenth grade when Charlie was forced to go as my date because Aiden was taking one of my friends.

Marjorie and my mother had made us a big tray of lasagna and platters of cookies, and I would still argue it was more fun than the actual dance that followed.

I remembered feeling so awkward when Charlie would put his arms around me for photos, and how I much preferred the group pictures when things felt more normal - like we were all friends and Charlie wasn't my *date*.

A small part of me wonders if I would feel the same way now, and an even larger part of me wishes there were some dance to escape to that would get me away from the judgmental eyes of Beckett Grant.

"Are you moving home?" Aria asks me without hesitation or social graces.

I aspire to obtain the amount of candor young children possess.

"No, she's not Aria, you know that. Now stop asking," Charlie corrects sternly, saving me from answering.

Tonight, instead of a plate of lasagna, a bowl of spaghetti sits in front of me, and aside from Aria's sporadic questioning, the meal is filled with little more than the sounds of fork scraping.

"How was work, Dad?" Charlie tries for polite conversation, and Mr. Grant obliges, telling us about his day.

"How are things in New York, Harper?" Mr. Grant asks.

I can't help but feel pity welling up in my chest when looking at the shell of a man sitting to my right at the table.

I didn't get a chance to really look at him at church the other day, but it's clear Mr. Grant has lost weight since I left, and his forced smile doesn't quite reach his eyes, but he seems more present than I ever remember him being when we were growing up.

It's almost as if his loss grounded him to the earth in a way sheer goodness never could.

I've come to realize tragedy has a way of doing that to people.

"They're good. Awfully cold this time of year, but good." He nods without a response.

"It gets cold here too!" Aria chimes in.

"She knows that smart one, she's lived here before," Bex rolls her eyes, and I note the way Charlie's grip tightens on his fork.

It's some of the first words I've heard her say since I've been home, and they are laced with an expected amount of teenage sarcasm.

"How are things going with the ballet girls? Charlie told me you guys have parts in the annual *Nutcracker*." Aria gives me all the details of her part in the production, and I let her talk, her bright voice filling the silence of the small dining room.

"That's great. And Bex, are you going to the winter formal?" I ask, looking at the girl across the table from me.

The winter formal has been a tradition ever since the founding of Pinecrest High, and just like every other holiday tradition in this town, it's sort of a big deal.

Forget homecoming or prom, the peak of high school life for Pinecrest students is this dance, right after Christmas, in honor of the New Year.

"Yeah," is the only confirmation I get as Charlie's oldest sister pokes absently at her bowl of pasta.

"Do you have a date?" I try for a saccharine tone I hope will somehow make me come across as "one of the girls"; Instead, it is only met with a look of sheer disgust.

"Ew, no, why would you even ask? You're like, *old*," she grimaces.

Awesome. Now I'm old.

"Beckett take that back *now*," Charlie commands.

"Why should I? Why are we all suddenly acting like we're happy to see Harper, as if she's some long-lost friend, when in reality she hasn't given us a second thought since she skipped town!" Beckett slams her fork down on the table with a shocking force, sending our glasses rattling.

"That's not fair – she's had a lot going on." Charlie is trying to defend me, and though I appreciate the sentiment, she's not wrong.

"What's she been so busy with? Getting rich and famous, while we get left here to rot?"

"I don't know what has gotten into you tonight, but you know full and well this is unacceptable–" Charlie is about to continue but I cut him off.

"It's okay Charlie, she's right. I have no business being here, I'm sorry girls, Mr. Grant," I nod in their direction, "have a good evening. I hope I haven't disturbed you all too much. And... I'm sorry for your loss." Pushing my chair back, I place my bowl in the sink and make for the door, avoiding the gaze of my former dining partners.

I hear Charlie calling my name as I walk outside, but it doesn't matter, because Beckett was right: I *don't* belong here, and I don't deserve a warm welcome into the lives of these people whom I've essentially deserted.

When I'm nearly halfway to my car, I hear the front door open behind me.

"Harper, where are you going?" Charlie calls after me. I don't turn and face him, because then he might see the tears welling up in my eyes.

"Home," I tell him.

"Why? You were planning on staying."

"Because Charlie, I don't have a single reason to stay," I hate how thick my voice sounds. "At least at home I can hide in my room till I go back to New York, instead of disrupting everyone's *perfect* lives that seemed to be just *fine* without me," Charlie grabs my arm and pulls me to face him, before cutting me off.

"*My* life was not perfectly fine without you. So, if that counts for anything, then there's one reason to stay."

I don't fight his grip, or his gaze, as we stare up at each other.

One moment passes.

Another.

I'm not sure when I took my last breath, but I am positive I don't want to let go or look away from Charlie right now... or maybe ever.

Taking another breath is the least of my worries.

"You don't have to go back to dinner, but at least stay and help me finish the quilt."

I try to loosen a breath since it feels like my lungs are constricting in a horribly unnatural manner (totally justifying the way my heart is racing right now... right?), and I add this moment to a growing list of others that make me wonder what I'm going to feel when I go back to the city.

"Fine, if you're sure it's okay?"

"Always."

Releasing my arm, he stuffs his hands into his coat pockets and glances around, "Oh, and by the way, Aria has decided you're volunteering at the soup kitchen with us tomorrow night." With a wink and a gentle laugh, Charlie turns to head back to the house to grab the quilting supplies before going to the cottage.

"Of course, I am," I say flatly.

"What? Think you're too old for it?" He teases.

"I mean, according to Bex I'm old – which means you must be *ancient*," I emphasize.

"Absolutely am," he calls over his shoulder, "I wake up with back aches every morning from carrying the weight of all the fun and joy in this friendship!"

"Very unfortunate for you grandpa, you sure you can make it up those steps okay?"

"Pretty sure," he grins at me from atop the porch. "But you know, I *really* think she was talking more about those wrinkles you have from frowning, more so than your actual age." I gasp, shocked by the fire behind his playfulness.

"Rude!" I try to yell, but there's no way he's listening over the din of his laughter, so I attempt to protest by flinging a snowball after the closing door, thankful we once again are acting like ourselves – like the way *friends* should act, and I know all hope is not lost for my heart.

* * * *

Snuggled under one of the Grant's old fleece blankets, I listen to the sound of Charlie preheating the oven. Due to our impromptu, mid-dinner exit, we're both hungry, and we agreed the only answer is cookies: the proper meal for movie watching and quilt making.

After putting in the old DVD of *A Christmas Story*, I rummage through the tub of Marjorie's belongings to find the sewing kit, and the remaining squares needed for the quilt.

"So, I have this theory," Charlie announces without introduction, plopping himself down beside me on the couch as he presses play on the movie.

"And what's that?"

"I believe there are two kinds of people in this world," I nod for him to continue as he looks at me expectantly, "There are those who watch *A Christmas Story* and those who watch *White Christmas*!" I can't help but laugh as he makes his final declaration with such confidence you would think he just determined the sky is blue.

"Okay...? And where did you get the evidence for this theory?" I pose, secretly eager to hear more of his ideas. He shrugs as if he can't fathom why this never occurred to him before.

"Simple: you ask anyone what movie their family watches for Christmas every year, and they will answer with one or the other, but never both. Because no one watches both!"

"But why?" I press. He throws his hands up, equally as flabbergasted.

"I don't know! That's the great mystery! I don't know what it says about a person, or what it all is supposed to mean, but I know it's the truth, and it's probably connected to Darwinism or Freud somehow!"

I nod solemnly doubting he knows what either of those concepts means.

"Definitely. So, what if two people are in a relationship and they watched different movies growing up, who wins?" I can tell by the look on his face that I've stumped him now.

"I don't know... I guess they just decide on a case-by-case basis. I've never met two people who didn't watch the same movie growing up..."

As if in sync, we instantly lock eyes and I whip out my phone, emphatically texting Rose what her family's signature Christmas movie was.

Both of our legs tap impatiently waiting for a response, while in the background Ralphie tells us about the Red Rider BB gun he wants for Christmas.

After what feels like an eternity, we get a response.

R: We normally watched White Christmas, why?
H: No reason, just curious!

"I mean, what do we do? Do we tell them to call the wedding off?" Charlie asks. I shake my head solemnly.

"I don't know, but one of us should break the news to Aiden..." I say, agreeing with Charlie before a new text pops up from Rose.

R: Okay! You know what is such a good Christmas movie though? A Christmas Carol! I grew up LOVING the Muppet version!

A memory resurfaces of Aiden sitting in front of the television, all too obsessed with the *Muppet Christmas Carol*. A smile spreads across my face as I relish this match made in dork heaven.

"I think they're going to be alright," I say, feeling my lips spreading into a smile. It's Charlie's turn to nod in agreement, as he too, had to live through the *Christmas Carol* phase.

"I think so, but you know what this does mean?" I arch an eyebrow as I speak, setting to work on the quilt. If there is any domestic skill I still possess, despite many years of patriarchal resistance, it's sewing (thank you sophomore year home-ec). "It means your theory is wrong."

Charlie yanks his attention away from the movie to give me a look of deep hurt.

"And how did you come to this conclusion?" He says, the offense ringing through in his tone.

"Because, Aiden and Rose didn't watch the same movie growing up, but they seem to be getting along just fine." It's his turn to roll his eyes at me.

"I never said that if you watched different Christmas movies you weren't compatible, I was simply stating there are two kinds of people in the world."

"And these two different kinds of people can still have a happy ending?"

"Yes, *obviously*, they can," he drags out.

"But what about the people who *did* watch the same movie growing up?" I insist.

Charlie ponders this for a moment.

"It just means they're the same deep down," he says thoughtfully, "like you stumble upon somebody by chance, who didn't have the same upbringing as you, and you have to really work to make it something. But those others, the ones with the same movie, they just fit."

"Oh yeah? What about me and you? We both watched *A Christmas Story* growing up and we're completely different." He shakes his head, lips pressing into a firm line.

"Nope. You and me, Harper Marshall – we're the same. We, to some degree, will always understand each other."

"Is that so?"

"It is."

I don't like this game anymore, and I don't want to press for more information; not when there's already blush spreading its way across my cheeks; so I nod and return to sewing.

We continue like that for some time: me sewing and Charlie watching the movie, but after one finger prick too many, I give the quilt a break and lean back into the couch to enjoy the movie.

I like the way the whole couch seems to shake with Charlie's laughter when one of the kids gets their tongue stuck to the flagpole; and at some point, without realizing it, Charlie wraps his arm around my shoulders and I find I actually don't mind. Instead, I lean into him and the endless warmth radiating from his body. In response, he rests his head on top of mine with a contented sigh.

In my head, I imagine what an onlooker would say or how I might describe this scene in a novel: it's rather domestic and… *warm*. Cozy even.

It's like looking through a camera lens and seeing everything filtered with a sepia glow.

I'd go as far as to guess that's what the world probably looks like to Charlie every day: the warm glow of endless opportunities. And it's a visual I find, well… somewhat, incredibly, beautiful.

When I catch myself romanticizing the simple perspective Charlie Grant might have on the world, or the way I would describe our actions in a book, I stop myself, because it is *wrong*.

I don't need to think about what this is, or why we are doing this, or how my body feels more relaxed right now than it has in ages, I just need to let it be.

I try to allow myself to enjoy it.

"Hey Harper," Charlie's sleepy voice speaks above my head as I too begin to nod off, neither one of us looking away from the screen. "I triple-dog-dare you to not go back to New York."

My skin runs cold, a bomb detonating in my gut, waking me from any sleepy daze or fantastical fantasies I could be in.

It's like I had fallen into some drunken stupor and had a bucket of ice water thrown on me: I am instantly sobered up.

Lifting my head off his shoulder, I meet those ocean blue eyes – they're dimmer in the dark than their usual midday sparkle, but beautiful and heartbreaking pools nonetheless, and they're now staring down at me.

"What?" My voice is barely above a whisper, wondering if I heard him correctly.

"Don't go back to New York."

There's a yearning in his voice that strikes me hard in my chest.

His gaze is so strong, so insistent, it could make me do whatever he asks, be whoever he needs.

It's terrifying and tantalizing all at once.

He presses on, "Today, in the dress shop, seeing you..." he doesn't finish, and I say a silent prayer of thanks because there's no telling what I would agree to if he did. "I just want you to stay here. With me... so we can have more of this."

More of *what*? Playing pretend? Watching childhood movies? Hurting everyone in a 100-mile radius by letting them get too close just to leave all over again?

My mind immediately begins to race through every single way this could go wrong, regardless of what my heart feels.

"Charlie...." I don't know what I'm trying to tell him, what my heart is screaming for me to say, but my body feels frozen, my mind blank.

I knew the cost of what I was feeling, but *leaving New York?* For what? A few meaningful glances and some handholding?

As I am sitting in a state of panicked confusion, Charlie starts leaning towards me and I can feel my eyes closing in some automatic, primal response, defiant towards any contradicting thoughts within my mind - my body naturally gravitating towards his without a conscious decision.

He is going to *kiss me.*

And I think I might want him too.

No matter what logic is for, or against us, I think I want to know what it feels like to kiss Charlie Grant – a thought that makes my inside shake with fear and anticipation.

My body screams and protests for me to flee. But I am trapped, my legs are useless, and I am entranced by primordial instincts that far surpass reason within the 21st century: I am a fly caught in a web I'm not sure I will ever want to leave.

And as his wonderfully perfect lips are mere centimeters from mine - the smoke alarm goes off.

The magnetic force of confusion, desperation, and longing that drew us in is shattered as we break apart and jump into action.

Running into the kitchen, we see smoke beginning to billow out of the oven: *the cookies.*

How long ago did he put those in? How long have they been burning?

Some sick part of me wants to laugh because *Mr. Perfect burnt the cookies.*

I wonder if something within me has snapped as a little cackle almost makes its way out of my lips.

Charlie doesn't look at me as he beats the smoke down with a towel and reaches up to turn off the smoke detector. Instead of allowing myself to laugh, I crack open a window, letting the winter chill outside cool my reddening face, and I stay there, staring out the window for some time.

"I always hate when that happens," Charlie tries to joke, but I still can't bring myself to look his way. A small smile twists its way onto my lips though, at the idea of the Hallmark King having a hard time baking store-bought cookies.

"I know the pre-packaged baked goods have always been your downfall," I try to joke, but it comes out sounding more like a person whose recently been deprived of their air supply speaking for the first time. Our laughs that follow are forced as we try to move past the last fifteen minutes.

"I'm sorry about that Harper," Charlie says softly. I finally turn and face him.

"Don't be. It's not like anything happened."

He chews on the inside of his cheek.

"Right... you're right," he waves his hand – like he can swat away the fact that he almost kissed me in the same way he swatted away the smoke. "I'm just tired, I don't really know what came over me anyways," he offers.

I nod, ignoring the pain spreading through me at his words, wondering where the confidence and desire I felt a moment ago went.

"I mean, it's been a pretty draining day, neither one of us is really in the best headspace right now," I say, trying to reassure him, despite my tone sounding hollow.

Now is when I remind myself, that he and I are merely mammals who have been left alone for too long: of course, we would jump at the first sign of meaningful companionship. It doesn't mean there's anything truly *meaningful* about it. It doesn't mean anything I just felt mattered – it wasn't even real.

"Yeah, for sure," he agrees.

The air in the kitchen grows stale as we stand there, basking in our silence.

"So, um... friends?" I propose, in what's possibly the most awkwardly stilted manner imaginable.

We can't meet each other's eyes at my words. I want to gag after saying it, or maybe take back the offer entirely and walk back to the couch to see if maybe there were drugs laced into the quilt fabric.

Exhaustion. Instinct. Long day.

Friends.

All of those words sound so disgustingly simple now, no matter how proper and needed they are.

Because I know the truth: if Charlie Grant wants his happy ending, then we need to remain friends at all costs.

When I finally look at Charlie, I see his skin has lost its color, paling in the moonlight.

I wonder if he's going to be sick, right here in the kitchen.

We are friends, we are friends, we are friends, I try to will him to believe it, screaming my internal thoughts his way. I *need* him to believe it. I need to believe it.

I can't lose my only friend to something as foolish as *love*.

Finally, after an eternity of waiting and forcing myself to be still, he nods.

"Yeah, friends."

14

For as long as I can remember, ever since Charlie could walk, the Grant family served as one of the many families in Pinecrest at the church's soup kitchen.

Struggling families found a safe place to gather together each Friday night in the brightly lit basement of the church and its fellowship hall. It was there they could be offered a homemade meal and community with others who could offer a kind smile and a listening ear.

Some nights, business owners in the area serve alongside the cooks and wait staff, offering free haircuts and business consultations; and often, a local nurse or doctor held appointments while the teenagers in the congregation provided childcare.

It's the epitome of small-town living: relying on one's fellow man when one stumbles and being the Samaritan who would pick someone up.

I'm thankful that despite all of the changes that seem to have taken place in the church, this element has remained the same. I feel confident Marjorie would appreciate it.

Marjorie Grant felt it was important her kids be raised around people who had less than them; I suppose her family continued this tradition even after she was gone to keep fulfilling her wishes.

Often, my family was busy at the library, but there were still many nights spent at the church alongside the Grant's.

I was never big on childcare, despite being stuck there year after year in the pastor's chagrin.

Now, I've been promoted to the role of Food Server #5 beside Charlie.

We don't talk about what happened last night, there's no reason to because we are *friends*. Friends who serve together.

"It's lovely seeing you dear," Mrs. Nilson smiles at me in the sweet, old lady manner only grandmas can do.

Mr. Nilson passed my sophomore year of high school, and it was at that point the entire congregation insisted Mrs. Nilson be served, instead of helping with the soup kitchen.

This didn't stop her from sneaking into the kitchen or nursery, but you can bet everyone tried. I smile back at her involuntarily, surprised she remembers me.

Another young family comes through, and I note they're short on a father.

The youngest boy smiles at my offer of mac and cheese, but it's a shy smile that speaks of hesitancy. Charlie knows the mother by name, and I marvel at the way he greets everyone with such kindness.

As families pass through, I'm washed in waves of emotions: confusion, and sadness, and *zeal*.

"Harper, you're looking lovely darling," my old Sunday school teacher tells me, coming around the table to hug me. I'm surprised she can recall my name.

It's not just her either: nearly every vaguely familiar face has called me by name.

Pastor Mark even came over and talked to me and Charlie for a bit, helping us serve food before returning to ministering to the families eating.

I get comments about people being grateful they saw me in service Sunday, wishes that people would get to see me more often, and several congratulations on behalf of Aiden's engagement.

It's so very different from New York, where within the big cities and book tours I'm just a number. This feeling of being known makes me itch in my skin, like an old wool sweater: the most comforting discomfort you can ever feel, that still smells ever so faintly of something familiar.

I've never wanted to burrow deeper, and take something off, so badly as I want to tonight.

"Not used to being somewhere where everyone knows your name Turkey Chaser?" Charlie notes, alternating between spoonsful of green beans and carrots. I glance his way: he's so amused by my discomfort, reverting back to old nicknames.

It's infuriatingly charming and familiarly brotherly.

It's the way things should be. But I still can't help but hear his words from last night in the back of my head: *leave New York*. My stomach churns again as I survey Charlie.

His hair has grown shaggy through the busyness of the holidays, with his thick, blond hair starting to cover his ears.

He's scruffy and alive, embodying a backwoods-mayor type as he chats with each family, and eventually, it begins to rub off on me, easing my nerves.

I catch myself finding warmth in my metaphorical wool sweater that's been forced upon me, and I'm reminiscent of a girl from long ago, as I begin chatting with people passing through the line. The smile on my face can't be disguised because I'm beginning to realize it's *nice* being a part of something bigger than myself.

Something that actually matters.

And deep in the pit of my gut, I feel embarrassed and ashamed of the way I've judged the people of this town for so long. They didn't deserve that.

Charlie comes around my side with another tray of beans, looking me up and down before remarking, "You know, if I didn't know any better, I'd say you're actually enjoying yourself."

I roll my eyes, looking out at the people milling about, eating together. I can hear children laughing in the daycare down the hall where I know they're in good hands (Anna is with them), and I smile because the reason I'm even aware of that is because she came to hug me when she first arrived.

It overwhelms me, rising inside me like a tide, it's a sensation I could get lost in, so I smile at Charlie and tell him:

"You know, if I didn't know any better, I'd say you might actually be right."

* * * *

Once everyone has been served, the workers are allowed to eat whatever is left.

Charlie and I don't bother removing our aprons as we sit down with a family who offers us empty seats and genuine smiles, and Charlie tells me about the repairs he did on their car the other week.

"Charlie is really just heaven-sent; he helps coach our son Eli's t-ball team in the spring!"

"Oh, does he?" I say with an arched eyebrow. Charlie's face reddens at the praise, and I begin to wonder what he *doesn't* do in this town.

"Yes! He's so great with the kids, but it is such a shame, we never have enough hands to help with team snacks."

"You know," Charlie adds between bites of his dinner, "Harper and her mom used to make the nicest little snack bags for me and her brother when we were younger and would finish up practice. They'd always have some kind of theme - it was the best." The couple smiles at this amused.

"Well, if you're ever looking to spread the love, we'd appreciate the help once the season starts!"

Before I can respond, Charlie answers for me.

"I wouldn't bother, she'll be back in New York by then." My face flushes red with embarrassment, unable to meet the couple's eyes as they smile politely.

It's the first comment Charlie has made all evening to hint at what conspired last night, and though I can't say I blame him, his words still catch me off guard. For all of his social nuance, he seems oblivious to this, smiling along as we change the subject to the state of the church and plans for the holidays.

"So, how long have you two been seeing each other?" The father inquires. I cock my head confused at the man's question.

"I mean, we've been friends since we were little..." I offer hesitantly. It's now the couple's turn to look confused. The woman places a comforting hand on her husband's arm as she clarifies.

"I'm sorry, my husband and I thought you two were dating, since you two work so well together and seem to have known each other a long time."

"Oh," another embarrassed flush, "I see," I stammer out.

Charlie shakes his head on my behalf.

"Don't worry about it, we are *just* friends. Always have been, always will be."

He's grown *awfully* comfortable with that word in the mere hours since our moment in his kitchen. I push for another change of subject, asking the couple about themselves, and their son, and what brings them to Pinecrest, but most importantly I avoid looking at Charlie, whose emotional whiplash nearly has me in tatters.

It's exactly what I wanted, what I *needed*, but now that I have it, I hate the foul taste it leaves behind in my mouth.

As dinner progresses, people begin to move about the fellowship hall, greeting one another, and taking turns savoring each other's company. Eventually, we pass out dessert as the business owners spread out and begin their consultations. In the distant background, someone turns on an old radio playing the crackling kind of Christmas music that makes you want to dance around a living room with a cup of cider.

I set to work, wiping off a table, when Charlie saddles up beside me. "I'm glad you came with us tonight," he smiles at me, pausing to scrub hard at a mysterious stain on the table.

"Well, there's no way I could say no to Aria. Have you seen those eyes?"

"Those are very convincing eyes," he nods solemnly. "But I'm serious, it's nice working on something non-wedding related together."

"Yeah," I say with a tight smile, "it's nice." I wring my rag a tad aggressively.

"Is everything okay?"

"Mhm," I nod, none too convincingly. "You were just very *friend*ly tonight." He shrugs.

"We said we were going to be friends, didn't we?" I nod in agreement. "I thought you'd be happy with me. No mention of staying here, no hints of any kind of relationship between us, it's what we agreed to."

"I know." It comes out more rude than I intend and I don't understand *why*.

Why am I so upset? I'm the one who *suggested* we just be friends.

I try to reason with myself, knowing I don't want to be reminded of all the things I'm forbidding myself from feeling, while still *needing* to be reminded of why they *can't* happen.

"Thank you for inviting me tonight, it was nice being back," I try changing the subject with the truth: it *is* nice being back, belonging, and Charlie has a right to know that.

"I knew you were enjoying yourself – I'm glad," Charlie's smile is genuine as he says, "We might remind you of your small-town roots just yet."

I smile coyly as I tell him, "Maybe so".

We keep cleaning till the awkward tension dissipates for the millionth time since my homecoming, making sure each table is spotless, and all the dishes are washed.

When we pause and take a seat, I begin to hum along with the music playing through the fellowship hall. I don't have the same kind of confidence Charlie does, a fearlessness to sing out of tune, especially seeing as my voice is plenty more off-key (I never was asked to sing in the church choir on Sundays), but I think it suits me just fine.

As I glance around the room, tune on the tip of my tongue, Charlie asks me to dance.

"What? You can't be serious," I say dismissively.

"I am 100% serious." A jazzy song plays through the radio, and it does make me want to dance... a little.

"No one else is dancing," I point out.

"Has that ever stopped us before?" Charlie asks.

I was not prone to impromptu dance parties growing up, but they were one of Aiden's favorite things. He and Marjorie would often break out in random dances, no matter how old we were, and try to drag me and Charlie into whatever private party they seemed to be having.

"It's never stopped *you* before, it has stopped *me* plenty of times," I argue, crossing my arms and pursing my lips in the attempt at defiance I can muster in response to Charlie's outstretched hand and puppy dog eyes.

"Come on Turkey Chaser, live a little," he says with a wink.

It's a challenge. I know it is, and for once, it's not because of some dare or desire to learn about happy endings. I just want to do it for fun.

Rolling my eyes, I take Charlie's hand and allow him to guide me to a clearing in the fellowship hall.

We dance like children, forgetting people might be watching us, sashaying back and forth. Charlie pushes me away and pulls me closer, and I imagine we are doing our own convoluted version of a fox trot or a waltz.

We laugh, and my cheeks ache with the strain of smiling for so long.

When the song ends, I stop to catch my breath, pushing my hair behind my ears with a laugh just as the fellowship hall erupts in applause. I look to Charlie who is equally as red-faced at the sudden attention but he recovers quickly with a mock bow. Gently, he nudges me with his hand before commanding me to, "take a bow, Heartbreaker," and with a laugh, I do.

* * *

When the crowd begins to disperse, Charlie offers to walk me home, in favor of letting his dad ride home with the girls. Hesitantly, I accept.

The town is quiet, as flakes of snow begin to fall from the sky, putting on a glittering show for only us to see. The streetlights cast a golden light on the icy sidewalks, and I hear the jingling of bells in the distance as Karl and Edmund make their final lap for the night.

"Do you ever wonder what those sleigh rides are like?" Charlie seems to ask of no one in particular.

"Staring at a horse's butt for twenty minutes while you take a lap around the town square? No, it's never crossed my mind." I say with a laugh, pulling down the beanie I have on, fighting against the cold.

"But I mean, *surely*, there has to be some kind of appeal, right? Otherwise, people wouldn't pay to do it."

"Maybe," I shrug, "Or, maybe those people are just tourists who think there's some hidden holiday magic in that horse's butt, that they'll absorb via proximity; when really, it's just a smelly and uncomfortable money trap Edmund tapped into twenty years ago."

"You're no fun," Charlie pouts, glaring down at me. Snowflakes have begun collecting on his eyelashes, coating them in tiny crystals his eyes reflect. Fear clenches my gut when his pout turns playful, glancing up to the sound of jingle bells. "There's really only one way to settle this..." I roll my eyes.

"No Charlie, first the soup kitchen, then the dancing – I am not going on a sleigh ride with you! It is downright taking advantage of me and my good nature!"

"But you enjoyed all of those things!" He throws his hands up as if that proves his point. "Have I steered you wrong yet?" He asks.

I don't respond.

"Charlie, I'm tired, it's cold, I'm sure Edmund wants to go home..." I whine, trying to reason with him.

He looks me up and down weighing his options: on the one hand, I can be an absolute terror when angered, but on the other, he *really* enjoys making me angry.

"Hey Edmund!" He calls to the approaching sleigh, which slows beside us, as Edmund looks down at the bitterly frozen pair we are becoming standing in the middle of town.

"Charlie my boy, what are you doing out here, causing this poor lady to freeze to death?" I throw up an exasperated hand, thankful Edmund has confirmed my point.

"Edmund, do you and Karl possibly have one last ride in you for the evening? I'll throw in a free polish and tune up of the sleigh if you make all my Christmas wishes come true!"

Edmund's wrinkly jowls break into a grin as he produces a thermos of hot chocolate and a pile of blankets, and pulls Charlie into the sleigh.

Saying Charlie is thrilled would be an understatement.

"Come on Harper, you have to now..." He says.

A few grumbles, groans, and eye rolls later, I am being tucked in the backseat of the sleigh beside Charlie.

Snow crunches underneath the horse's feet as we ride through town, and as we go, I note the little lights shining through the windows of the businesses and homes: a flash of people's private lives.

It feels deeply personal in a way I wouldn't expect, and I'm struck by just how beautiful my hometown really is. A small smile spreads its way across my face as the sleigh jostles, pushing me closer to Charlie.

Through the window of a little brownstone on the edge of the town square, parted curtains reveal an elderly couple in their living room where they sit reading.

I feel a twinge in my heart I can't quite place, and I think of my parents at home, probably doing something very similar.

Some part of this routine strikes my core, but I push it away like I've done a dozen times since leaving Pinecrest, a dozen times since coming home.

"What's wrong?" Charlie asks me, reading the look on my face.

"Nothing," I shake my head, "just thinking about my parents."

He quirks an eyebrow up, "Are you guys still fighting?"

"I don't know... I mean, my dad has always been more of a lover than a fighter, but my mom..." I pause at a loss for words. "I just don't know what our relationship is anymore."

"You'll get through it," Charlie shrugs in response, "you always do."

I chew on my lip before saying, "I don't know... this feels different. Like we've come to this great divide that just seems so insurmountable now, and I'm not sure there's a way across it." I loosen a deep breath thinking about my outburst when I first came to town and was drowning in the shock of losing Marjorie, "I think I've gone too far this time... I said some pretty unforgivable stuff just because she was trying to care for me."

Charlie considers this for a moment, nodding along as he listens.

"Harper, why did her caring upset you so much?"

That's the question, isn't it?

Why does anyone's attempt to get close to me transform me into a snarling beast backed into a corner?

Because I don't want to be a burden.

Because I can't be fixed.

"I don't know," I say with a shrug, "I think it just felt like too much pressing after finding out about Marjorie."

It's a half-truth, but it's as much as I feel like confessing right now. Charlie processes my answer in silence before replying.

"Well then, if your greatest issue is crossing the divide of where you are, compared to where you want to be, then you get to experience the wonderful thing about great divides."

"And what's that?" I ask.

"You get to find a new way across," he pauses, "When it seems like there's no way out, like you've gotten too far off the beaten path, you chart your own path and find your way back. It may take longer than you planned, but most of the time, it ends up being even prettier than the easier way across would have been."

Oh Charlie Grant, so full of kindness and sage wisdom despite not even knowing the full story; I can't help but smile.

In the mind of Charlie, I can find a way over this divide, and that thought gives me a small burst of hope.

"You're enjoying this aren't you?" He says haughtily, already knowing the answer to his question.

I feign surprise at his observation, "Nope, not at all. Still just a cold carriage and a horse's butt, stuck here with you." He shakes his head in disbelief, a smile crossing his face, utterly baffled.

"Between my wonderful advice and Karl, you're ready to deck the halls and spread good cheer."

"No sir, I am not, you are definitely mistaken."

He laughs at my insistence, "That horse butt is transferring its holiday magic to you – I can see it all over your face."

"Oh yeah? What does it look like exactly?" I say, teasing him, a smirk of my own on my face.

"Well," he says, taking my face in his hand and running a thumb across my cheek, "It looks a lot like you when you're happy." My smirk falters, but his touch persists, goosebumps popping up on my skin, something telling me they're not from the cold...

"I'm always happy," I whisper, quieter than I mean to. His eyes seem darker now, as the sleigh crosses into a shadow, with no light shining on this corner of the street.

"No, not really," he confesses with a slight head shake, "Not the kind of happy where your smile fills up your face and it just kind of oozes out of you."

"You think oozing is synonymous with happiness?" I try to joke, to shake the liquified feeling from my insides, but it doesn't work.

"I know it is. It's rare, but it's the way you looked tonight."

As we cross into a new patch of light I pull away from his touch, taking a shaky breath.

"Speaking of tonight, you were rude to me." The holiday magic around us evaporates at my words and my insides re-solidify.

"What?!"

"When we were talking to that couple, you lost all sense of your manners, and were rude about me going home."

"You mean New York," he states, his mouth a straight line.

I huff out a frustrated breath, "I mean my *home*, Charlie. You know the place I've lived for nearly a decade?"

He rolls his eyes before returning with, "That doesn't make it your home."

"See!" I say, throwing up my hands, "This is exactly what I mean! You get angry every time New York gets brought up, and I don't understand why."

Charlie's jaw slackens as if I've slapped him: "You know exactly why."

"Seriously?! Like you have any right to get upset about this? You're the one who made it abundantly clear we are *just* friends!"

"Because you asked me to!"

I'm not sure I've ever seen Charlie like this: voice gravelly, a wild look in his eyes I can't quite decipher. I glance at Edmund, who has sat only a few feet away with no comment this entire time.

I wonder how many late nights like these he's had...

"Charlie... it has to be this way."

"Even if it's clearly not what either of us want?"

"Yes," I say with far more determination than I feel. "All we are going to be is friends."

Charlie sits back in the sleigh staring ahead. His jaw is tense as if he is biting his tongue in concentration.

"What if I'm not sure how to just be friends with you?" Charlie's eyes pin me to where I sit, challenging me to answer him.

"You seemed to manage just fine for eighteen years... just do that again. Then in a few more weeks, I'll be gone, and life will return to normal."

Charlie is quiet, obviously hurt.

That was a low blow and I know it, but it needed to be said.

He never thought twice about me until all of this wedding planning got into his head; what he feels isn't real. It can't be.

Finally, he breaks the silence: "So much for crossing those insurmountable divides, right?"

There's no response I could give him that would appease him or solve this problem I am so determined to avoid. So instead, we sit in the quiet for a little while longer, accepting this door I am trying so desperately to close.

Charlie nods as the sleigh comes to a slow, signaling the end of our ride. Despite the angry tension hanging between us, he offers me his hand to help me down. We thank Edmund and give Karl a quick pet before continuing our walk.

"So... *friends*," he begins as we turn onto my street, "are they allowed to accompany each other to their little sisters' ballet recital?"

I consider this for a moment before hesitantly responding, "I would hope so."

"Good," Charlie smiles, satisfied with at least some normalcy.

It's no miracle salve for our unresolved situation, but it's a start.

It's just further confirmation for what I already knew: these feelings, for both of us, are merely a momentary lapse in judgment. A sudden surprise brought on by the outside, romantic pressure, of planning a wedding.

We will not fall into the age-old cliché of the girl who goes home and falls for her childhood friend. We won't because that's not how our story ends.

I watch him chew on his lip with a smile, a nervous expression reminiscent of him in high school, before he says, "Horse butt magic really is something isn't it?" He glances up as if there's evidence of sleigh ride magic in the sky, and I swat him playfully before rolling my eyes. I appreciate the obvious attempts at changing the subject and lightening the situation.

When he laughs, I know this can be good; this feels safe. We will make it through the next couple of days, and then I will go back to New York and this will all feel like a very strange dream.

"You are simply impossible Mr. Grant," I tell him, letting our laughter fill the night around us, knowing even when this ends, in some way, we will still be okay, because there will always be this: laughter, and sleigh rides, and snowflakes.

15

The few frantic days leading up to the all-consuming Christmas chaos of Pinecrest pass by in a blur of pricked fingers, bridal bouquets, half-written pages, and infrequent exchanges.

Charlie gets busy with work and PTO preparations for the winter formal, and I avoid the subject of the ballet in fear of adding something else to his plate – possibly tipping over the carefully balanced routine we've orchestrated amongst ourselves to make it to the wedding.

We've learned I can handle logistics if Charlie runs interference – encouraging Aiden to call Charlie with new "to-do's", giving me space to make calls and arrange drop-offs, while I leave the heavy lifting to Charlie: working out semantics with people in town who view him as mayor, being there for the delivery of tables and sound systems, and jointly splitting up the finer tasks of taste testing and answering the questions of family members and friends trying to find Pinecrest on a map.

Our system works like a well-oiled machine; it just also happens to be a system that keeps me and Charlie separate most days.

I try to hide my simultaneous disappointment and relief at this fact, as the ballet inches closer and closer, and I remain even more in a gray area of feeling for Charlie Grant.

These aren't my sisters.

He's not my boyfriend.

Inserting myself without the presentation of a ticket simply seems wrong.

Maybe, Charlie has changed his mind, no matter how well we've played this game.

Maybe, he thinks it's better to leave me out entirely than confront these feelings that we can no longer deny since that moment at his house.

Charlie's absence has also eliminated anyone I can talk to about the persistent discomfort around my house.

Despite Charlie's advice in the sleigh the other night, my mother and I remain on opposite sides of our canyon, refusing to build any kind of bridge to help us get across (and I'm fairly confident that to chart one of those beautiful paths he mentioned, someone needs to be willing to lay aside their stubbornness and take the first step).

So, instead of trying to solve the larger issues in my life, I deal with the tasks directly in front of me: finishing Marjorie's quilt (without the help of Charlie), finishing the wedding plans (also without Charlie's help), and writing (which yes, again, doesn't include Charlie, or his stupid garage, or any of the little charms I'm remembering about Pinecrest that I refuse to admit exist).

When I write, I refuse to look over the pages, despite taking a painstaking amount of time to write them, because I know I'm only giving pieces of myself to the project.

I can't bring myself to fully sink into it, to share the vulnerability a true happy ending demands, and I know my writing reflects that.

Nearly every morning now, I'm greeted with a passive-aggressive message from my agent Lauren.

And nearly every morning, I flag it to read later and ignore it.

It's wrong, I know, but reading more threats about the impending termination of my contract will do nothing to inspire me. In fact, I'm not entirely sure much of anything will.

So, I drink more cups of coffee and convince myself the brief caffeine rush is inspiration; then I spend my time mindlessly typing away at whatever words will come out of me – even if I know my story still lacks direction.

It makes me wonder what happened between Charlie's garage when I was able to write with ease, and now.

It reminds me of when I first started writing, just an unsure and scared little girl, with an unreasonable amount of anger at the world, wondering if she could create something.

It was writing before the world cared. And deep down, there's a part of me that missed it; when writing was just a silly thing I did for fun, without the pressure of it being some professional bestseller.

That's how I find myself at my usual perch in the kitchen, the day before Christmas Eve, drinking mug number four, when my mother places an envelope on my desk... or counter?

The lines of my creative space should remain undefined.

I look up, surprised, and mildly disgruntled, but she's already busied herself in the kitchen, pouring herself a cup of coffee from the pot I brewed this morning.

"What's this?" I ask her.

"You do know at a certain point, caffeine has adverse effects, don't you?" She says, her words striking me as rather patronizing for so early in the day.

"Yes," I hold up the envelope, "but what is this?"

My mother continues walking around the kitchen, sipping her cup, ignoring my questions.

"And there comes a certain point where you over-caffeinate and end up depressed and exhausted..."

"Dually noted, but what's with the unmarked envelope?" I try once more.

She carries on as if I'm not even there, or maybe I am here, asking for a lecture on my coffee consumption, instead of why I've been handed an envelope: "Insomnia, nervousness, restlessness... it's probably why your attempts at writing aren't going well."

"Mom!" I cut her off mid-lecture, "Why the sudden tirade about coffee, instead of answering my question?"

Finally, she stops to lean against the bar, holding her mug with both hands: it's one Aiden and I got her for Mother's Day a few years ago... she still has it.

My mother looks at the envelope with meaning, before looking up at me, a fierce sympathy in her eyes.

"My point is, there are certain good things that lose their goodness after you have too much of it... Too much can become a bad thing." She chooses her words carefully as if weighing each one of them in her mind.

I've surpassed confusion, palming the envelope in my hand, feeling its weight and the shape of something inside of it. A card? A check? Neither of which makes sense...

"Okay?" I reply.

She lets out a long-held breath before saying, "Charlie Grant is *not* one of those things."

With her final word, my mother takes her cup of coffee and leaves me alone.

Utterly baffled, I open the envelop, stopping short when I see what's inside:

A ticket to the ballet.

* * * *

Every town has an institution nearly as old as the town itself. For some, it's a particular football game in a specific stadium. For others, it's a certain parade in a town square.

For Pinecrest, it's the church, and right behind it, for no reason in particular, is the theater with its Christmas ballet recital.

I was never the ballerina growing up, but each year, I vividly recall my friends preparing for months in advance. Sore feet and busy schedules consumed the lives of the Pinecrest Dance Company, and everyone else waited with excitement for Christmas Eve.

My world was consumed with coordinating the 12 Books of Christmas, whose final reading always followed the recital.

It's a night for miracles and magic, bringing out the good cheer in even the most determined Scrooge.

In the nine years since I've been gone, absolutely nothing about this has changed.

I still feel the same flutter of excitement putting on my pearls to go to the ballet that I felt when I was twelve, and I can hear my mother humming as she moves in and out of the house throughout the day, preparing the library for tonight's crowd.

Nothing, however, could really prepare me for the rush of butterflies I get when my eyes land on Charlie.

It's been days since I saw him last, and the pale blue button-down he's wearing only brightens the blue in his eyes, his trim sports coat making him look comfortably oblivious to his devastating good looks. Almost as if, he's stepped out of the pages of my fairytale for a moment, to remind me of how I continue to torment myself with resisting him.

Internally, I hear a fourteen-year-old Harper making gagging noises, obviously horrified by the recent change in our perception of Charlie Grant - if only she had known what was to come, maybe, life would look a lot different now.

"Evening Ms. Marshall," he says with a nod, offering me his arm to take as we ascend the steps of the theater.

"Mr. Grant," I say, trying much too hard to resist the urge to hold on to his arm just a little bit tighter, feeling safe beside him, holding on to the bulging muscle covered by his coat. "I wasn't sure I would still be invited after I didn't hear from you for a few days..." I venture as I take the tickets out of the small clutch I hold in my hand.

"Why? We agreed we're still friends Harper. You said it yourself: friends can go to the ballet together. Besides, it's not like you're just here for me, the girls always appreciate the support..." Charlie's face remains friendly and composed as he presents the usher with our tickets.

Removing my hand from his arm, I follow him to our seats, and as we try to cram in the aisle, his hand briefly brushes against my lower back, guiding me – as if it's an involuntary action we've taken a dozen times over.

I try my very best to pretend it doesn't happen.

"Besides," he says when we take our seats, "I've missed you." I can't hide the surprise on my face, as his lips quirk up in a half smile. "What?" He asks like I've made a joke.

"You've missed me? Me and all of my crazy?" I tease.

His soft laughter sends a thrill through me, well worth ignoring. As the lights of the theater begin to dim, and the first dancers begin to take their position, Charlie's hand brushes against my knee as he leans in to whisper a response, nearly rendering me speechless.

Why the sudden, casual affection? I thought we agreed we wouldn't do this.

Why is he making my heart squeeze, as if holding it in a vice?

Does he know what his proximity does to me?

I realize now I don't care.

He missed me as desperately as I missed him, and I don't care if he can read all over my face what I feel, or if he ever knows the depth of what he stirs in me.

Charlie stole my heart a long time ago, whether I wanted him to or not, and I never thought of any stipulations for getting it back.

And maybe, I secretly hoped I would take up residence in his heart in the same way he'd taken root in mine; that what we felt might grow into something more than friendship. Its secret wants like that, that make my lungs constrict, like a vice tightening around me.

I know deep down, that the tightening in my chest is merely a symptom of my sickness – a side effect of believing maybe happily ever after's get a chance.

When Charlie finally whispers a response to me, it shakes me from my thoughts:

"You've always been the best kind of crazy, Harper Marshall".

Maybe, my heart stops.

And if it does, it doesn't truly matter, because the music is drowning his voice out.

* * * *

The dancer's movements are fluid and well-timed, executed with such precision and grace that for a brief moment, I don't think about Charlie Grant.

It's a glorious moment of peace.

I feel my heart swell with pride as the girls dance across the stage, giving in to the rhythm of the music.

I rejoice at their triumphs and feel this strange sense of unity with the people sitting around me: these people I know, who have now grown up in the most magnificent ways.

This has been happening year after year without me… and a small twinge in my chest reminds me of how many moments like these I've missed.

Some part of me is tired of missing them…

I ride with Charlie and his family to the library; whose warm light serves as a beacon to the town now that the ballet has let out.

The comforting smell of chocolate greets us as we remove our coats in the doorway. The hot chocolate bar my mom and the library staff have set out is in the corner, and there is a table of baked goods *Written Comfort* has provided beside it.

Charlie grabs us a disconcerting number of ginger snaps, while I find candy canes for our cups of cocoa, and my laugh rings out, sudden and uninhibited, as Sleet runs by in a Santa hat someone has strapped on him.

Stepping out of the way as children begin to pour in, Charlie and I tuck ourselves into a crevice between the bookcases.

I'm immediately enveloped by the scent of aging pages and leatherbound books, with a hint of motor oil - even beneath the fine coat and slacks, Charlie is still himself.

"How's the writing?" He asks me, staring down at me as he sips from a Styrofoam cup. I wait a moment before sipping mine, burning my tongue, trying to avoid the possibility of bumping into Charlie, whose closeness is quickening my pulse.

I try not to blush as I think about the casual way he touched me in the theater, resisting the urge to ask him to do it all again: *tease me like there's nothing you'd rather do, brush against me like it doesn't require a second thought.*

I shake my head, attempting to clear my mind.

"Uh, yeah, sort of... it's going slow, but I'm finally getting something on the page which is better than when I got here." My laugh is strained, with the dim lights and closeness in the heat of the library.

This is different than the darkness of the theater, where I could pretend things were normal between Charlie and me. But now I question whether things have ever really been normal.

From the moment I got into town the thin fabric of normalcy that laced our pasts has evaporated like permafrost, leaving nothing but this... *newness* to embark on.

In a world where I thought nothing had or could change, maybe it was the people here who have been changing all along.

"And is it a happy ending?" Charlie asks with a wink, "I've got to hold my Heartbreaker accountable".

I roll my eyes at his nickname, realizing that though I once despised it, it now evokes within me a sense of comfort.

It's a joke for just Charlie and I, like verbally squeezing my hand.

Finally meeting Charlie's eyes, I smile at him hesitantly, "I actually think it could be..." He quirks up an eyebrow in surprise.

"Really? I wasn't sure you had it in you."

"Well, I am certainly full of surprises," I tease, "Especially when I've had such an excellent coach."

I'd wink at Charlie if I believed in my ability to do so, so instead, I embrace his nod of understanding. The corners of his mouth pull up into a smile as if a ribbon tugs them gently. It's a look that makes my heart tighten.

"I'm positive it's amazing, just like everything else you've written," he offers.

I scoff at his compliment, disagreeing, "I

t is *far* from amazing – it most definitely embodies the spirit of a "rough draft", but it's a step... I'm just hoping it's enough to satisfy my publishing house: I haven't exactly stuck with my deadline."

Charlie attempts to ease my mind, questioning how serious a deadline can really be.

"What about you?" I try, changing the subject, "How have you been handling your mayoral duties?" He shrugs his shoulders with a laugh, and I use now to glance around me: in the time we've been talking, the library has filled with people.

"It's nothing too out of the ordinary, just getting ready for the holidays. I wrapped up the lighting for the wedding!"

"Good! I'm sure it's wonderful." Another smile and squeeze of my heart.

"Can you believe Aiden and Rose aren't having a rehearsal dinner?" Charlie asks me. I shake my head in disbelief, shrugging my shoulders.

"I guess when your planning is as exact as theirs, and this season is just as busy, you can't blame them. Feels like a very "Rose" thing to do anyways."

Charlie laughs in agreement.

"Oh, and speaking of finishing things for the holidays," I continue, "I have the quilt in my car at the theater if you want to pick it up tonight. That way you can give it to the girls on Christmas Day." Charlie mulls this over for a moment.

"I'd actually really like for you to be there, if that's okay?" He asks. "You were a bigger part in finishing it than I was – Mom would have wanted you to be there."

My gut twinges at the thought that no one wanted me there for the biggest thing of all, but now I will take what I can get: being present for this.

"Okay, I'd like that."

Smiling, Charlie whispers, "Good".

So, like an idiot, I smile and whisper "good" back.

A syrupy warmth spreads from my stomach to my toes, as Charlie looks down at me with such warmth, I wonder if I'm melting like the snowmen in spring.

I like this Charlie: the flirty, kind, unattainable one I will never have, and I savor his undivided attention while it lasts.

Before either of us can do anything to break the tension, my mother clears her throat, drawing attention to the reading chair, seated in front of the fake fireplace, where she now sits holding *The Night Before Christmas*.

As my mother begins reading, I feel the knot that's taken up residence in my stomach tighten. So tight I fear I might split in two, and then, as the rope of guilt and anger draws taught within, I let go.

I release a shuddering breath that holds all the confusion I've felt the last month, and it gives me no answers.

Not a single resolution, but it feels good.

To acknowledge that I have no answers for what comes next.

To know that in more ways than one, I am reaching the fullest extent of what I can hold in.

That eventually, I will have to come to terms with what has been, and what is here now; what I've tried to avoid feeling for so long.

I let a silent tear fall, as my mother's voice washes over me, and I wish, not for the first time, that I could be a child again: staring up at my mother with a face full of hope and faith in something magical.

Charlie wordlessly slips an arm around me, pulling me into his warmth, and squeezing more tears out of me.

It breaks some of the anger apart.

It brings me back to reality and holds me together for a moment longer.

And I can't help but smile.

A snotty, delirious smile of holding it in for too long.

"How about we just be here now... okay?" Charlie whispers in my ear.

I nod. That is something I can do.

16

Aria has fallen asleep on the floor of the library by the time the evening comes to a close. As I watch Charlie carefully pick her up, I try to blink away the image of him as a father.

Blond hair, fading to gray, chasing little ones around the yard. They'd have their mother's eyes and Charlie's boisterous laugh, and he would know just the right face to make to get them to laugh when they're sad.

He is going to be a great dad someday.

A great husband.

Just not *mine*.

With a sad smile spreading across my face, I pick up Aria's stuffed reindeer she dropped on the ground mid-nap. As I run out to the parking lot, I wrap my arms around myself, wishing I had brought a warmer coat, and carefully tuck the stuffed animal into the crook of Aria's arm.

"Here, you must be freezing," Charlie says in a rush, wrapping his jacket around my shoulders.

Beckett closes the door to the car without batting an eye in our direction, but as Charlie towers above me in the dim light of the streetlamps, our feet sinking into the frosty ground, I feel her watchful eyes on me from within the car.

Charlie's face is nearly impossible to read right now, basked in shadows, and I try so hard to read his mind the way he always seems to read mine.

"Better?" He asks, rubbing my arms with his hands, which I know must be freezing without a coat on.

"Charlie, you don't need to do this, take your coat back," I try slipping it off my shoulders to give it back, but a whiff of his scent brushes past my nose and a few tears prick at my eyes.

It's been a long evening.

"No, it's the gentlemanly thing to do." He brushes it off like it's meaningless, but I draw the line when he tries to open the door for me.

No matter what lapse in judgment this evening has been, it has to stop before someone gets hurt *again*.

We said we were just friends and that's what we need to be now.

This story is ending whether we like it or not, because I am not the girl for Charlie Grant, and he has to accept that.

I have to accept that – just like I have to accept a million other things about the little broken shards of my life: they need to be picked up first, long before I'll be capable of giving my full self to someone.

"Charlie, please…" He hears the pleading in my voice, as my eyes pool with tears. "Please stop." My begging elicits nothing from him, and it makes me wonder if maybe I've read too far into this evening: the casual brushes and lingering stares.

"It's really nothing Harper. I heard you the other night, *just friends*. I'm not going to force you to take my coat, or let me open a door for you, because I get it: *we aren't going to happen*. I'm sorry if I've made you think otherwise – it wasn't my intention."

Now I know I haven't imagined a thing.

When I think back to Charlie in high school, I know his statement might have been true if we were sixteen again: him being the type to pointlessly flirt, when his actions and affections stemmed from nowhere but friendliness and boredom, but looking at the man before me now, I know it's simply not true.

Charlie Grant doesn't do anything without intention.

That's why I know he's lying - but it's still a lie; a lie I desperately need and want to believe.

So, I do.

I tell myself he's right and I'm wrong: Charlie Grant feels absolutely nothing for me.

He is just a flirt with manners.

I hate this stupid little town I grew up in.

I can't wait to get back to a city that suddenly seems far too loud for my thoughts to be heard.

And I ignore the shuddering within me, like something has shaken loose the very foundation on which I've built myself.

Wiping my eyes, for what feels like the hundredth time tonight, I offer Charlie my very best smile; the one I've used on book tours and in meetings to discuss contracts: my face for the people who can't shake me, and I tell him I'll be over tomorrow morning for pancakes and presents with the girls.

He offers me the same polite smile back, before opening my door for me and dropping me off at my car. And for a brief moment, I consider taking the coat with me. Like some memento of this night will make it all feel more real, but as I open my door, I'm not sure I want any of this to be real.

I want to wake up in the morning and find out I made it all up: the perfect plot to a story that will never get told.

When I start my car, I feel exhausted; cracked open, and drained, as if I'm an egg someone has tried to separate from the yolk.

I left the jacket, and I quietly waved goodbye to Beckett who was nodding off alongside Aria, and I didn't hug Charlie goodbye. Because that's not what friends do. And the cold coating me now, where Charlie's jacket once hung, is simply the winter night trying to cling to my skin.

I'm too tired to cry on my way home. I just drive surrounded by silence: the same way I came into town. As a new round of snowflakes falls, I think back to a time, long ago, when things were simple and there was still such a thing as happily ever after... when they were real...

"You have to catch the snowflakes, Harper," Marjorie says with a kind smile, gesturing to the powder she's caught on her glove.

"But what if it doesn't work?" My questions are interrupted by the startling screams of Charlie and Aiden as they pelt each other with snowballs.

Our attention is briefly captivated by the two boys, brothers really, as they run from snow mound to snow mound beating the absolute snot out of each other.

I resist the urge to roll my eyes, a new expression I learned the other day - Mom isn't crazy about it, which only makes me want to do it more.

"Well then, you just have to try it for yourself and see."

There's a twinkle in Marjorie's eyes that makes me believe in miracles, like anything is possible, but not as much as I believe that no matter how many snowflakes I catch, the sixth grade will still be terrifying.

"You know Harper, there are miracles all around us if you're willing to see past the boring lies the world likes to tell you."

This has grabbed my attention.

"What do you mean?" The skepticism is written all over my face, but I'm game and she knows it.

With a slight smile, Marjorie looks around us before pointing up,

"Every snowflake is unique and one of a kind – and if you can catch one, you can see all the little details in it. Like all the details the Lord crafts in your life."

"There's that many details in my life?" I ask.

"Yep, like going to the third grade or facing mean girls at school – and each snowflake can be a reminder that God is taking care of those things." She glances around as if we are sharing a secret before dropping her voice, "Trust me on this one – I'm an adult, I know stuff," Marjorie nods with a straight face.

"Okay," I muse, thinking I'll be able to trip her up now, "what's a prayer you prayed on a snowflake and it came true?"

"Easy," she tells me, a smile spreading across her face, "I can tell you two: the first one, was that Charlie would have a brother."

"But you're pregnant with a little girl! Charlie is going to have a sister!"

"Nope," she shakes her head, "I'm watching him play with his brother right now." She nods her head in the direction of Aiden and Charlie: so different, and yet, so alike.

They must be brothers separated at birth! They say they are my protectors and will always have my back – or at least they do when we play princess and dragon, and they are the dragon slayers rescuing me from my tower.

They work so well together, taking down all the dragons and monsters under my bed, it would only make sense for a miracle to have some hand in this.

"You're right! Miracles are real!" I exclaim. Marjorie nods her head emphatically agreeing.

"And what's the other prayer?" I ask. Her smile broadens as she squeezes my mitten-covered hand.

"That Charlie would find a good friend – one who sticks closer than a brother, would follow him anywhere, and love him as fiercely as I do."

"So, Aiden answered two prayers?" She shrugs her shoulders.

"I'm not sure yet."

"But you said both prayers got answered!" I practically shout.

She laughs, its musical sound carrying above the winter wind.

"You'll understand when you're older," she offers with a wink.

"That's not a very good answer," I say, crossing my arms, fully prepared to pout till she tells me what this adult thing is.

"Mm, sometimes miracles appear in unexpected answers, whether we think they're very good or not." She winks at me, encouraging me to catch more snowflakes regardless of my desire to pout.

"Okay, do you know what miracle you want to pray for?" She asks. Nodding my head yes, I tip my head up to the sky, per her instructions, and wait.

I stick out my tongue and let the little white ice crystals collect, reciting prayers in my head as they pile up, one by one.

It's not long before Marjorie tells me to swallow, and I do, quickly closing my mouth and swallowing the snowflakes down. I squeeze my eyes shut and imagine I'm swallowing their power down, feeling it seep into my skin and spread throughout my body, so nothing but goodness will radiate out – angel sugar crystals or not.

Laughing and giddy, Marjorie and I fall to the ground and begin making snow angels.

"So, Harper, what did you pray for?"

There's no hesitation in my voice when I tell her, "I prayed for happily ever after".

* * * *

"Do you want chocolate chips in your pancakes?" Aria asks me, jumping up and down excitedly from the opposite side of the island in the kitchen.

"Sure, why not?" I say laughing, looking to Charlie to make sure he heard. I stifle another laugh as I take him in: Christmas tree pajama pants, a *Christmas Vacation* shirt beneath his candy cane striped apron, complete with the finishing touch of a Santa hat, as he ladles pancake batter onto the griddle. He looks up at me smiling, confirming my pancake order, and it's now I notice the batter smeared on his cheek.

How does this man keep getting food on his face?!

"Hey Charlie, I uh, I think you got a little something there," I tell him, gesturing to his cheek with my finger. Eyebrows raising in surprise, he tries to ask Aria for a napkin, but she's already run off to wish Beckett a merry Christmas. Batter bowl in one hand, ladle in the other, Charlie looks around frantically for a way to clean up without burning the pancakes. Finally letting out a sigh, he asks for help.

"Sure thing," I say as I take the batter bowl from his hands. Holding a damp paper towel now, Charlie asks again where the batter is at on his face.

"Oh, right there, on your cheek," I try to direct, but my directions do nothing to help as he wipes the completely wrong spot. "Here, let me just get it," I offer, setting the batter bowl down on the island, positioning his face with one hand while using the other to wipe off the mess.

For a moment, we pause, frozen in a position that feels much too comfortable.

He stares down at me, seeking answers in my eyes to questions I've never been willing to answer. It's broken, however, when Charlie shakes his head, letting my hand drop.

"Thank you," he says hurriedly, getting back to flipping pancakes, bubbling up as they finish cooking on one side.

"You're welcome, it wasn't really that big of a deal… are you alright?" I ask cautiously. I know we made it clear last night that we are keeping our distance, but something seems off with Charlie, and I care more about making sure he's okay than protecting my heart.

"Mhm," he nods without meeting my eyes.

"Charlie, are you sure? You seem a little stressed." He rolls his neck cracking it, before looking my way to answer.

"I'm fine Harper, just a little preoccupied. Trying to give the girls a great Christmas is all…" I nod, trying to understand. Charlie's dad has been sitting in the living room all morning, only going out once to shovel the driveway. Surely, he could help Charlie with some of these things…

"What about your dad? Or me? Is there anything we can do to help?" Charlie looks around frantically as if seeking out something for me to do.

"Yeah… I guess. Uh, set the table if you'd like?"

With a smile, I follow my orders, and begin gathering up the dishes to set their dining room table: a fresh bowl of winter fruit salad, a pitcher of orange juice, the first round of pancakes, which look ever so slightly tree-shaped, a pile of eggs – all the makings of a Christmas smorgasbord.

In the morning light filtering through the kitchen window, I observe Charlie. Carefully stirring, and spooning, and flipping, glancing up to check on the girls in the living room, quickly turning from the pancakes to scramble the eggs on the stove beside him, then a brief pause to sip his coffee.

Black, I remember.

He simultaneously appears both present and completely removed.

He's thinking about his mom. He doesn't say it, but he doesn't have to.

He wears the apron, and makes the pancakes, and does the song and dance for the girls and his dad, but it's a mask. One I completely see through.

One I'm not entirely sure I'm supposed to see in the first place...

When the pancakes are done cooking, he sits beside me, attempting to finish the coffee he's been working on for over an hour.

"So, are you ready to talk about what's really going on?" I ask him carefully, taking a sip of my own sugar cookie-flavored caffeination.

"What are you talking about?" He responds gruffly.

"I can tell today is hard for you," he silently raises a brow at my observation, "I just can't see past your Santa exterior far enough to know what's going on deep down." Playfully, I tug on the cotton ball at the end of his hat, wondering if I've said too much – been too transparent.

Are friends allowed to talk to each other like this?

I suppose so, because Charlie lets out a sigh so deep, I know it comes from his soul.

"It's that exact thing actually..."

"What do you mean?"

"This Santa-exterior," he remarks, gesturing to his ensemble. "I do it for the girls, because I know the holidays are hard for them, but I can't help but wonder if this is the right way to be doing it."

"How else would you go about things?" I lean back into the table, my mug warming my hands.

"I'm not really sure yet, but it's something I've been talking to Pastor Mark about," he sets his mug down to remove the Santa hat atop his head. He holds it in his lap looking forlorn, and even a little disgusted, as if perhaps it were sheered from a dog instead of a factory made in China.

"This whole town is so focused on "Christmas" – we have ballet recitals, and book readings, and dances, and parades – we do nothing but exude holiday cheer nearly the entire year, and I still can't shake the feeling that it's not supposed to be this way."

I'm shocked to hear Mr. Hallmark admit such a thing aloud.

"What about all of the things we've been doing, do you regret them?" There's a hurt in my voice I wish I could conceal because this is supposed to be about Charlie and what he's working through – not me.

"No, I don't," there's a meaning behind the look in his eyes I don't completely understand. "That's the tricky thing about all of this: I think so much of it is *good*. It brings the community together, it gives people something to celebrate, but it just seems so far from what the Bible says."

"In what way?"

"Well for starters, there weren't any Christmas trees in the manger – I'm not even sure that they should be a thing. And, Jesus wasn't even born in December."

"So, you'd do away with them?" I ask, wanting to understand what he's been learning. He pauses, debating this thought in his head.

"Maybe? Would that be wrong?"

"It would make you a social pariah in Pinecrest," I say, halfway joking, while trying to mask what we both know is the truth.

He nods his head as if this is something he's already considered. "Or, maybe, it would change things for the better," I try.

In an attempt to offer a more positive perspective, I suggest, "Maybe it could lead people closer to the Lord and the way we're actually supposed to do things. Help us find a way to honor his birth without making a spectacle of it." I shrug my shoulders because who's to say Pinecrest's mindset about the holidays couldn't be changed – it's a small enough town.

"I don't think there's anything wrong with people gathering together to eat cookies or giving someone you love a gift simply because you love them. It's great to support arts programs and feed children's imagination, but lately it has just seemed like people are more preoccupied with the presents and a fictitious man in a red suit than they are with talking about Jesus' birth," Charlie continues.

I nod along, long ago having realized these things myself. Charlie is on a roll, finally being able to confess all he has held in for so long, "What we were doing at the soup kitchen the other night: helping those in need, actively serving and loving on people – we need more of that. It felt good and right. It's what this season should be about. I just think there's more beneath it all, something deeper than that, and I just haven't figured out how or why yet. But I know I *want* to know."

I try my best to comfort him: a man facing the many questions the world poses.

"Then maybe there is more to know," I offer rather simply, "It's always something worth looking into, especially if you have a check in your spirit about it."

He nods in agreement, seemingly bolstered by my support, "All I know is I want my family to be different. I want us to do the *right* thing, the God-honoring thing, even if we have to do it alone."

I've always admired Charlie's boldness; his desire to do what's right and fair.

It's what made him never cheat on a test in class, what made him the best student body president our high school had ever known, why he was a good teammate on and off the field – because his goodness simply set him apart from everyone else.

It's that boldness and desire to serve the Lord that tells me he is going to do this, no matter what "this" is – because it's the right thing to do.

He'll do the research, chart the path, make the changes – he'll do whatever it takes to do what the Lord is calling him to.

What makes me curious, is why he isn't doing it already.

"What's stopping you from doing it now?" I ask.

"What do you mean?" He says defensively, like he can hide the truth from me.

"I mean, why the Christmas tree? Why the abundance of cheer?" I press. Charlie hangs his head now, and I realize we've reached the root of the issue.

"Because it's what my mom did."

Caution aside, I wrap my arm around Charlie because I know for all the ways he's tried to honor his mother, this would be one of the first times he's ever disagreed.

He doesn't protest as I rub soothing circles across his back, instead, he continues explaining, "Mom loved holidays, Christmas most of all – if I stop celebrating it, or try and change it, or downright disagree with it, what does that say about her memory? Removing the one thing the girls could always have to still feel her cheer – would it make me a terrible son? Would I be a failure?"

I know Charlie loves his mother more than nearly everything: he was by her side every step of her sickness, and he wants to do everything to keep life normal for the girl's now, to let them still remember their mother as much as possible. But I also know Marjorie was my friend too, and though I wasn't around in the latter years, I knew her at her core: the woman who prayed on snowflakes for her son's happiness.

"It would make you a *God-honoring* son, and there is nothing terrible about that."

He looks at me, hope and fear clear in his gaze.

"Your mom was a wonderful woman, she made amazing memories for this family, and she led a *wonderful* life – but that doesn't mean you have to lead the same one." I pause, taking a breath before continuing, wanting to offer Charlie the words I know he needs to hear: "You are allowed to chart your own path and lead your family the way *you* want to lead them, no matter how counter-cultural it is. If it's what the Lord gives you peace about, and what He convicts you of, then that's what you need to do."

I don't know much about convictions or peace from the Lord these days, but I do know the Grants, and I know that is what Charlie needs to understand: he is *good*. His mother knows she is loved. God is going to do something amazing with him.

"Thank you, Harper, I really appreciate it."

"Always, you know that – besides, you would say the same to me."

Trying to work up a smile, Charlie squeezes my hand twice.

"Why is doing the right thing so hard?" He asks, the exhaustion coming through his voice.

"Because it's the right thing? If it was easy, more people would do it." He nods. "You're going to figure this out Charlie, when the time is right, you'll know. And the minute you decide to start changing the world, I've got your back."

He offers me a lopsided smile. "You mean you won't allow me to be a social outcast, all alone?"

"Never," I shake my head emphatically, "we down-trodden-half-weirdos have to stick together, remember?"

Finally, he laughs, and instantly my whole body feels lighter.

"Of course, how could I ever forget?"

* * * *

When breakfast is done, I help Charlie clean the kitchen. As I wipe down the table, vigorously trying to remove the more-than-likely permanent syrup spots, I watch him: he's moving about the kitchen lighter now as if our conversation helped him take some of the weight off his shoulders.

I try to imagine what it must be like being him, carrying everything inside like he does.

It makes my heart ache and I wish I could take away some more of those troubles, hear out every hurt that plagues him, and remove each chain one by one.

It can't be easy carrying the weight of the world with you and still keeping a smile on your face.

I decide to add that to the ever-growing list of traits that set Charlie apart from everyone else I've ever known.

"He's crazy about you, you know," I jump, startled by Beckett's sudden appearance by my side and intrusion on my thoughts.

"What?"

"Charlie," she says with a nod in his direction, "don't hurt him, okay? He's lost enough as is." I stare in shock, at the young woman before me, who though only a girl, carries herself in a much older manner – who now seems to be threatening me?

"I – I know," I stammer out.

"You're good for him. Ever since you came home, it's the first time we've seen him really enjoy himself again... since Mom. He deserves happiness, and we like you, so don't mess this up," she says with a finger pointed at my chest.

They... *like me?*

All this time I thought they held nothing but hate for me, when really, they *wanted* Charlie and I to be together.

I want to tell her that I've pushed him away too hard; there's no coming back from the things I've said, from the inevitability of the hurt a long-distance relationship would cause.

When someone has lost so much, they shouldn't be willing to take a risk on forever, with a girl who has never believed in them.

But what if...

I think of Marjorie and her snowflakes and wonder what she would tell me to do.

"Make nice with your mom", *"Take a chance on my son"*, *"Write your happy ending"*, a million options run through my head, her voice parroting each of them to me, but it's Aria's announcement of more snow that draws my attention to the window once more.

Crisp, white, fluffy flakes flutter to the ground, adding to the mounds of snow already blanketing the neighborhood, and something draws me outside with the girls, away from the warmth of the kitchen and Charlie's side, and into the flurry.

"Catch one! Catch one!" Aria screams with childish glee, sticking out her tongue to catch as many flakes as she can. Even Bex laughs at such child-like innocence; such child-like *joy*.

So, we join in.

We dash into the yard, running around, tossing snow. I'm not entirely sure what exactly overcomes us, but the snow brings with it a cleansing; a brilliance to the world we've lacked for so long.

At some point, Charlie's dad coaxes him outside and away from the kitchen, and Charlie ends up standing beside me in the freezing cold, wearing nothing but his pajamas and an apron.

Flakes of snow gather in his blond hair, Santa hat now gone, and I fight the urge to brush them away with my hand. I funnel my energy into smiling, numb to my core in my thin red sweater and jeans, but regretting absolutely nothing about this moment.

"Catch one! Catch one!" Aria cries again.

I am tired of resisting; of trying to force myself upward in a world that simply wants to fall – so, like the snowflakes, I let go.

I meet Charlie's gaze, so filled with promise and hope and adoration, just as I tip my head back, and as the first flake collides with my tongue, I know exactly what Marjorie would tell me:

Believe.

* * * *

Catching snowflakes devolved into snow angels, laughter, and chattering teeth, which though fun, required everyone to change so we wouldn't catch colds. Charlie lent me one of his old sweatshirts to change into, and I couldn't help but savor the smell that enveloped me, like a blanket or comfortable spot beside a fire.

It's warm and inviting, familiar and lived in: it smells like home.

Like him.

After breakfast, we watch the girls open their presents from Santa and their dad, joy and curiosity radiating through me as I watch the excitement on their faces.

This might be the last time they do something like this, but right now, in this moment, the sheer giddiness is infectious.

It makes me want to share this feeling all year long – not just in December.

I adjust myself, leaning against the doorway, rotating the cup of coffee in my hands, and take a sip. As Aria sends more wrapping paper flying, Charlie comes up beside me, pressing into my back to whisper, "Ready?".

I smile, nodding my head yes, and watch as he disappears down the hall to get the girls' final present.

"Okay girls, this is a gift from me, Harper, and well... mom."

The girls look confused as the large box is set before them, but it doesn't stop them from readily tearing into the package to find what's underneath.

A shocked silence envelopes the room when the girls pull the quilt out of its box.

I search the faces of each person in the room trying to understand what they might be feeling.

I'm a writer. I should be able to fathom a million different emotions that could be passing beneath the sisters' unreadable faces, but I can't. And I don't think I want to, because some things are simply better left felt.

Beckett is the first to rise on shaky knees and look around the room with watery eyes, "I- I..." she tries to stammer out some kind of response, but all words seem to fall short on her lips. Instead, she runs to me and Charlie, wrapping us in a fierce hug.

I feel my sweatshirt growing wet with tears as Bex presses into me, and I wrap my arms around her. I try to squeeze her back as hard as she's gripping me.

Stroking a hand down her back soothingly, I feel a love so strong it overwhelms me. I try to imagine if this is what a mother might feel for her child, and I realize this is an earth-wrecking kind of feeling, so encapsulating you know you would, and will, do anything to make sure this person is safe and loved.

It makes me understand why Charlie stayed.

I don't know if it's moments or hours, but somewhere between Aria joining us in our group hug, Charlie wraps us up in his arms. Beckett pauses to catch her breath. With watery red eyes, she stares up at me, and thanks me and Charlie for the quilt.

"Mom wanted you two to have it, she wanted to be here for you, so you could always have a piece of her, even when she feels far away," Charlie chokes out to them, fighting tears of his own.

"This is what I prayed for," Aria pipes in. We all swing our heads in her direction.

"What do you mean Aria?" Charlie asks her carefully.

"I asked God to let mommy be with us this Christmas," she says simply, "and now she is, and she always will be." It's my turn to get misty-eyed.

"Yeah sweetie, she is," I tell her softly.

You were right Marjorie: the miracles are real.

A sob from the other side of the room shocks us all, as we remember Mr. Grant is still seated on the couch, clutching the blanket as if it can give his wife back to him.

"Dad? Are you okay?" Charlie moves to take a hesitant step towards his father, but Mr. Grant shakes his head back and forth violently, causing Charlie to stop short.

"I'm so, *so* sorry son," Mr. Grant looks at each one of us slowly, tears streaming down his face. I hold the girls close to me as they watch their father fall apart before their eyes.

Charlie crosses the living room to crush his dad in a hug, similar to how Bex did minutes before. Must run in the family…

"Dad, you have nothing to be sorry for – "

"No, I do. I do… I have been a shell of a man since your mother passed, and all this time you've carried the burden alone. And I am so sorry…"

Charlie tries again to protest, to tell his dad he's wrong, but Mr. Grant persists.

"How much life have you missed out on trying to keep this family together? How many years have you sacrificed, playing father for two children who aren't even your own?"

"But they *are* my family," Charlie insists. I've never seen such fierce determination in his eyes. "They are not just my family by blood, they are the family I *choose*, and no set of circumstances can change that."

No one moves to disagree.

"I love you Dad, and I love the life I chose, okay? Whether life is here, or Tennessee, or halfway across the world, the only place I want to be is beside the people I love."

For a moment, Mr. Grant can't respond, he just holds his son as if he's a little boy again, hoping he can somehow transfer back all the lost time with a touch.

Charlie knows he can't. But maybe that's what you do for family... you forgive them.

It's what Charlie has been trying to teach me this entire time, and now he's shown me.

"Thank you, son. Thank you for everything," and like the wonderful man he is Charlie tells his dad:

"Always."

Love can hurt you.

It can leave you hollowed out and empty inside.

It can fill you up to the point of breaking, and you could still be wanting for more.

But love can also heal you.

It can welcome you home with a warm embrace and show you how to fit all your broken pieces back together.

Love can be beautiful and healing. Love can conquer all.

* * * *

The rest of the morning passes by in a wintery blur of warmth and familial love.

The girls love their presents (and their older brother even more), and we play a card game to let the snow finish falling.

When the blizzard begins to break though, and we've long since made it past the soup and grilled cheese we had for lunch, I begin to make my way to the door.

"You should come to the dance with Charlie!" Beckett shouts, as if the idea has dawned on her as I'm halfway out the door.

"What?" Charlie quirks up an eyebrow at the idea.

"The winter dance is tomorrow night, and Charlie is chaperoning. You should come and keep him company so he's not all weird and big brotherly." She explains calmly as if this is the most logical explanation for things and not her attempt at covering up her desire for me and Charlie to be together.

"Oh yeah, totally," Charlie throws in offhandedly as if I'm offering to help him shovel the driveway or clean the kitchen. As if it's nothing. Which it is. So, I agree.

"That actually sounds fun... meet you at the school?"

Now, Charlie finally stops cleaning up wrapping paper from around the living room and locks eyes with me. He seems frozen for a moment, processing the reality of what he's gotten himself into.

"Uh... yeah, sure thing. I'll text you the details?" I smile and nod my head, wrapping my scarf around my neck once more before walking out the door.

As soon as I close the door, my phone buzzes in my pocket:

C: 8 pm, school gym, wear something nice Heartbreaker ;)

17

The last time I was in the Pinecrest High gym was for my high school graduation.

They lined all of us up before marching us out onto the field; I remember then, feeling much like a soldier, marching out into a brave new world of adulthood.

I wonder if there is some way, I could warn the past version of myself about what's to come: how she'll go off to the big city, and still somehow find her way home, but not just home – home as in the halls of a high school she had no plans on returning to. *Ever.*

Let alone as Charlie Grant's date to the winter formal... *again.*

I laugh at the absurdity of it all studying my reflection in the trophy case outside the entrance to the gym: the light glittering off the deep blue material of my dress making it look like the sky on a clear winter night, and I gently sway to the pulsing beat of the bass of the speakers in the gym.

I wish I was out under the sky instead of these fluorescent lights.

I wish I were outside and far away.

Far, far away from the nervous knots twisting in my stomach at the thought of Charlie coming to meet me.

I twist the snowflake necklace dangling from a chain around my neck, as Charlie opens the door to the gymnasium. I hear voices, and laughter, and music from the lower half of the gym where the basketball court sits.

As Charlie wordlessly offers me his hand, I take it, and allow him to lead me down the stairs. I wonder how this is even the gym of my youth: coming to basketball games for the boys, or the far and few dances I allowed myself to socialize at.

A new state-of-the-art scoreboard hangs on the wall, and plaques boast the achievements of the school's sports teams. New speakers have been brought in to loudly project a song I've never heard of. All too lifelike decorations cover the gym, making it look like we've entered a winter wonderland.

And for the first time in my life, I've never felt so *old*.

After watching the gradual horror spread across my face for a few minutes, Charlie can no longer contain himself and busts out laughing.

"It's awful isn't it?!" He exclaims, looking around the gym himself and making note of all the girls in dresses far too short to meet dress code requirements and the boys with outlandish suit colors. "I don't know if I'm horrified or jealous," he continues, "but this was most certainly *not* what a winter formal looked like back in my day."

"That's right you old man," I tease him, attempting to divert my own horror at the state of teenagers today, "it's certainly been a while since your old glory days, hasn't it?"

He rolls his eyes, "Ha-ha, yes, make fun of the old man who is only a few years older than you."

"Years? Based on the way you're talking; I'd say it's more like *decades*."

"I've aged remarkably well, can't you tell? I take my skincare routine very seriously," he notes before giving me a wink and a crooked smile, which automatically leads to an eye roll in response from me.

"Clearly, I know plastic surgery is a pricey investment," I reply. Charlie clutches at his heart in mock horror at my response before scolding me with a pointed finger.

"Now, now missy, didn't you ever hear you're supposed to respect your elders?" I can't help but laugh at the severity of his tone.

"You're right, my apologies, should I get you a cardigan and a warm glass of milk? I know it's almost your bedtime." He nods somberly.

"You know, that's not a bad idea… this old thing is clearly not appropriate for such a man as me," He says, tugging on the lapels of his dress coat, and I laugh. I do. Because there's no other response that is remotely acceptable at a time such as this.

Because he's right, he does look utterly inappropriate, but not in an *"old-man-whose-overdressed"* kind of way, more like a *"he's-so-handsome-I-could-cry"* way.

The thought does cross my mind when I look Charlie up and down, as he laughs in his perfectly tailored suit, that maybe I could cry.

The deepness of the blue and the starkness of the white.

He compliments my dress perfectly and I hate it.

I hate it so much, because deep down, I don't hate it one bit.

"You know, you outdid yourself tonight Heartbreaker," it's Charlie's turn to look me up and down, slowly, savoring every dip and curve of the dress as it hugs my body, flaring at the hem of the skirt.

It's a little much for a chaperone of a high school formal, but it's all I could acquire on such short notice, thanks to the assistance of Anna, my resident fairy godmother who just so happened to have a few dresses for black-tie events in her shop.

"You thought a high school winter dance necessitated black-tie?" Charlie asks after I hurriedly explain that "this old thing" is nothing really, just something to borrow for the night.

"Well, I don't know, it's not like I really spend all of my time doing philanthropic service at high school dances," I say, quick to defend myself. He nods.

"I suppose that's acceptable considering the fact that you're *totally* breaking dress code."

I glance down, an internalized and automatic panic setting in, that I, the grown adult, will be dress coded in the same manner I once was in high school.

"Why? What for?" A once-over reveals my dress is just long enough... I'm not really sure what the problem could be. "Scared my knees are going to distract someone?" I quip.

Again, Charlie's eyes rake over my body... over *me*.

I long to know what he's thinking; it's the same part of me that trembles with fear at admitting the truth.

The look he gives me when he quickly bites his lip in thought before speaking is *not* a friendly one. There is no brotherly goodwill in his eyes – only *want*.

"I don't know about someone, but it's most certainly distracting me."

With that final comment, Charlie turns to get us punch, leaving me alone as my insides turn to mush.

* * * *

I have never been a jealous girl, but I can't help but wonder if "jealousy" is what this bitter acid is racing through me as I watch him flirt with one of the young, pretty teachers also chaperoning the dance, and I am left to stand along the wall sipping from a plastic cup.

I thought he would come back after going to get punch.

Which, in his defense, he technically *did*, except instead of hanging around and talking, maybe sharing a dance or two, he handed me my cup and told me to "enjoy myself" before striding across the gym to chat up the teachers.

Enjoy myself?! As if he's doing me some kind of favor by dragging me along to some high school dance.

Charlie Grant's "date"? I am his shadow at best – no different than the girl I was in high school (she was at least smart enough to fight against going to these dances in the first place).

I try to connect the Charlie he was moments ago, with the man before me now, and can no longer find the warm, mushy feeling he filled me with.

Now, all I feel is simply the purest and most honest kind of blind, raging, jealousy.

Of course, he's not interested in me. Or at least not anymore... not after I've pushed him away so many times.

I begin to wonder if there's something wrong with me and the way I interact with people. Maybe it's because I don't know how to flirt. Certainly not in the same way this teacher knows how to, batting her eyes and twisting a strand of hair around her finger while she laughs at some joke Charlie has made.

Maybe I should have done that after Charlie commented on my dress, instead of staring at him like the dumbstruck idiot I am.

Maybe it's my constant need to run away the moment someone gets close.

What would have happened if I never said no?

Another high-pitched laugh echoes across the gym, causing me to cringe as it carries itself over the din of the music.

It's disgusting really.

They should get a room or something so the children aren't badly influenced.

I begin to wonder if maybe this whole thing was payback: retribution for turning Charlie down. My punishment for muddying the lines between friends and "other" has landed me as a wallflower once again at a Pinecrest school dance, doomed to watch the most amazing man in the world slip through my fingers because I was too scared to say anything else.

I suppose though, the first rule of *not* letting something slip through your fingers, is learning how to hold on. Something I never really did for Charlie.

We don't get a happily ever after because since day one, I've told him they aren't real.

I go back to New York and he stays here, and we run into each other again ten years from now when he'll probably still be charged with saving me from whatever disaster I will have landed myself in by then. Why should he expect anything else?

I've been erratic, emotional, and generally unfriendly.

Heck, at this rate, I'd choose the peppy blonde cheerleader too!

Another comment from Charlie makes her laugh so hard, she tips her head back and touches him on the arm.

Definitely a cheerleader in high school.

Besides, I've talked to Charlie, and he's not *that* funny.

To prevent myself from gagging, I look around the room.

I search for anyone, anything, to get this visual out of my mind. But instead, I see them happily married with two blonde-haired, blue-eyed babies, and a golden retriever.

It suits Charlie. Good for him! I never wanted those things.

No way, not for me: no babies by the fire, or small-town life, or quiet nights at home.

I'm going back to *my* home – the city, the place I'll always be running away to.

Then, I see her: a young girl, maybe a freshman, sitting on the bleachers reading a book. Her dress is as black as her nails, and her face is completely clear of any makeup. Craning my neck, I try to see what book she's reading and think I can make out the cover of *Wuthering Heights*.

I like this girl.

What I don't like, is that she's utterly alone.

In an attempt to save us both from ourselves, I make my way across the gym to her and take a seat.

"Mind if I sit here?" I ask, trying for my friendliest voice possible.

"It's a free country," she informs me without looking up from her book.

She's not hostile, just lost in a world that's not here, and I for one don't blame her. A decade ago, I would have been in her place.

I remember always hiding a book in my purse when I'd go to school functions, knowing if all else failed, I could retreat to a world of fiction. I currently wish the little clutch I had brought with me was big enough to hold at least an e-reader or something.

"What are you reading?" I try again, ignoring all social cues clearly saying I should leave her alone.

"*Wuthering Heights.*"

So, I was right.

"Hey, you're that author lady, aren't you?" She asks, a mild, but ultimately bland amount of interest crossing her face.

I laugh, "I suppose I am, yes."

"Cool," she nods, "I was at your book reading the other night, you have some pretty good stuff."

Surprised, I smile at her. "Thanks! Now what's your name?"

"Rita," she says as she adjusts the book in her lap, "and I'm going to be a famous author like you one day." She says this with her head held high - I have no doubt she will be.

"I'm sure you will, shaking the dust of this crummy little town off your feet?" I ask. I've pinned her so well - she seems shocked like I've read her mind.

"Yes, actually, I am."

I nod, in silent understanding. "I was too."

Neither of us says anything for a minute before I ask her why she got all dressed up for the dance, only to sit on the sidelines.

"Because my mom wanted me to go... she even tried to get me to go with one of my guy friends just so I'd have a date," she makes a gagging motion with her hand as I laugh. "I can't believe her, she just wants me to stay in this town and be like her – it's like I'm some project for her to fix or a doll to dress up. But I don't want to be fixed – I'm not broken. I just don't fit in."

Sounds familiar.

Shrugging my shoulders, I tell her, "Moms just want to bond with their daughters, it's all they think about from the moment they find out they're having a girl. Just have a little patience with her: they don't always realize that sometimes they can love too hard. They're just people trying to learn how to relate, just like we all are..."

Somewhere, in the back of my mind, I hear Charlie's mocking tone say something about calling the kettle black.

"I guess so, but that doesn't justify her need to control my life, or *more specifically*, put me in a poufy dress," Rita objects.

She's right, the taffeta on this dress is a bit much by some standards, but I imagine it looks pretty if she were to stand up and swish, like a goth princess. I tell her this, making her laugh.

"Maybe... but come on, you wouldn't wear something like this, would you?"

"I don't know," I tell her honestly, shaking my head, "I hated the whole dressing up thing when I was younger, but now, I think I have a newfound appreciation for it. Life is better with glitter," I say with a wink.

Rita ponders this for a moment before concluding that she might just have to test this concept of spinning out on the dance floor.

"You're only young once Rita, why not dance while you can?"

"Then I should, but not before I hear how the heck you ended up here." Leaning back and crossing her ankles, Rita props her Doc Martins on the bleachers, making herself comfortable.

"Oh no," I say, brushing her off, "Go have fun, I don't want to hold you back." She looks indignantly at me as if there is no option other than telling her how I ended up back in Pinecrest.

"No way! You've heard my sob story, what's yours? We wallflowers have to stick together you know," she says before gently nudging my shoulder, like we are longtime friends and not strangers. Laughing, I concede.

"Well, *technically*, I came back for my brother's wedding, but..."

"But what?"

But what is the question, isn't it?

Why *am* I still here? Why did I come so early?

At the time, I told myself I was running away from my writing; seeking an escape, and just making up for lost time, but with who?

I haven't spent a minute with my parents since I've been home (unless you count fighting). I've hardly written anything despite hours of trying.

Every second of every day has been taken up by Charlie: wedding planning, baking, dancing, laughing, and playing in the snow

- everything down to thinking about the guy has consumed all of my energy since I came across that stupid turkey.

But what if I hadn't?

What if Charlie wasn't the guy who came to my rescue that wintery day? What if he was just the guy who was helping me finalize details for my brother's wedding?
Something tells me that even then, I'd still be sitting here watching him across a crowded gym... because some things are simply inevitable.
"But then things got complicated," I answer Rita, who has been waiting expectantly for a beat too long.
"So, you met a guy?" She clarifies. I laugh at her sudden assumption.
"What makes you think that?" I say knowingly. She rolls her eyes as if it's the easiest answer in the book.
"Because it's *always* about a guy." I quirk up an eyebrow at her response. "What? I'm a reader," with a shrug of her shoulders she tells me, "You know it's the truth."
"Mm, maybe so... but that's beside the point. There's more to life than just a boy."
I say it like it's nothing, but deep in my heart, I feel the same pang of heartbreak and jealousy I get every time I look in Charlie's direction.
Every time I look at him and he's not looking at me.
"You can tell yourself that all you want, and it *is* true, but that boy sure is into you." I look at Rita in surprise as she tells me, "He hasn't stopped looking your way since you sat down."
I fully look over at Charlie where he stands so casually across the gym, eyes darting between me and the woman in front of him.

When I catch him staring, he pauses and smiles, frozen and ignoring the conversation taking place right beside him.

When he breaks my gaze, it doesn't take a second for me to know there's a blush spreading across my face - and Rita sees it too.

"I'll leave you two to work things out, I believe *I* have an appointment with a dance floor..." Rita winks at me before setting her book down and marching off to the ensemble of kids, moving in time with the song playing through the air.

Chaperone job: done.

Or so I think until Bex marches over to me. "What are you doing?!"

It's my turn to lean against the bleachers, crossing my ankles, careful not to crush the half-up-half-down hairstyle Anna helped me put together before coming to the dance.

"Chaperoning."

Her response is a glair that could kill, which quite frankly, is rather terrifying given how intimidatingly beautiful she looks in her silver dress.

She reminds me of an ice princess, capable of freezing me in place with a single look.

"You know for a *fact* that's not why I told you to come."

"Yes, and I told *you* Charlie's not interested, otherwise he wouldn't have spent the entire night talking to Teacher Barbie," I say gesturing to where Charlie stands, now surrounded by not one, nor two, but three of the teachers charged with "keeping an eye" on the students littered about the gym.

Based on the way they all seem to hover around Pinecrest's most eligible bachelor, I'd say they really just want to keep an eye on a certain Mr. Grant. Bex rolls her eyes.

"All of them are just desperate for any single dads they can get their hands on, single older brothers included! Did you really think you wouldn't have any competition?"

She sits on the bleacher in front of me, a deep conviction filling her words as she continues, "You've been gone for almost *ten* years! But you're the one he wants Harper, I've seen it. You just have to want him back."

She makes it sound so simple… I wonder if it is.

When the first slow song of the evening comes on, Beckett's date comes to retrieve her, and as she is drug away by one hand, she emphatically points between me and Charlie, mouthing FIX THIS!

And so, I do.

Or at least, I have every intention of marching with full-force determination across the gym and stealing Charlie away from those greedy teachers, but he's already walking my way.

When Charlie gets to my side, he joins me in the bleachers, and for a moment, neither of us says anything.

"You seemed to be doing a pretty good job chaperoning tonight," he says with a sly glance my way.

"I've been known to dabble," I smirk, "I'm not sure if the same thing can be said for you though, sir."

"Me?" Charlie says innocently, "Why would you say such a thing?"

"Hm," I raise a finger to my chin, pondering, "Maybe it has a little something to do with the pack of she-wolve teachers drooling over you as if you're a fresh cut of meat."

"Have you seen this suit? I'd certainly say it's fresh," he replies, not entirely addressing my statement. I roll my eyes, thinking *that's one way of putting it.*

"I suppose some might think so," I offer nonchalantly, causing Charlie to arch a brow.

"Would *you* say so, Ms. Marshall?"

I consider answering Charlie, flirting back like he seems to do so casually, acting like those women who still stare us down from the other side of the gym, but that's not who I am.

If I am going to do this with Charlie, then it's going to be authentically me – no more pretending. So, instead, I ask him a question:

"Would you like to dance with me, Mr. Grant?" A small smile of surprise works its way across his face.

"I thought you'd never ask," he tells me as he stands.

Charlie flourishes and bows, offering me his hand, and I take it, letting him lead me to the dance floor.

"I thought you weren't much of a dancer, Heartbreaker – what changed?"

I shrug, entwining my arms around his neck, allowing his familiar scent of snow and engines to wash over me, bringing me more peace than I've felt all night.

"I believe, someone once told me to live a little."

He laughs softly before saying, "You really are something else, aren't you Harper Marshall?"

All I can do is smile, as Charlie pulls me just a little closer, planting a gentle kiss on my forehead.

As his lips brush my skin, I close my eyes, melting into the music and the warmth of the shield of safety known as Charlie Grant.

It sends chills through my body and drives a knife through my heart.

It was supposed to be good, finally having Charlie this close to me, in arms reach, and all I have to do is say yes.

But now the cliff is right in front of me and jumping only seems to promise a plummet down.

Images of every moment leading up to this flash through my mind: the book reading, the baking, the night on the couch; the ballet, the library, and Christmas Day – and now this. Each moment pushing me closer and closer to this ledge in my mind.

"Harper…" Charlie says, his voice nothing more than a whisper amidst the cacophony of the gym.

I don't want to look up into those deep blue eyes and be absolutely destroyed; I can't.

Because if I look up, then I'll want to stay. And no matter how much I want Charlie, staying is something I'm just not sure I know how to do.

"Harper…" he tries again, "please look at me".

So soft, so gentle Charlie pleads with me, as we continue swaying in time with the music.

I risk it, raising my eyes to his, noting how soft his lips look, how close they are to me at this moment…

"We need to talk about this," he hesitates before adding, "About us".

I shake my head emphatically, tears welling up in my eyes.

How could I think about doing this? To him? To us?

"I'm so sorry Charlie," tears begin to stream down my face as he tries to protest.

"Harper, no, let's just talk this out. I know we can find a solution –"

"No," I beg. "No."

Silence.

"I have to go." The song isn't over, but my time here is.

It's time for me to leave Pinecrest.

To leave Charlie Grant and let him move on with life; to find love with someone who will stay, and to forget I ever came here and wrecked his world.

I'm done toeing the edge.

I'll explain to Aiden on the drive to New York, or maybe I'll call my mom.

I can come back on the day of the wedding and be gone by the time the reception starts, whatever I have to do, I just need to go.

I burst into the night and am met by a sudden gust of cold winter wind, realizing I left my jacket in the gym.

I don't care, I'll buy another.

"Harper! Harper come back!" Somewhere behind me, Charlie is calling my name, and though every part of me aches to answer, I cut across a snow-covered field by the school instead, hoping it'll get me to my car faster.

I'll get in and I'll drive.

Drive and drive and drive, and never look back.

Never come back to Pinecrest, or *Written Comfort*, or the library, pretend this month never happened.

"Harper!" Charlie runs across the field catching me, as I move painstakingly slow through the snow in heels. "Harper, stop!"

Anger, hurt, desperation, a whole host of emotions carry with Charlie's words as he reaches for my wrist and pulls me into him.

I try to push him away, to signal that I'm a mistake.

A *mistake* of the most epic proportions.

"Let me go, Charlie!" I yell at him.

"No!" His eyes are wild as he watches me wrench against him, trying to get away. "Why did you run Harper? Why did you run when I asked about us?"

"Because I can't stay!"

"Why not?!" We pause, breathing heavily from the cold, running, and yelling. "Why can't you stay with me, Harper?"

"Because you have a whole host of other girls you could be with!" He looks around as if this is some kind of joke.

"And? I don't want them! I just want you! You're all I've ever wanted," he cries throwing his arms up in the air.

"That's a lie and you know it, Charlie Grant! You haven't looked at me twice in our lives until I came back home," I'm not even sure it's the truth anymore.

How long have Charlie and I played this game of wanting and leaving?

Has there ever been a time *before*?

"Maybe I haven't looked *twice* Harper, but it's only because I've never looked away. From the moment I met you, I have never been able to take my eyes off you, let alone stop and consider *maybe* what I felt for you wasn't just *brotherly* love."

I shake my head, crossing my arms, trying to stop the tears that flow so readily.

He continues, "I've never known anyone like you Harper – when we were kids, and even still. There is no one else who *feels* as deeply for everyone around her as you do; the way you see the world and people so transparently and long to see people get justice. The way you've brought out in me a vulnerability and honesty that I haven't felt with anyone since my mom died. Your willingness to love my sisters the way that I do; to help friends and family at the drop of a hat – even if you insist you're nothing more than a frozen heart. You're the best person I know, Harper."

As he speaks, my eyes fill with more tears that threaten to spill over.

How is he saying these things? This can't really be the way he sees me – I am not these good things he's listed; I'm a mess.

"What are you trying to say, Charlie?" My voice trembles as I watch him step toward me hesitantly, eyes unbreaking as he watches me resist falling apart.

"I'm trying to say I'm in love with you." He moves slowly as if I'm a wounded animal, frantic to escape, "I am *in love* with *you* Harper, and I know you love me back, and I want us to make this work."

Now it's out there. He's said it. *Love.*

"I have been falling in love with you over and over every day, from the moment you first got scared of a turkey. I have never been so thankful for such a stupid bird."

Charlie gets misty-eyed, as he draws me into him, paralyzed where I stand. He cups my face with his hands.

Gosh, those hands.

So gentle and rough all at the same time, I'd do anything to never let those hands go.

"Every challenge, and cry, and laugh I've had with you has filled me with life I never even knew I lost. And I don't want to lose it again, Harper. So, stay. Have a happy ending... with *me*," he begs.

I open my mouth to speak, but no words come out.

There are no words to encompass what I feel for this man, so vulnerable before me, and yet a voice in my head screams I *still* can't stay.

Every moment with Charlie makes me inch closer and closer to the taught edge of the tightrope of my life: on the other side sits hope – and no matter how many times I try to cross it, I just can't let myself do it.

"Charlie.... I- I-" I keep trying to start something, anything, to rip these words from my lips, but they hang there on my tongue, trapped in my throat, choking me, squeezing the air out of my lungs and I wonder if I'll faint. "I love you."

The words fall out of me like a whisper, like if I say them too loudly then one of us will spook.

"I love you Charlie and that's why I can't stay. I can't be your princess."

I don't get the happily ever after, because I never made the wish.

Because there's no fairy godmother, and all I'll be left with when this comes crashing down is a pumpkin and a pile of tears.

I've seen this story before, and it didn't end well – not for me.

My prince didn't come back, and every pile of broken promises said I wasn't worth the fight.

"What?" The air seems to deflate out of him at my words. "Please, just tell me why?"

The tears begin flowing as I shake my head, biting my lips, because the truth just hurts too much to say.

It's self-sabotage – I know: not giving myself the chance to try again, closing myself off to the possibility that maybe *someone* will fight for me.

I've written dozens of characters who do the same thing – my attempt at a cathartic release – at healing.

I kept hoping one day I would finally change the story, and yet every time I reach the end, I don't do it.

I can't.

I'm not strong enough.

"Because happy endings aren't real. I know so, I've been told so, time and time again –"

"By whom?! By me? By your brother? Your parents?"

"By the world Charlie!" I explode, throwing my hands up, and letting out all the things I've carried with me for so long. All the anger I tried to squeeze out of me with my writing, all the words I was never able to say. "I don't know if you've looked around lately, but the world isn't a fairy tale! People get sick, and they die, and they starve, and there's war, and poverty, and a million other things every day that proves just how very *wrong* the fairy tales are!"

"But... I thought we were making progress. Your happy ending..."

"Is a wash! I doubt the publishing agency will even take it, besides, what am I if I'm not a heartbreaker?"

I can see Charlie grappling so hard with himself, fighting the urge to shut down and shut me out, to walk away or stay.

"You'd be mine."

I don't say anything, so he continues, "I thought I was changing your mind –"

"You can't change what's burned into me, Charlie," I tell him, my voice void of any gentleness, "The first lesson I learned in my very first creative writing class was happy endings don't sell. They aren't real, and if you aren't real then you'll never be taken seriously as a writer."

I feel the fight fading out of me as I tell him the truth, "All I ever wanted was to be taken seriously as a writer, and now look at me," I weakly toss my arms up, my voice breaking. "I did it. I proved everyone wrong. I'm one of the best *freaking* writers in the U.S. today. I've got the fame, and the money, and a whole brand to go along with it, and I am *broken*."

Charlie shakes his head gently, "But you were never broken to me". My responding laugh sounds utterly insane, and he looks like I've slapped him.

He shakes his head again, finally understanding: "You're never going to change your mind, are you?"

He's looking at me the way he should: like he's just realized what I've been trying to say this whole time – *I'm* the villain.

There's no dragon to slay or damsel in distress – there's just me.

Charlie is looking at me like he sees right through me.

"You're scared of what a happy ending looks like, but you don't need to be afraid –"

I cut him off, "I'm not scared!" Tears begin rolling down my face again because even at my worst he's still trying to save me. I catch my breath, "I'm not afraid, I'm just done wasting time on things that aren't real." He bites his lip, straightening his shoulders: shutting down.

"Fine then. You're not changing your mind, you're not scared, and none of this was real." He nods, running over everything one more time in his head. "You know what you *really* are Harper?" I can't answer him, otherwise, a sob might slip out of my quivering lips. "You're a *coward*, too scared to leave your comfort zone – too afraid to *live*, so you write fiction instead. And one day, it won't be enough; because the world you live in isn't *real* - but this was."

Charlie finally walks away, leaving me in the snow – the truth of his words stinging more than the biting cold tethering me to the ground.

Alone is the way I was meant to be – finally playing out my proper role.

And as I embrace this, I realize several things.

Charlie Grant plays a million roles: he's a friend, a brother, a mechanic, and a terrible dancer. He's a golden boy, a best man, and the kindest human I've ever met.

Charlie Grant is the love of my life.

He would give me a lifetime of hope and happiness I could never deserve because I am *hopeless*.

Because a happy ending isn't a part of the story I wrote for myself, and it never will be.

This is the ending I deserve – it's the ending I earned.

18

Harper, I am sorry to break this to you on such short notice, especially after Christmas, but I felt you should know: the house will not be accepting your newest manuscript. It doesn't fit the image they were looking for – they really want something more "classic Harper".

On the bright side, they are giving you a second chance! If you can deliver the first few chapters of a new project by New Year's Eve, then they'll extend your deadline into the new year.

They did find it of the utmost importance you understand the significance of this manuscript and the urgency with which you deliver it.

I look forward to hearing from you,
Lauren

I'm not surprised when I read the email – not really. It seems rather fitting actually: *poetic justice.*

Those words seem to curdle in my mouth now.

The thing about poetic justice is it doesn't account for love or the heart.

It doesn't lend grace to those who take sleigh rides or believe in the magic of snowflakes.

It merely happens and expects humanity to survive, and maybe even laugh at how opportune its timing is.

I don't think I'm the biggest fan of it these days.

Regardless of how I feel (because I've never let that matter anyway), I know what I need to do. I've done it a dozen times: cut my losses and move on.

It's been easy in the past – using words to put a temporary balm over the emptiness I feel inside.

This will be no different... right?

* * * *

In the first 6 hours of life without Charlie Grant, I think, despite having done everything to protect *him*, I did nothing to protect *myself*.

I am convinced that maybe being awake for open heart surgery would be less painful.

And I consider it as an option: hospitals need organ donors all the time. Maybe someone could take my sick and twisted heart, give it to some poor girl who would know how to use it, and let her go out into the world to try again, since clearly, I don't know a thing.

I mean, that's what I've already done, isn't it?

Cut my heart open and ripped it out of my chest; thrown it away like every failed story idea I've ever had, left it pulsing there while I bled out, and then had the audacity to wonder where I went wrong.

I went wrong by thinking maybe I could change.

In the second 6 hours, I get three calls from Aiden, one from Rose, a knock on the door from my mother, and another email from my publisher.

All of which I ignore.

I don't eat, I don't sleep, I don't even think I cry, I just exist.

I wallow in my pool of self-pity, and I stare at the wall, and I contemplate breaking the mirror because then I wouldn't have to look at myself: The Heartbreaker.

Whoever said words can't hurt you was full of crap, because I now see I am a well-trained mercenary.

Come hour 18, I fall into a restless, nightmare-filled sleep, in which nutcrackers chase me and the gum drops are poisonous; and I watch over and over again as Charlie walks away from me - as *I* push him away.

He was right: I am a coward.

An unfinished manuscript chases me down and I think it'll eat me alive.

An oversized wedding cake towers above me, and the life-sized groom figurine comes toppling down, and just as it's about to crush me, I wake up in a pool of sweat and tears.

Numb, I stumble down to the kitchen, scrolling through the many notifications on my phone while I brew a cup of chamomile.

I see a message from Rose, a photo of her and a few of her girlfriends in Chicago celebrating her bachelorette party, tagged with the caption "wish you were here!!!".

How she is able to put together a whole bachelorette party of women, and not a single one of them can be her maid of honor, I will never understand, but there are some mysteries in life I am choosing not to pursue these days.

The clock on the stove reads 3:33 AM: December 28th. I don't know whether to be impressed or concerned by my ability to spend a whole day locked away in my chamber moping.

The 28th... one more day until the wedding.

I dip my tea bag in and out of my cup, and re-read Lauren's email.

If I'm going to have a manuscript come New Year's, then I have to start writing – and fast.

Even the roughest of drafts need a little time to come to life.

Seeing as now is as good a time as any, I grab the nearby yellow legal pad Dad keeps on the counter and start scribbling story ideas: a ginger-haired cult takes two young bakers hostage; snowmen come to life and try to take over the world; a high school dance goes horribly wrong.

Every story I come up with reminds me of Charlie.

But as I write, I soften: a boy saves a girl from a savage turkey; a golden-furred dog has a fun day in the snow; two little ballerinas dance their hearts out on stage.

Deep down, beneath the surface of anger and angst, beneath the brokenness I have convinced myself defines me, I'm still standing outside with my tongue sticking out, hoping to catch a snowflake.

And it's that part of me that I can't deny has been revived since coming home – but choosing to acknowledge it simply leaves me conflicted.

Crumpling up the piece of paper, and finishing my tea, I try to toss the paper in the trash, narrowly missing it.

Oh well, I was never an athlete.

Deciding it's probably a sign I should give up on thinking for the night, I decide to try again after some sleep. As I begin my assent up the stairs, I repeat the same words over and over again: *tomorrow*.

Tomorrow we'll try again.

19

"Wake up."

With no gentleness, my mother flicks on the lights in my bedroom and tosses a crumpled-up piece of paper on my bed. Squinting, I read it, my eyes adjusting to the mid-day light, eyes blurry from the exhaustion of my late-night cup of tea, and I see it's my discarded story ideas from last night.

"Do you mean those?" She asks me, as I read over the paper once more.

"Yes, Mom," I answer with as much sarcasm as I can muster pre-caffeination, "I legitimately meant evil snowmen come to life and try to take over the world. It's one of my deepest, darkest fears."

She doesn't even try to hide her eye roll as she counters with, "No, the rest of them. Like the one where the mother and daughter make up."

Oh.

I see where I scribbled it at the bottom of the paper: a fleeting and unrealistic thought, written in a sleep-deprived state.

An unrealistic thought, that I meant every word of.

"Yes."

My mother doesn't say anything, she just nods her head, and in a much softer voice replies: "Get dressed, I have coffee waiting downstairs when you're ready to work towards a happy ending."

It's an invitation, and one I readily accept.

I may not ever be brave enough for Charlie, but I can at least make things right with my mom – *I have to.*

She's sitting in her rocker, sipping her coffee, when I come downstairs.

Creak, creak, creak.

I think back on our fight when I first came home and feel the all too familiar guilt in my gut as I sit down on the couch, where a cup of coffee beckons me.

My mom lets me get a few sips in before speaking, "I'm sorry about you and Charlie".

I stifle a scoff. "No, you're not, you're just sorry you missed out on getting the dream son-in-law."

"Would you stop?" The pleading in her voice takes me aback.

"Stop what?" I ask.

"Assuming the world is against you."

I swallow hard, her eyes frantically searching my face for something.

"I'm sorry," I whisper.

My mom doesn't know what to say for a bit, so she shakes her head. Hanging her head and closing her eyes she takes a deep breath.

"It's not something to be sorry about unless you plan on changing it."

I nod, knowing she's not wrong. "I want to change it."

"Want and will are two very different things Harper Marie Marshall – you of all people know that." I nod again, hanging my head, waiting for the lecture to come, but it doesn't.

Instead, my mother ever so softly asks me, "What happened to you?"

She's tried to ask me this very question a dozen times; each time more infuriating than the last. But this time, the softness of her voice shatters my heart in two.

Sensing my trepidation, my mom reaches out a hand, squeezing mine tight: "I love you, no matter what it is," she offers with a hesitant smile.

I don't know if it's the question, the answer, or the comforting hand of my mother, but I let out a sob startling us both. A deep pain I didn't even know I'd been holding on to, as I quietly whimper out:

"I don't know."

"Then maybe that's where we start," she tells me.

And so, we do:

F, I see the grade glaring up at me in red ink. I've never failed something before in my life, let alone something as simple as writing a short story. In the tiny margins, I note my professor's comment "Happy endings aren't real".

My ending wasn't all that happy either, just realistic.

Or what I had always considered to be realistic.

"Fairytale Fiction is a dying art; one you are not an artist of - stick to the real stuff".

I tell myself this is one professor out of the dozens I'll have in college, and this is great practice for one day when people will leave critical reviews of my work. All I have to do is make it through this semester.

Then the leaves fall from the trees, and it's a new semester.

I barely made it through the last one, but I am still me. I stuck to my guns and knew the truth about my work - I have a story worth telling, just not everyone is meant to listen.

F, another one, this time a little more costly.

"Real writers don't do fluff," they tell me. My classmates judge me for not seeming to understand the "proper principles of writing". I argue romance novelists and children's authors are real writers too, they just don't have someone die at the end of every novel. "But they aren't taken seriously in the writing community", "is that the life you want?" and quite frankly, I'm not sure anymore.

For the summer, I move in with some girls from a poetry class I took.

They are the kinds of people I always said I wanted to be friends with: they speak so eloquently, and dress so edgy, and they go out to underground speakeasies on the weekend.

I start too as well.

They wear lots of leather and talk about being "one of the greats", and I begin to wonder if this is what you need to do to be successful.

A new year, a new chance to try again.

My friends tell me I should dress more professionally, so I buy lots of tweed and black, I go out drinking with them, and smoke a few cigarettes, and we watch as the world judges us for it.

I begin to see why they have such a chip on their shoulders.

That chip follows me back to Pinecrest and I get in a fight with my mom; my parents cut me off and I spend the remainder of the semester tutoring to have enough money to travel over Christmas break.

I take a trip to London with my friends and they introduce me to their upper-class friends: "Students at Oxford who write like Shakespeare", "the kind of people who really have something to say", but all I see is judgment in their eyes, and all I hear is their critiques of the lighter things in life.

I start to wonder what ever happened to Charlie Grant who always had such kind eyes, or a girl named Anna who always remembered everyone's birthdays. On quiet nights, I almost message one of them, just to see how they're doing; but they've moved on with their lives – they wouldn't want to talk to someone like me anymore.

I start forgetting to call my mom and dad, and I wonder if there's always been this tightness in my chest.

I lose sleep and I fail another essay, and I wonder if maybe there is some way to make this easier.

At the start of the spring semester, I run out of a lecture hall when my professor criticizes my writing in front of the whole class, and I have to take fifteen minutes in the bathroom to make my heart stop racing.

Has it always done that? Has the world always been this mean?

I stop going out.
I stop drinking.
I stop eating altogether.
I stop writing. Until I have to.

The doctor tells me the pain is anxiety and I need to find a way to decompress, but I tell no one. They can't deal with my mess. They shouldn't have to.

Writing used to be my way of decompressing.

My friends tell me about how the world has fallen apart, and the economy is in shambles, and we should probably flee the country.

They curse the government, and I never stop to question why they never do anything about it.

If the world is ending, wouldn't you at least want to try and save it?

I get called into the dean's office: "You are at risk of losing your scholarship if you keep failing". Failure is no longer an option, I have to write something, so I give in. I think I'm too tired to fight it anymore.

I write a story so tragic I wonder if it'll be over the edge: **A.**

They like it.

I write another: **A.**

"You have such a gift", "so moving", "the kind of story the world needs these days".

Is it?

Does a broken world crave brokenness?

The people I thought were my friends leave: "You're too tortured", "You should get some help". I know they're just jealous, but maybe they're right.

Aren't all tortured artists considered "tortured" for a reason?

No one tells me I am still whole; I am not too broken to be pieced together.

No one tells me I am not composed of pieces to begin with.

Over the summer, I get my first publishing deal and the critics love it.

Heartbreak apparently sells, and the world around me confirms every day just how right I am.

I go numb to the sensation of pain I used to feel at writing such darkness, and people praise me for it.

They encourage my craft, and I stop asking if this is right, if this is what I want.

Why would you stop doing the thing people praise you for?

I am a good writer, and now the world knows it.

The anxiety begins to ease, but the pain doesn't when I look at the mirror, because all I see is broken.

I feel empty.

Junior year, I start dating a guy in one of my classes.

He doesn't shrink away from my jagged edges; he sharpens them and tells me I can do more.

I try to fill my shattered pieces with him. I wonder if this is love, but I don't stop to ask myself, how can this be love if it leaves me feeling so alone?

He's here, but he's not.

He encourages me to get a place on my own, so I do, but when my parents come to visit, I don't tell them about him.

He doesn't want to meet them and says, "Parents only create problems".

How would they feel seeing me with someone clad in all black? Someone with a cigarette dangling between his lips, who carries a notebook of poetry he lets no one read.

How would my parents feel seeing their perfect girl slip out of small-town safety - gone off the rails?

All seeing them reminds me of is just how far I've fallen, and I begin to think the distance is too far.

There is no healing for me, only hurt.

And I am quite good at it - just ask the New York Times Best Seller's List.

That guy promises to marry me, but never buys a ring; he tells me they are an outdated concept anyway.

I tell myself that this is it: this is the future I wanted, with the guy I always pictured.

But then he breaks his promise.

When he breaks up with me, I don't cry. I dismiss it as a product of my actions.

Why stay for someone who is such a mess?

I don't deserve happily ever after, even if they are real...

And so, the story goes.

Time moves on, I graduate, I re-new my publishing deal, I find some friends who don't tear me down as deeply, but I never let them in.

I never let anyone into my world of hurt and brokenness, because what good would it do?

Until now.

I spill my story before my mom in a series of cries and runny noses and wonder how I held this in for so long.

I might have stopped wearing all the black, but what got left behind still feels just as damaged.

I don't think I ever really stopped seeing myself that way, and I have pushed everyone away as a product.

I convinced myself no one could want a mess like me, without even stopping to ask myself if I was really such a problem to begin with.

I was a person in pain, so it's what I've inflicted upon others, and I never even stopped to say sorry.

I became convinced there was no safety outside of my broken tower, and every fleeting happiness that could bring me closer to the edge of my comfort zone just seemed too far.

It required a strength and a hope I didn't have, something I never thought I'd be able to reach.

I still don't.

When I finish, my mom doesn't say anything, she just gets up from her chair and hugs me. I cry into her clothes like I'm a child again and feel so very small.

"I'm so sorry you carried that alone for so long, Harper. But you don't have to anymore."

I think about the grief over Marjorie being added into the mix and my journey of healing having a long way to go, but I also know this: sitting here, with my mom, whose eyes I can finally look into for the first time in years, is a first step.

"I'm sorry, for the way I've behaved for the last couple of years. I was just afraid if I let you all in and told you the truth, you'd... I don't know... be disappointed in what I'd become? I'd be too big of a mess for you to deal with? I didn't want to be a burden."

"You have *never* been a burden to this family Harper," My mom says fiercely, "That's what we signed up for in being your family: to carry the burden of life together." I nod my head, trying to let myself be convinced.

My mother pauses for a moment, seeming to think something over, almost as if she is listening to someone giving directions. "You know what, Harper? Whether we ever accepted you or not, you're still not alone."

I look up at her confused, feeling a slight pinch in my chest.

"Harper, the Lord loves you and wants a relationship with you that is *far* greater than any love or acceptance we could give you."

The knot in my gut tightens again: *The Lord*.

Jesus Christ the Messiah.

I had thought about Him in passing over a dozen times in the last decade and steered far away because I knew about the hellfire and brimstone I was preached growing up, and I certainly wasn't worthy of pearl streets and golden gates.

"He doesn't want me like this," I tell her.

My mother shakes her head with insistence.

"He has *always* wanted you like this. Every day from the moment the Devil convinced you that you weren't worthy: The Lord has been chasing after you because He will never leave you."

"No Mom, He *can't*," I insist, "Not after everything I've done."

My heart is racing in a way I haven't felt in so long. The only other time I felt like this was sitting in the church beside Charlie reading that verse...

"For everything, there is a season", that's what it said: I was worth the wait.

My mom takes my hand and squeezes it.

"Harper, the Lord asks us to come to Him broken. To give our burdens to Him and let Him put us back together because He is the answer to all of the brokenness, the anxiety – the hurt in our hearts. He heals it. And He is waiting for you whenever you want to return to Him." My whole body feels warm and my eyes prick with more tears.

He still wants me.
He'd wait for me.
How? How? How?

How can He still choose me again and again, offer me a salvation I don't deserve, a comfort I haven't earned, after all the ways I've strayed from Him?

I think about the ways I've fallen away from Him over the years: the way I'd give my body to every guy I dated hoping to feel something, the way I'd drink and smoke to numb my pain, the hate I'd carry in my heart – how can someone so perfect still want me after that?

I do. I always have.

The voice speaks so clearly to me that I wonder if someone has said something aloud.

My soul aches to hear more.

You have never needed to earn your way to me. You just needed to say "yes".

More tears fall from my eyes as my whole body trembles before the Lord.

I want to say yes.

I want that perfect healing in my heart.

I want Him to clean out all the filth the world has left behind and replace it with Him.

I'm ready for Him to take this broken mindset away.

Father, I need you, I cry to the calling in my heart. Like an orphan calling out to their dad: never needing to see their face, simply *knowing* you're home.

"Mom, I want to ask the Lord back into my heart. I want to go back to how things used to be when I was a kid. When I got baptized, and read my Bible, and first said that prayer. I want Him to come back."

Ruefully, my mom softly shakes her head. "He never left Harper, you just have to repent of your sins, and return to Him. God isn't the one who moves away, He never will be. How close or far we are to Him is up to us and what we want the relationship to look like."

"That prayer you mentioned," my heart is beating harder than I ever thought possible in the most glorious way, "What do I need to say?"

Another squeeze of my hand as a smile starts to spread across my face.

This is what hope feels like.

"You say whatever is on your heart," she tells me.

Bowing our heads and closing my eyes, tears dripping down my face, I begin talking to God for the first time in a while.

Dear God... Father? Jesus? It's me, Harper. It's been a while since we last spoke... I'm sorry. I'm sorry for all the ways I've sinned and stepped away from you.

I was just so afraid.

I didn't want to disappoint you in your perfection. But you knew, didn't you?

I don't remember a lot about Sunday school, but I do remember that you know our hearts better than we do.

I was never broken, was I? I was just a sheep who wandered off. Thank you for finally taking me home.

I'm so sorry it took so long, but I'm ready to come back now. To do things for you, <u>your</u> way, not mine. My way is human and flawed.

I want to do everything to grow closer to you, to your heart, and your plan for my life.

I love you. Thank you for loving me. Amen.

Salvation is not pretty words – and I'm a writer. It is a genuine heart change.

It is repentance. It is returning to the God who perfectly loves you after you wandered away for far too long because He's still there recklessly seeking after you.

Putting turkeys, and failed manuscripts, and snowflakes all in your way to remind you that you need Him.

* * * *

When I open my eyes, I'm smiling: the deepest, most genuine, soulful smile I've had in such a long time.

My mom hugs me tight, not even trying to wipe away her own tears.

For a moment, we just pause and celebrate – in one way or another, I've come *home,* and it feels so, *so* good.

I am going to heal from everything that's happened to me because the Lord is doing the healing now. All my broken pieces will be used to build something incredible and glorifying to Him.

And the fact that my mom got to be here to share this with me feels so *right.*

I want to jump around, and dance, and find my Bible, and tell everyone I know.

There's a zeal racing through me I didn't know I could feel ever, and I almost reach for my phone to call Charlie.

I have what he has now, what he, my mom, and Marjorie all get to feel every day.

Marjorie.

I take in a deep breath knowing I'll get to see her again, and a shudder races through me at the realization that I almost didn't.

My fate could be something so much worse than anything I've ever experienced. But now, I'll see her again: healthy, happy, **healed.**

A question comes into my mind though, something I truly need to ask my second mother, but will never be able to. At least for some time…

So instead, I ask the mom who is here with me now. Who just led me through salvation.

My mom.

"Mom, if you all wanted to be there for me, and would have loved me regardless, why didn't Marjorie let me come see her? Why didn't anyone tell me?"

My mom's smile falters as her brow creases in either confusion or disappointment at a memory I can't see.

"We tried to convince her to let us call you, but she always insisted otherwise. It was one of her final wishes. She seemed so sure of it for some reason. And then when she passed, I guess... I don't know. I think we thought maybe it would make the pain easier?" It's the same answer Charlie gave me, which means it still leaves me just as unsatisfied. But my mom isn't done talking.

She takes a deep breath, the years of exhaustion truly showing as she continues talking, "We couldn't stop ourselves from hurting, but maybe we could protect you. I'm not sure... we got so bogged down in our grief that we didn't think about how *not* telling you might hurt worse than telling you the truth. It was hard letting you live your own life, off and independent of us. But I thought that was what you had wanted, and I now see I was incredibly wrong."

My mom is holding my hand like that can transfer all the words and feelings she's trying to articulate now with a touch. "I wish I had reached out, or called, or done what a mother should do and simply *sensed* her child needed her. I am so *sorry*." Tears well up in her eyes as I shake my head, now being the one to comfort her.

"I think everything happened exactly the way it was supposed to. The Lord is intentional like that."

He is. I see that now; how my falling away wasn't right but allowing Him to save me was.

And a part of me knows this is exactly how I needed to be broken down to see just how desperately I needed to rely on Him.

My mom and I sit in silence for a bit, letting everything settle, feeling the goodness of God in the room. Taking in a deep breath, I tell her my final confession.

"Mom, I love you." She smiles at me kindly as she says: "I love you too." She squeezes me a little tighter before also mentioning that "I think it's a great thing you love Charlie."

I let out a dry laugh at her observation, "Not so great that I totally messed things up with him though." She shrugs.

"I don't think you totally messed things up. I think you have some work to do on yourself in figuring out the Lord's plan for your life, and a lot to learn about loving someone in a way that's healthy and God-honoring, but I don't think things are so broken that there's not some room for a happily ever after."

"No Mom, you didn't see his face. It's over," I insist.

She sighs before locking eyes with me,

"Harper, the thing about truly loving someone, the way God loves us, is showing grace. And grace forgives all things. You already know that."

Somewhere in the back of my mind, is Marjorie's voice, reciting 1 Corinthians 13 to me:

"Love is patient, love is kind. It does not envy, it does not boast, it is not proud. It does not dishonor others, it is not self-seeking, it is not easily angered, it keeps no record of wrongs. Love does not delight in evil but rejoices with the truth. It always protects, always trusts, always hopes, always perseveres. **Love never fails.**"

Deep in my soul, I know that's the way Charlie loves me.
And it's the way I want to love him.
I want to love him the same way God loves me.

"So, what do I do? How can I fix this?" I ask, desperate to know more.

My mother's eyes search mine for a long time. I could grow to appreciate this contemplative silence. It holds a peace this house hasn't known in a while.

Carefully, my mother smooths out the scrap of paper, and hands it to me, gesturing to my story ideas.

"You do what you've always done dear: you write it out."

Taking the paper from her hands, I know I've come upon a clear and dangerous precipice in my life: the publishing house wants another tragedy, but that doesn't mean I have to give it to them.

I can choose to rewrite this ending.

And I know I've said those words before.

I know I've probably said them a dozen times in the course of the last couple of months, trying again and again to change myself to save the relationships in my life.

I've counted on Charlie to save me, I've sought validation from my writing, but never once have I done any of it for myself – nor did I do it for the Lord.

Never, have I tried to let the Lord guide my pen.

That's why I know, as I climb the stairs to my room, armed with a fresh cup of tea, and a renewed sense of purpose, of *hope*, this time will be different.

Because this time, I'm doing this for something bigger than all of us.

* * * *

Sitting down at my desk, with my laptop open, I begin to write.

Truth blurs with fiction as I pour out my heart onto the page, and I write till dark.

When I stand to stretch my legs, I'm dizzy, but deep down I feel an unbeatable level of satisfaction.

It feels like the first time I finished a novel in middle school, and I printed it for hours off of our home printer. Dad was so mad I used up all his ink, but I didn't care.

He could yell all he wanted to, but what mattered most was I had created this thing. This beautiful and magnificent thing, full of sweet, grammatical flaws.

I imagined that was what mothers felt like after giving birth to their first child; something they made all on their own.

Evidence of God and the power of the mind – a product of my own time, sweat, and tears.

This moment, right now in my room, feels the exact same way.

I take a step back from my desk and pace a lap around my room before sitting back down and scrolling through my manuscript.

Page after page of incredibly mediocre writing, but for once, it's writing I'm proud to have produced.

I know come morning, I'll proof it before the wedding, and then I'll print it, and it'll be something for me.

Mine.

My story. Not anyone else's.

I think back on the one piece of writing advice I heard in college that just might actually be true: "Write the story you need to read".

I need this.

And deep down, I know someone else will too, and that makes it worth it.

20

The wedding festivities begin early the next morning, and promptly on time, in a manner I have come to expect from my future sister-in-law.

We begin with brunch in embroidered silk pajamas, and I try to mask the mix of emotions in my smile as Rose's photographer snaps away. Pure, unadulterated joy from my newfound salvation, and nerves of what's to come from the ceremony.

In the end, only two of the original bridesmaids could make it, and I find myself pleasantly surprised by their company.

They are more girly than I might have personally chosen for myself in the realm of friends, but they are here for Rose with the purest intentions, and I can respect that.

By lunch, we begin hair and make-up while ever so carefully snacking on finger foods to tide us over till the wedding reception, where Rose and Aiden have arranged for a full charcuterie table.

By the time Rose's timer is trilling, we are efficiently moving towards our dresses like the proper little bridal bots we are, and when I wriggle into the dress I tried on in the shop, I'm hit with the same familiar awe that surprised me the first time I let those sequins touch me.

Is it wrong that I'm still so surprised I can see myself as beautiful? As an intentional creation from the Lord, carefully crafted, more worthy than the rubies adorning my body now.

Was it really only days ago, and not years, Charlie watched me twirl in the mirror... that I tried on a wedding dress?

Now, I understand what his look meant, what it was he wanted so desperately: Me.

And me alone.

Worthy. Beautiful.

Fanning myself, I wonder why I've begun sweating, ignoring the obvious answer: this will be my first-time seeing Charlie since I shut him out, and I want, no I *need*, for him to take me back. To see that I am not whole, but I am healing, and one day, I will be the woman he deserves.

He needs to see that my heart is his – now and always, no matter what this journey looks like.

Despite this deep desire though, I hear a new voice in my head, one that's been silent for far too long: *even if he doesn't, I'll be okay.*

Even if he doesn't choose me, I am still worth choosing.

"Ready?" A bridesmaid asks Rose, grounding me to reality: today is about her and my brother, not me and Charlie.

Rose fans herself frantically, trying to keep her makeup from running as tears prick her eyes.

"I just- I love him *so* much. Is that normal? To like, I don't know, feel like you've been struck by lightning? Like you're some kind of princess?"

It's shocking, seeing the perfectly composed Rose crumble like a cardboard box left out in the rain, but I suppose, there are multiple sides to everyone.

Wedding magic tends to put that on display...

Her friends try adamantly to soothe her as she stands there, a vision in white, with her ballgown ballooning around her small body, her blushed cheeks growing rosier as she dabs at her lashes. They all look at me for guidance, which confuses me until I remember that I'm supposed to be the *maid of honor* – preventing a bridal meltdown is my main job.

Hesitantly, I crouch down in front of Rose, take her hands, and softly beg, "Rose," she looks up at me, her doe eyes fluttering furiously, "it is far from normal in the most wonderfully unusual way. It shouldn't feel *normal* – it should feel exactly like every fairy tale you ever dreamed of because your prince charming is waiting for you." She sniffles softly as I finish with, "Rose... that makes you a princess today."

More tears brim in her cerulean eyes and I wonder if I've said something wrong.

Knowing myself, I probably have.

"*Thank you*, Harper," she whispers, before grabbing me around the neck and giving me a fiercer hug than I thought her capable of. "Thank you for making my fairy tale possible."

"Of course," I offer with a shrug, wiping away the tears that have surprisingly popped up in my eyes, "that's what sisters are for, right?"

With another emphatic nod she agrees, before we suddenly are both hugging and crying. As she squeezes me tighter, I know this – *this* is the beginning of something good.

Something real and lasting, that feels like having a family.

"Alright you two, break it up before someone smears their makeup!" A bridesmaid jokingly cries. "We've got to get you married!" And so, we march out of the dressing room in the chapel to meet the wedding planner, who will line us up for the final march.

* * * *

Before lining up, I tell the girls I need to go to the bathroom, but once their backs are turned, I slip down a separate hallway that leads to the groom and his groomsmen.

Rose had a strict "no boys" policy during girl's time, but he's my brother! How could I not wish him well on his big day?

I knock gently on the door labeled "Groom" before stepping inside.

Aiden, not so shockingly, is staring at himself in the mirror.

"You do know you'll have to actually look at someone *other* than yourself today, right?" I chide from the doorframe.

He smiles, noticing my reflection in the mirror as I stand in the hallway.

"Good to see you too, little sis," he turns around and welcomes me in with an embrace.

I squeeze him tight, the reality of this moment setting in, and tears prick at my eyes again, surprising me once more.

Who knew accepting Jesus would make me so emotional?!

As a sniffle escapes me, Aiden pulls back, "Hey now, no crying on my wedding day – I demand it!"

I laugh through the tears, which only makes more fall, "Gosh, you two really *are* perfect for each other, aren't you? Rose already told me the same thing today!" His lips twitch up into a smile. "I mean, I'm really *really* glad you found her," I finally stumble out while dabbing away the remnants of tears. He laughs again.

"I'm certainly glad you've had a change of heart since we kind of accidentally thrust planning our entire wedding upon you," he offers sheepishly.

"Whaaatttt," I play coy waving a hand in the air, "I mean, it was nothing, I plan random weddings all the time."

He nods while conceding, "I'm sure you do". Quickly, he glances around as if looking for someone before saying, "Besides, from what I can tell you certainly weren't doing it alone." He winks at me, and I wonder if maybe Charlie hasn't told him already.

"About that... Aiden, I'm sorry. I don't know how much Charlie has told you, but I did exactly what you asked me not to do: I hurt your best friend. But I'm going to make it right, I promise."

Aiden's smile is still easy as if nothing I've said is news to him.

"Charlie already told me, but it's not something you needed to apologize for, because I already knew you'd fix things."

"I mean, I'm going to try..." I try to explain, "But I already told Mom, I'm not sure how much I can truly *fix* things." That familiar thread of doubt is beginning to lace its way into my gut as the time to face Charlie draws closer and closer.

Aiden's smile broadens, "Trust me: I know my sister, and I know my best friend – and I listened to him last night. He's upset, but something tells me, you and I both know there's always room for hope."

It's the most serious I've seen Aiden... possibly *ever*, but for the first time I don't want to disagree with my eternal optimist of a brother, because for the first time – I know he's right.

"Annnd, Mom told me about your little conversation with her yesterday, and I just want you to know I love you, and I'm happy for you – happier than anything else in the world could make me."

My vision begins to cloud again at his words, "I'm sorry for everything the last few years Aiden, I didn't mean to push you away or create so much distance," more tears trickle down my face as he wraps me into another hug, "you were just trying to love me – I'm sorry it took me so long to accept ."

He laughs into my hair as he holds me – ever the protective big brother.

"Does this mean you'll start drinking green juice with me?" He tries. Laughing, I shove him off.

"No, and quite frankly, I think Jesus would agree with me on that." Aiden's laughter is loud as he adamantly disagrees.

"Harper!" I hear a voice call from down the hall – *shoot*, I've been in the bathroom a suspicious amount of time.

"Okay big brother, you ready to get hitched?" I ask. Aiden adjusts his bow tie once more in the mirror before nodding.

"Never been more ready."

* * * *

If I know anything, I know this: Charlie Grant looks good in a tux.

And maybe, in some alternate reality where I am a far more confident person, I might actually tell him this. Except I wouldn't just say that - I'd also tell him I love him; that I'll probably always love him, but most importantly, I'd tell him I was wrong.

But that's not who I am.

I am a woman of words – none of which are spoken aloud.

So instead, I line up beside him like the wedding planner tells us to, and we watch Aiden walk down the aisle.
Charlie won't meet my eyes anymore, which is honestly colder than I expected, and as I watch the guests find their seats and get situated, I realize just how many people are at this

"small-town wedding".

A mixture of people from both Pinecrest and Chicago fill the seats of the Old Chapel (Aiden's choice so they could be close to Marjorie): these are people I don't know, who just might judge me, and for a moment I'm scared.

All the options run through my head as to how everything could go wrong: *I could trip and fall, drop my bouquet, photo bomb the photos, or* - Charlie takes my hand, silencing my thoughts. Surprised, I look up at him, but he still won't look down at me.

Our fingers intertwined is the only thing telling me this moment is real.

Two strong squeezes remind me: no matter how broken we seem, we are okay.

In some strange, perfectly imperfect manner, we always will be.

"Thank you," I whisper to him, as the wedding planner nods, giving us our cue to walk.

Charlie offers me a nod, letting me know he hears. And that's how we walk: hand in hand down the aisle.

He gives me another quick squeeze before I dare to let him go and am left standing alone beside the bridal party. All heads turn in attention as the bridal march begins to play, and I watch what feels like our entire town stand as Rose makes her debut.

No exaggerations are necessary when saying the air seems to be sucked out of the room as everyone audibly gasps.

Layers and layers of shimmering material bury my brother's bride-to-be, and I resist the urge to even look in Aiden's direction as I hear him crying aloud.

I do, however, steal a glance at Charlie, who is already looking at me.

Of all the beautiful things he could cast his gaze upon in this chapel, he chooses me.

That's why I don't look away when my eyes meet his.

Instead, I smile, and hesitantly, he smiles back.

In unison, we turn back to watch Rose walk with her father, to be given away to Aiden.

We cry when they read their vows, and Charlie presents the rings he's kept tucked away in his pocket this whole time.

When the newlywed Mr. & Mrs. Marshall have their first kiss, I'm the one to fan her dress out like Anna taught me, and I pull the officiant out of the way when the photographer steps out to take a picture.

It's a perfect moment.

And then snow begins to fall from the rafters of the church.

Aids had been tucked away with buckets of snow-like confetti, and it rains down as the couple runs down the aisle.

As it shimmers in the fading light of the afternoon, I begin to notice the flecks of glitter mixed in.

Rose arranged for it to *quite literally* rain glitter on her wedding day.

I respect her just as much as I fear her.

What did I truly do for this wedding?

To have been put in charge of a lot, I'm not really sure what I contributed.

The lights for the reception.

It dawns on me that I never asked Charlie what his plan was. I look over in his direction where he stands grinning with the other groomsmen, just as enthralled as everyone else is by the snowstorm in the church.

He's got this.

Charlie Grant has never failed me before, why would he ever start now?

* * * *

I follow the rest of the bridal party into the church garden where the reception is supposed to be and am blown away by the transformation of the backyard of the church.

Where post-service potlucks were once held decades ago, there's now an exceptionally large cream tent and full-sized dance floor arranged on the grass area.

When one enters the tent, they are transported to a different world of fairytales and magic.

To the right of the dance floor is a table full of charcuterie and finger foods, along with the cake table where the towering masterpiece Charlie and I selected proudly resides.

To the left of the dance floor is the DJ (who is actually just our old high school computer teacher who likes to believe he's a DJ) softly playing iconic love songs for the wedding party that has spread out across the lawn.

Heat lamps are stationed about the dance floor, warming the tent and its partygoers, but what truly stops me in my tracks, is directly in front of me: a series of neon signs lit up in a golden color, each a cursive script reading something different: *"it was always you"*, *"be mine"*, *"forever & always"*, but most importantly – *"happily ever after"*.

Charlie Grant: the romantic.

A sweeter love song is played as the newlyweds are announced and make their grand entrance.

I'm thankful Rose didn't have a big enough bridal party to have some grand entrance for us, I'm not sure how much more attention my inner introvert could handle.

So, I cheer, and I clap, and I yell for my brother and my new sister, and I try to blink away the tears I cry during their first dance.

I watch them, spinning so gracefully: a perfect pair. And I wonder if someone would have thought the same thing of me and Charlie.

We have our differences, he and I, but when we let down our walls, he's shown me more gentleness and love than I've ever deserved.

When the DJ begins playing a song for everyone to dance to, I notice my dad take my mom's hand and lead her on to the dance floor.

They're still so in love after so many years.

Could I ever have a love like that? Maybe.

Loving someone, I've come to realize, isn't something that just falls in your lap and stays with you forever.

For most people, it's easy to fall in love, like breathing.

But staying in love? When the world creeps in and things get tough, when things get *real*, that's when love becomes a choice.

Every day, choosing to forgive and grow instead of running away. Giving up your fears and desires, to give of yourself the way the Lord does.

I have a lot to learn about staying in one place, since my whole life I've been running from myself, but I'm ready to face my fear with a strength that's not dependent on *me*.

So maybe, it's Charlie and I one day. Or maybe it's me and a man I've yet to meet.

Regardless, when it's me and whoever the Lord has planned for me, the thing that will matter is when I find them, I wake up and I choose to stay every day.

To keep the story going even when the "Happily Ever After" has come and gone.

Loving is choosing one another when the storybook has closed.

Chapter 1: Harper admits maybe there is hope for humanity after all.

Chapter 2: Her fairy-*mother* reminds her she doesn't need glass slippers to be worthy of a fairy tale.

Chapter 3: Harper finds the real person who can save her *and then* finds her prince.

Chapter 4: They live Happily Ever After...

Chapter 5: They keep choosing each other, every day, always, till death do us part.

My story is just beginning, and it is far from over because now, I know the one writing it.

"Care to dance?" I ask Charlie, with far more confidence than I feel.

My question doesn't garner a smile from him like it once did before; rather, I earn a skeptically arched eyebrow.

"Where have I heard that one before?" He asks, avoiding my eyes.

"Please," I beg, offering him a hand. He looks at it without taking it, his face guarded.

"The last time I agreed to a dance with you Harper, I ended up chasing you out into the snow and getting my heart broken... I'm not exactly looking for it to happen again."

Fair enough, I feel myself begin to deflate at his rejection.

I knew this would happen; how could he forgive me after all I've done?

No.

Having a heart means being willing to have it broken. It means staying.

"I'm not asking for you to come after me on a white horse, I'd just like a dance... and to talk." He shrugs, his hands shoved deep in his pockets.

"A dance I can do... I'm not too sure how I feel about the talking part." But he doesn't fight me any further, taking my hand and leading me onto the dance floor.

As we find a spot and begin gently swaying, I try to not get lost in savoring Charlie's touch. I didn't think I'd get to feel it again.

"Your lights look incredible," I offer, trying to break the ice. Charlie glances around the room with a satisfied smile.

"They really turned out great, didn't they?"

"Yeah," I nod, happy to be sharing this moment, "how'd you find them?"

"I know a guy," Charlie tells me with a secretive smile, and I wonder if one day I will ever know how he really found them.

Some part of me secretly hopes he just ordered them off Etsy.

"I'm particularly fond of the one that says "Happily Ever After" ..." Charlie's smile falls from his face at my comment as if I also suggested we clean the floors with our tongues once the wedding is over.

"What is it you wanted to talk about Harper?" He asks brusquely.

Oh right. We still aren't on good terms. I have to do the whole apologizing thing first...

"I wanted to say I'm sorry for the way I've acted the last couple of days. I haven't been a good friend by any stretch of the word, and I shouldn't have yelled at you... multiple times. But I'm trying to do better, and I'd like to start over –"

"Start over? How can you of all people say that Harper? It's not that easy." He seems shocked I even have the audacity to propose this.

"Why not? I had a heart-to-heart with my mom, and she and I worked things out, and I- I gave my heart to the *Lord* Charlie, and I'm ready to turn over a new leaf! So, why can't we do the same thing?" I feel like a child, debating with my parents on whether or not I can get what I want, but I persist.

Charlie's eyes soften at my words, "Listen, I'm glad you and your mom worked things out, and you're trying to work on yourself, and that you've reconnected with the Lord, but I don't want to be your collateral damage."

His comment hits like a punch to the gut. It's what I always feared, and even expected, I just didn't know he had realized the same thing.

But I have a renewed sense of purpose – I need him to listen.

"I know, which is why I'm telling you things are going to be different. I apologized for getting angry, you're just not listening -"

Charlie looks as if I've blown his mind.

"You think I'm mad because you *yelled* at me? Harper, married couples fight all the time and work past them. I *hear* you loud and clear, but I can't keep fighting for someone who doesn't believe we are going to work out because things are *too good*."

"I never said that," I try to protest.

"Yeah, but you did say we weren't real. How different are the two things?" He pauses for a breath, his blue eyes the color of a snowstorm. "You showed me I'm not worth the risk."

He's caught me.

How do I prove to him my heart has changed?

I am absolutely terrified of whatever life lies ahead of me, but I don't think I can live it fully if he's not beside me.

How can he know my heart has changed when I've already pushed him away so many times?

"I finished the novel."

"I know," he says with an eye roll, "and it probably got rejected by the publishing house".

"It did," I nod my head, "but now I have a different one. I made some revisions." He doesn't respond. "I think it would make things a lot clearer."

"I don't have time for more make-believe Harper – I can't just be a character in your stories forever".

"I don't want you to be…"

But I know I'm losing this battle, so as the song comes to a close, I tell him the only thing I know he really wants to hear: "I truly am sorry for everything I've done Charlie, and I hope one day you can find a way to forgive me. I was ashamed of the person I had become, and I thought there was no hope for me to ever change – I thought I didn't deserve something good because I was too broken for it. But you've helped me see that nothing is so broken that it can't be healed by the Lord – that no ending is so bleak that it can't be re-written," taking a deep breath, I pause before saying, "Thank you for reminding me that happy endings are real."

We drop each other's hands when the music ends and stand at a semi-awkward impasse between songs: neither staying nor going, just staring at one another. Charlie's face is a masked whirlpool of emotions, trying to sort through everything I just said, but no words ever leave his mouth.

I'm the first to walk away when a new song starts, wiping away the tears in my eyes as I leave the wedding.

I make sure to hug Aiden and Rose on my way out and briefly stop by Charlie's truck in the parking lot.

He may not want to hear me out loud, but speaking has never been my strong suit.

In his trunk, next to the wrappings he'll need to transport the neon signs, I lay my latest manuscript in a jet-black binder.

I know when he opens it the first thing he'll see is the dedication page: *for Marjorie.*

What he does with it from there is up to him, but for now, I know I'm going home.

Wherever home is…

21

"I've got to go home now Marjorie," I tell the gravestone I now sit beside. "Or, at least, I've got to go back to my apartment."

It's the day after the wedding: Aiden and Rose have left for their honeymoon, the library will return to its regular hours, and my car is sitting idle in the cemetery parking lot.

I had one last stop to make on my way out of town before it was time to watch out for turkeys and piles of snow and hope I don't get stuck in the city traffic for New Year's Eve.

"I didn't change the ending, just so you know..."

Saying the concept aloud still feels traitorous, but empowering.

"I wrote the ending I wanted."

Those words feel more liberating than I ever thought possible, and Marjorie being the one to hear them feels right.

I left the ending to my story alone, and I'm now going back to New York for a meeting with my publishers tonight, where I suspect things will not bode in my favor.

Then, I'll go back to my apartment, and go from there.

Maybe I'll get a house plant or a cat... maybe I'll sign up for some sessions with one of those grief counselors Charlie told me about...

I'll need to start going to church somewhere, and maybe, I'll finally figure out who Harper Marshall was supposed to be before the world told her who she was.

And I will write happy endings, and be broke, and it will be okay.

But I'm getting ahead of myself now; that's not why I came here before leaving town.

Carefully, I tuck my bouquet from the wedding into the hole in front of Marjorie's headstone and scoot back onto the damp grass before finally pulling out the old, faded letter she wrote me before she died.

"I need to know what's been left in my past if I'm ever going to move on," I explain to no one in particular, and carefully break the seal to the letter.

* * * *

Harper,

If you're reading this, I'm hoping it's because I have long since gone, and our families have respected my final wishes: you not see me till I've passed.

I have some explaining to do, but first, let me start with a confession: I am a coward.

And more than likely, a little vain. I have always seen you as a daughter, I have loved you as my own and would consider our friendship the kind of thing families are made of.

Which is why, I must apologize for keeping my illness a secret.

You see, when we found out my illness was terminal, the doctors suggested I say goodbye to everyone who mattered to me, whom I didn't get to see often.

Your mother and Charlie were the very first to pick up their phones and plead with me to call you.

And I said no.

For some reason, some part of me liked the idea of you, off living your life somewhere, not being burdened by the concept of me leaving.

I mean, you all always knew parents were bound to pass eventually, why add on the heartbreak of watching me fade away?

I liked someone not knowing this side of me.

It brought me hope to know there would at least be one person I loved, who would not have to carry this weight. Because Charlie, my sweet boy, watching him fade alongside me is almost too much to bear.

So, instead of bringing you home, I asked to read your books instead. And I did sweetheart, every word of them! And they were <u>beautiful</u>. Though, I do think I would like to see at least ONE story where they all live happily ever after!

Those were my favorite stories you wrote growing up because they were so far and few between.

I think you see the world in a very realistic way, Harper – true happy endings don't happen every day. But I think it's only fair I tell you, though realistic, that train of thought is <u>wrong</u>. Miracles happen every day, all around us, just as often as tragedies do. And tragedies, well, they are just happy endings that need a little shaping.

I believe you writers call it "vision"...

I'd like to tell you a story Harper: the sad boy with beautiful eyes, finally tells the girl next door how horribly in love with her he is.

Ring any bells? Perhaps, WEDDING bells?

I don't know what Charlie's story is supposed to be, nor do I know what yours will be, but I do know being able to share in one's loss, to find someone whose broken pieces so perfectly match yours – is rare. A story in need of vision perhaps, but potential for a story, nonetheless.

I wish I could give you more words Harper; that I could be there for so many more of your big moments. I wish I could be more to you than cursive on a page, but that's not my story, and that's OKAY! I am at peace with this being the story God gave me, and I want all of you to know that.

There is a miracle in there somewhere, my happily ever after in the making, we just have to trust the Lord to write it...

You're going to be okay dear.

Always yours,
Marjorie

* * * *

I sit on the ground for a while, stunned at the words I just read.

Marjorie knew.

She always knew.

She was not this fearless and flawless human being I made her out to be; she was human, and she was broken, just like me.

But she had hope.

I run my thumb across the Bible verse embossed at the top of her stationary:

Jeremiah 29:11 *"For I know the plans I have for you,' declares the Lord, 'plans to prosper you and not to harm you, plans to give you a hope and a future".*

These words have never seemed truer.

I still have a future no matter how much tragedy it's laced with, regardless of where I live, or whether or not Charlie comes with me.

I can have hope that things will get better and my story will write itself, no matter what the world wants me to believe.

Standing up, I brush my pants off, and take one more look at Marjorie's grave: we are going to be okay.

I glance over at the entrance to the cemetery, where Charlie walked me in, what feels like years ago.

I remember how I sat on the ground, and I cried, and he soothed me.

I think now would be an excellent time for him to come riding in on a white horse. To wrap my fairy tale up so nicely… but he doesn't.

Instead, I am walking out of here having accomplished the goal I set out to achieve: writing a happy ending.

"I want to write a happy ending and I don't know how."

Charlie looks exceptionally confused, positioning himself on the ground so he can face me.

"What do you mean?" I sigh before crossing my legs beneath me.

"You're right. I'm supposed to be here writing a new book, and I can't. I can't write another sad ending, not when the world is so full of it. Your mom deserved a happy ending Charlie, you deserve a happy ending. My agent expects another "classic Harper heartbreak", but I don't think I can do it. So, I want to write a happy ending, I have to try. I just don't know how."

"I'm going to help you." An arched eyebrow is my response. "Seriously, I'm going to show you the world is full of happy endings, and you're going to help me plan this wedding."

He says it with conviction, fully resolute: fully Charlie.

There's a spark igniting in his eyes, just like they would before a game in high school.

I imagine Aiden is here starting a chant, and I want to join in the battle cry.

"Okay."

The word "okay" seems like such a simple agreement now, as I turn my key in the ignition.

It was a small step in the right direction when all I knew was that I needed to do the next right thing. And it's what I'm going to do now as I embark on this next stage of life.

"Okay," I say to absolutely no one as I start down the road: *okay, okay, okay, okay.*

Every mile I distance myself from Pinecrest, from Charlie, from my home: *okay.*

22

On December 31st, while the rest of New York is playing in the streets, dancing about with sparklers and streamers, decked out in gold and silver - I am tucked away in my apartment packing up my things.

It just so happened that waiting for me in my mailbox when I got home, was my offer to renew my lease.

I politely declined.

I've had enough of city life for now and think it might be time to try some small-town living on for size.

This hopeful future doesn't make the packing process any less grueling, however; especially when Ryan Seacrest's *New Year's Eve* is a little less than "rocking".

Somewhere in the distance, I hear fireworks, and it makes me think of Pinecrest, where everyone would be gathering around the town square for the annual fireworks display at midnight.

Written Comfort would be out there with their little drink cart, offering hot cocoa to anyone in need, and every kid would be running around on the pure adrenaline only found around 11:47 at night, just before the clock strikes twelve.

I kick myself for wondering if Charlie will be kissing anyone at midnight, especially when I already know the answer: he won't.

Because it's Charlie.

Unless he is, because he fell madly in love with one of Rose's other bridesmaids after I left the wedding, and he decided he was tired of dealing with my crazy...

I can't help but fear the impending awkwardness we're bound to experience now when I run into him around town. But, if there's anything I've learned, it's that life is precious and short, and no one truly knows just how much time they have left, and I plan on making the most of mine.

Starting by surprising my parents with the fact that their daughter is coming home.

I go back to packing up my books, every last one I've both written and read, ignoring the underlying current of fear accompanying this new chapter of life, while simultaneously eager to seek it out.

Then, I get a knock on my door.

I jump up from the couch, getting out my wallet to pay for the Chinese I ordered, but everything falls to the floor when I open the door and Charlie Grant is waiting on the other side.

He looks as surprised as I do, gripping a letter in hand, appearing slightly out of breath.

"There's a lot of people out there," is the first thing he stammers out.

"Uhhh yeah," I nod at the obvious, "it's New York on New Year's Eve... they kind of take that stuff seriously around here."

He doesn't say anything for a moment, just nods before telling me, "I... I read your book. It was really good."

I can't help but let out a small, soft laugh and roll my eyes. "No, it wasn't. It was a rough draft at best."

His smile broadens. "Well, maybe I like rough drafts."

"I suppose you are entitled to that opinion," I commend, nervously laughing back at him.

A slightly dazed look is spreading across his face as if he's in a dream.

It's so different than the last time I saw him that I can't help but shake my head.

"Charlie, what are you doing here?" My words seem to stir him back into action as he snaps to attention.

"Right, well, I opened one of my mom's letters and this is what was inside," he says handing me the envelope.

Hesitantly, I take it, reading the outside: *"For Charlie"*.

Inside it, I see a letter and a small envelope.

Feeling the words to Charlie are probably personal, I pull out the other envelope, where on the back side, in Marjorie's perfect script is: *"for when you realize you're in love with Harper Marshall"*.

I look at Charlie, who nods approvingly, before pulling out the single notecard within the envelope. On it, there are only three words: "*Go. Get. Her.*"

It takes everything in me to not burst into tears – of what? I'm not sure.

Horror? Happiness? Both?

"So, you see, I felt like Mama probably knows best, and I should at least be man enough to ask you to come home with me, Harper Marshall."

Straightening his shoulders, he says, "You said you had changed, so let's give it a try. And if we need to go back and forth between New York and Connecticut until you get things settled, then I am more than happy to, but I don't want to walk away from what is possibly the *best* thing in my life, just because we feel like it might be *too* good to be true. I think that's exactly *why* you try and give it your very best, and if we crash and burn in the end, then there's no one I'd rather pick up the wreckage with."

He catches his breath, his eye alight with passion as he continues, "You have set me on *fire* Harper, you've given me *life*. And maybe, it seems like a fantasy to you, but that's only because it's a dream come true. So please, forgive me, for being so harsh, for not giving you a chance to change; just please don't stay here because of me."

I beam back at him.

"Well good, because I wasn't planning on staying."

Charlie's face is enough to make this whole thing worth it.

"You're what?!" he exclaims. Throwing the envelope down, I take his hands.

"I'm not staying in New York. I'm coming home – to Pinecrest, to my family, to *you*, Charlie Grant, if you'll take me?"

Charlie's mouth is gaping open as I continue to explain that, "I wouldn't do what my publishers wanted, so they terminated my contract. I'm going to look for a new publishing house closer to home, or maybe I'll try some freelance work, or I'll just publish online - I don't care just so long as I'm with you!"

"Yes," is all he can say.

Tears welling up in his eyes, he pulls me into the tightest hug of my life.

"Yes, yes, yes," he repeats over and over again, squeezing me tighter.

I want to melt into this moment, into *him*, but I know there's something I need to say first.

"Charlie, when I told you what we had wasn't real, I was wrong. I was trying to push you away because I thought I was going to hurt you. You were right, I was scared of what any other ending could look like for me. I didn't have hope or the strength to believe things could change and leaving my comfort zone – if it can even be called that – seemed like the most daunting task in the world."

I choose my words carefully, aching to convey just how much this man means to me.

"The truth is you give me *hope*. You make me want to do the hard things because life with you is better than any piece of fiction I could ever write – and I want to build that life with *you*! I want to do the most utterly mundane things like paint our kitchen, and name our kids, and argue over what movies to watch each night. I want to hear every theory about life you have and support you while you play Superman to everyone in your life. I want to do absolutely nothing with you because it always makes for the best *everything*."

Taking a breath I say, "You are my most comfortable silence, and the best party I could go to all in one."

"You hate parties," he interjects.

"Exactly!" I exclaim, "That's my point: I have never felt more at home than when I'm beside you, no matter where *home* is."

Gripping one hand, he uses the other to brush a tear from my cheek, ever so gently.

Swallowing down the emotions that threaten to overwhelm me, I continue, "I want the big things, and the celebrations, and the happily ever after, but I want the little things too. I want you on a quiet Tuesday afternoon because there's nowhere in the world I'd rather be than by your side. I want you when the storybook *closes*."

Pure joy fills his eyes as he leans in to kiss me, but I raise a hand to stop him – not yet.

"And I need you to know I'm a broken person," he opens his mouth to protest, but I wave him off, continuing, "I am broken in a *beautiful* way, and the Lord is healing me, but it's going to take *time*. I have to learn how to love you as well as you love me."

His lips close in the sweetest smile before whispering, "You love me?"

All I can do is roll my eyes and smile.

"Maybe just a little bit." He blushes – and something deep inside of me nearly squeals.

"Then I will give you all the time in the world," he reassures me. "However long you need, I'll be here every step of the way."

I know he means it when he says it.

The Lord is healing me, He is my salvation, *not* some guy, but Charlie Grant will most definitely hold my hand while we embark on this journey – *together*.

"Harper Marshall, do you know just how madly in love with you I am?"

I smile through the tears, shrugging my shoulders as I tell him, "I think I'm beginning to get the idea…"

"Good, because I plan on spending the rest of my life reminding you of it."

"I think I'd be okay with that."

And finally, as the clock strikes midnight, Charlie kisses me.

This time, I don't pull back when he leans in.

I don't try and deny how good his lips feel against mine – I don't do anything other than kiss my Prince Charming with every bit of me I can muster.

And I know, deep down, I've come home.

AND THEY LIVED HAPPILY
EVER AFTER ...

AUTHOR NOTE

I never sought out to write a "Christian Romance Novel".

In fact, I had no intentions of writing something "Christian" at all – I just wanted to write a story with a happy ending.

But when I dove into Harper's story, and ultimately my own, I became convicted of something very clear: there is no happy ending without the Lord. Faith is not something we can dismiss as magic or discount as chance; it is not a hindrance to fiction; but rather the foundation on which the story of my life is built. Without Jesus, I would be just like Harper: broken and hopeless.

While mine and Harper's story is not the same, writing her story taught me a lot about the way I want to view the world and the kind of love we should accept – and if there is anything, I can encourage you, dear reader, to take away from this story, it's this:

You are worthy of a love that is kind. Of a partner that is good. That is not just good because they're a nice person, but because they root themselves in the Lord and seek after Him daily; someone who is good because they love you like Christ does.

You deserve a happy ending.

Much like Harper, I often thought that my "brokenness" made me a burden; that I was too much for the people in my life, and that this brokenness inside discounted me from the lighter side of life. And much like Harper, I have learned that method of thinking is wrong.

I know that someone who picks up this book will think the same thing about themselves; whether it be the lie that they must stay in a situation that is bad for them because it's "what they deserve", or that they must feel shame for what their lives have looked like, or that they can't talk to the people in their lives about what they're struggling with because it'll be "too much of a burden", and my prayer is that Harper shows you that you don't have to think that way.

That every story can be rewritten, and that no amount of "mess ups" can discount you from forgiveness.

And for those of you who might want to receive that redeeming love in the same way Harper did, I want you to know that the Lord is waiting and willing the moment you're ready – all you have to do is ask Him into your heart.

The world is not so broken that we have to believe there is "no such thing as happily ever after". Quite the opposite actually; the world is broken and in need of a Savior that unlocks the happiest ending of all.

ACKNOWLEDGEMENTS

I have quite a few people I need to thank for making this book a reality, starting with my mom. You are my very bestest good friend – both me and this book wouldn't be all that we are without you. You were the one who told me "The world has enough sad endings – what if you wrote something happy", and because of that, I'm here today. You are my agent, my editor, my advocate, and my event planner (and hopefully one day my business partner) – quite literally none of this would have happened if I didn't have you beside me.

To my dad, thank you for navigating a broken world with me. You're the reason I know what the truth is, and the reason I know the Lord is victorious over every darkness. Thank you for providing me with a life where I get to make dreams like writing a reality.

To JT, you are the reason I know there is a lighter side to life. You are laughter and hope, even when it's hard, and I'm beyond grateful to call you my brother. There is no one I'd rather share Radio Roulette on long car rides with or stay up late to have movie marathons beside.

To Randy, thank you for all of the editing and revising you did to make this book all that it is. You have been my counselor and advisor on the world of Pinecrest – from everything to art and grammar, and this book wouldn't have made it to publishing without you. I'm sorry that the Turkey Chronicles did not include any mysteries to solve or ninjas – I will try to do better next time.

To the friends whose hearts and experiences added depth and life to Harper and Charlie's stories, thank you. The memories we've made are what have given this story the life that it has, and I couldn't have done it without you.

To the family that has been cheering me on since day one, thank you! Whether I wanted to be a veterinarian, princess, popstar, or lawyer, you have believed in my ability to do it, and I thank you for that endless love and support.

To the teachers and classes that made me the writer I am, thank you for advocating for my stories – no matter the genre, length, or quality, you have believed in my ability to succeed at every level. I wouldn't be the adult that I am without that.

And finally, to my readers: thank you. There is not a moment of this story where I didn't beg the Lord to use me, and if you read this book all the way to ending, then that means that prayer got answered. You're the person I did this for – without you, there would be no story to tell.

MEET THE AUTHOR

Emma Chester is a poet, author, and blogger living in North Georgia, who enjoys spending time with her family and finding magic moments in ordinary days.

When Emma is not writing, she can usually be found reading, drinking a cup of coffee, arguing with her dog, or stress-baking while listening to Taylor Swift. Her heart is to see people find their purpose in Christ, by connecting with stories, so that the world can see that a hope-filled heart surrendered to the Lord is the happiest ending of all.

For more of Emma's work, visit: emmawritespassion.com
Or follow along on social media @emmawritespassion

Printed in the USA
CPSIA information can be obtained
at www.ICGtesting.com
CBHW061125171124
17562CB00013B/245